Making Waves Down Under

After a few graceless hours in the water, Eliza had managed to lock down a routine of sorts:

Step 1: Paddle your arms really hard when Macca says "Go."

Step 2: Hop up on the board when Macca yells "Up."

Step 3: Wave your arms around frantically like a windmill.

Step 4: Careen into the water.

It wasn't quite surfing, but it was something.

Eventually she started getting the hang of it. That was to say, she got the hang of those four steps. *Paddle, hop up, freak out, fall over.* At least she finally stopped looking like she was being attacked by a swarm of bees each time she hopped back up onto the board. Soon she could even stay up on it for a few seconds and, yes, even "feel" the waves carrying her along.

The best part, though, was when they would take a break to catch her breath. She would climb up to sit on the board, and Macca would climb on behind her, resting his palms on her shoulders as their feet drifted in the surf. She would lean back against him until she felt up to another go. They'd wait for the right wave, Eliza lying on the board and Macca floating next to her, his hand on the small of her back until he would yell "Go!"

Eliza would paddle furiously and then hop up onto the board and, once in a while, the wave would catch the board and begin pushing it toward the shore. And there would be Macca, catching her eye, a smile on his face as big as the one on Eliza's.

STUDENTS ACROSS
A SUPER
SPECIAL
THE SEVEN SEAS

Up Over Down Under

Micol Ostow and
Noah Harlan

speak
An Imprint of Penguin Group (USA) Inc.

Acknowledgments

MICOL would like to thank: Noah Harlan, writing partner, handyman, film buff, best friend; Jodi Reamer, warrior princess; Kathi Appelt, southern gothic mentor-type; Angelle Pilkington, SASS-y editrix and gossip partner; and Kris Gilson, patient Puffin boss-woman.

NOAH would like to thank: Micol Ostow, writing partner, writing guide, and mentor extraordinaire, general inspirer, best friend; Angelle Pilkington, editor-o-rama; Kris Gilson; Clan Harlan (Josh, Trinity, Leonard, Fleur) and, especially, Elizabeth Harlan, the original Harlan family YA author.

SPEAK
Published by the Penguin Group
Penguin Group (USA) Inc.,
345 Hudson Street, New York, New York 10014, U.S.A.
Penguin Group (Canada), 90 Eglinton Avenue East, Suite 700, Toronto, Ontario, Canada M4P 2Y3
(a division of Pearson Penguin Canada Inc.)
Penguin Books Ltd, 80 Strand, London WC2R 0RL, England
Penguin Ireland, 25 St Stephen's Green, Dublin 2, Ireland (a division of Penguin Books Ltd)
Penguin Group (Australia), 250 Camberwell Road, Camberwell, Victoria 3124, Australia
(a division of Pearson Australia Group Pty Ltd)
Penguin Books India Pvt Ltd, 11 Community Centre, Panchsheel Park, New Delhi - 110 017, India
Penguin Group (NZ), 67 Apollo Drive, Rosedale, North Shore 0632, New Zealand
(a division of Pearson New Zealand Ltd)
Penguin Books (South Africa) (Pty) Ltd, 24 Sturdee Avenue, Rosebank,
Johannesburg 2196, South Africa

Registered Offices: Penguin Books Ltd, 80 Strand, London WC2R 0RL, England

Published by Speak, an imprint of Penguin Group (USA) Inc., 2008

1 3 5 7 9 10 8 6 4 2

Copyright © Micol Ostow and Noah Harlan, 2010

LIBRARY OF CONGRESS CATALOGING-IN-PUBLICATION DATA
Ostow, Micol.
Up over down under: a super special / Micol Ostow and Noah Harlan.
p.   cm.–(S.A.S.S.: Students Across the Seven Seas)
Summary: When sixteen-year-olds Eliza of Washington, D.C., and Billie of
Melbourne, Australia, participate in a semester-long ecology exchange program, Eliza's
plan to "cut loose" out of the public eye goes awry, while Belinda must consider
tempering her idealism in order to work within the system.
ISBN: 978-0-14-241056-1 (pbk.)
[1. Self-actualization (Psychology)–Fiction. 2. Foreign study–Fiction. 3. Schools–Fiction.
4. Ecology–Fiction. 5. Washington (D.C.)–Fiction. 6. Melbourne (Vic.)–Fiction.
7. Australia–Fiction.]
I. Harlan, Noah. II. Title.
PZ7.O8475Up 2010
[Fic]–dc22   2009027241

Speak ISBN 978-0-14-241056-1

Printed in the United States of America

For Jim Kane, always and forever our Aussie-in-residence!

Up Over
Down Under

Queen Victoria Market

Royal Botanic Gardens

Sorrento

FISH 'N' CHIPS

The Esplanade

St. Kilda

Georgetown

Potomac

Billie's Washington, D.C.

Adams Morgan

Capitol Hill

The White House

Smithsonian Institute

Ocean City

River

N
W E
S

Application for the Students Across the Seven Seas

S.A.S.S. Goes Green! **Study Abroad Program**

Name: Eliza Ritter

Age: 16

High School: Fairlawn Academy

Hometown: Washington, D.C.

Preferred Study Abroad Destination: Melbourne, Australia

1. Why are you interested in traveling abroad next year?

Answer: As the daughter of the assistant administrator of the Environmental Protection Agency, I've had the chance to be exposed to many high-profile environmental reforms. Now I'm looking for an opportunity to really dig in and get my hands dirty through the S.A.S.S. D.C.-Melbourne eco-exchange program.

(Truth: As the daughter of the assistant administrator of the EPA, I've been living in a fishbowl practically since the day that I was born. Much as I love my dad and all that he works for, I'm sick of being on my best behavior 24/7. I'm _dying_ to head somewhere outside of the bubble, and this exchange program with my father's office seemed like the perfect opportunity to do just that.)

2. How will studying abroad further develop your talents and interests?

Answer: My father always tells me that actions speak louder than words. That's why I think it's imperative to supplement my policy education with some hands-on time with nature.

(Truth: My "interests" are mainly spending time at the beach down under!)

3. Describe your extracurricular activities.

Answer: I have volunteered as an intern in my father's office, as well as serving on various student council committees.

(Truth: My internships earned me some extra school credit, and some credit with Dad, too. Also? Cute boys can be found serving on the student council!)

4. Is there anything else you feel we should know about you?

Answer: I am an outgoing person who loves to meet people with vibrant, diverse, and interesting stories to tell!

(Truth... especially if that means scoring a few months of independence from my parents and long-term boyfriend!)

Application for the Students Across the Seven Seas
S.A.S.S. Goes Green! Study Abroad Program

Name: Belinda Echols

Age: 16

High School: St. Catherine's School for Girls

Hometown: Melbourne, Australia

Preferred Study Abroad Destination: Washington, D.C.

1. Why are you interested in traveling abroad next year?

Answer: I've spent the past two years crusading on behalf of many environmental causes directly from the front lines. Now I'm hoping to get an up-close and personal look at the ways in which policies are formulated and enforced by the government.

(Truth: That is the truth! I love sunshine and fresh air, but I figure it'd be nice to try and effect some change from the inside. Washington, D.C., seemed like an obvious place to do that.)

2. How will studying abroad further develop your talents and interests?

Answer: The Environmental Protection Agency is the organization directly responsible for ecological policy. Any self-proclaimed "greenie" would be dead lucky to spend some quality time on the inside, learning how it runs!

(Truth: Fingers crossed that Assistant Administrator Ritter actually is the sort to "make time for the little people"!)

3. Describe your extracurricular activities.

Answer: PETA, ASPCA, the Sierra Club, the National Wildlife Foundation, track and field, recreational surfing, vegetarian cooking club.

(Truth: It's actually not difficult at all keeping up with the American environmental groups in this information age. Thank goodness for the Internet!)

4. Is there anything else you feel we should know about you?

Answer: I've never traveled outside of Australia, and am looking forward to broadening my horizons.

(Truth: Cheesy, but true. Pick me! Pick me! My bags are already packed!)

Chapter One

From: elizarit@email.com
To: billiesurf@email.com
Subject: S.A.S.S.

Billie—

Hi! This is Eliza Ritter, and I'm going to be the one exchanging with you this semester. S.A.S.S. said we should get in touch so . . . well, here I am! I'm not sure what there is to tell you; everything here is pretty normal, so I doubt you're in for any surprises. My parents may seem a

little strict at first, but don't take it too personally. Their rules are really just their way of making sure that Dad's public image stays intact. But I'm guessing you would never have applied to volunteer for a government official if you weren't prepared to do the whole "perfect, polished student" thing, right?

As for me, I can't wait to get down there! I've been obsessively Google-imaging pictures of Australia, and it looks warm and gorgeous!

Now for the important questions: Do you live near the beach? Oh yeah, and I am a total *Gossip Girl* addict—do you have that down there?

Also, your profile said that you have brothers. How many? And how long do they usually spend in the bathroom in the mornings? I'm an only child, so I'm sort of used to unlimited mirror time.

Anyhow, feel free to send a note whenever. If you've got any questions of your own, I'll try to answer them.

—Eliza

About twelve hours into her trip, it struck Eliza Ritter that Australia was *very* far away. She had left Washington, D.C., early that morning on a flight for Los Angeles, and after a six-hour "hop" and an hour layover in the L.A. airport she'd boarded this flight to end all flights. She had been on this plane for five hours now and wasn't even near the halfway point. It was an unholy fourteen and a half hours from

Los Angeles to Melbourne, Australia, and the initial thrill of traveling on her own was wearing very thin. She had read through her copies of *Star*, *In Touch*, and *Us Weekly* and now was examining the movie selections to see what could while away some more of the time. By her calculations, there were nine and a half hours left on this plane. If the average movie was about two hours, that meant four movies and a catnap and she'd be there. *Voilà!*

Eliza had been ready for this trip. *More* than ready. Not that she didn't like her home life—the truth was that seeing herself in news pictures alongside her father at various events made her prouder than she'd ever admit—but lately, she'd been feeling sort of...well, smothered.

Her parents weren't overprotective like some kids' parents were, but what they were was, in a word, *conscientious*. They were conscientious of how they appeared in the media, and conscientious of the image they projected, separate or together, each and every time one or all of them stepped out of their house.

While most girls Eliza's age were posting party pictures of themselves on Facebook, Eliza had to be 150 percent sure that any blog post she ever wrote was friends-locked to the nth degree. Discretion was key. And frankly, it was exhausting.

She'd been happy to play the part of "first daughter" because she was an unabashed Daddy's Girl, and, well... there were perks in the whole process. Like having a

private hairstylist and makeup artist to prep you for fancy Washington parties—or even attending those parties in the first place. That was fun.

But, yes—it was also exhausting. And what Australia promised was a chance to fly solo, even for a few blissful, if short, months. A chance to cut loose.

To be completely honest, Eliza wasn't totally sure that she even knew what it meant to "cut loose," so controlled had things been up until this very moment. But that was the whole point of this trip. And she was for darn sure going to make it her business to learn—*pronto*.

When Eliza had first read about the S.A.S.S. exchange program, she just knew that she had to sign up. She didn't know where she wanted to be placed, but at that point, anywhere other than Washington sounded like Shangri-la. Based on photo research conducted mainly in the form of celebrity gossip magazines, France and Australia quickly rose to the top of the list. Unfortunately, her father pointed out that two years of French lessons probably would not be enough to get her through a semester of classes in Paris.

Australia was the obvious choice, then. Besides, what could be wrong with spending a semester in the place that produced hotties like Eric Bana and Hugh Jackman?

There were several cities to choose from, and Eliza weighed her options carefully. She looked at the three largest cities: Melbourne—a funky city in the south,

Sydney—the biggest city and very cosmopolitan (and also home to that cool opera-house thing on the bay), and lastly Brisbane—near the Great Barrier Reef and a stretch of beach called the Gold Coast.

Brisbane sounded amazing—what could be bad about a Gold Coast? The only problem was that her school wasn't offering an exchange to Brisbane.

That left Melbourne and Sydney. To settle things, she decided to ask her friend Allison's mom for advice. To Eliza, there was something ultimately less objectionable in seeking parental advice from a parent who wasn't one's own. Mrs. Shifton was a deputy undersecretary of something or other and had traveled all over the world. She had a sort of know-it-all air about her and was prone to correcting Allison's grammar with annoying regularity. But again, she wasn't Eliza's mother, and therefore her advice to Eliza was welcome. Mrs. Shifton considered the question and then announced, quite definitively, that Sydney was the place she should go.

That settled it. Eliza went home and checked the box for Melbourne. After sixteen years of doing nothing *but* listening to her parents, it was time to make a decision completely and entirely on her own.

So here she was, pondering the future, at least as far as the next nine hours were concerned. She'd left a lot behind in D.C. She had been dating Parker Green since the spring of sophomore year. He was very cute, smart, and

charming, and he got along with all of her friends—not to mention, he was a parents' dream—but to Eliza, Australia was a big, life-changing opportunity, and she was determined to make the most of it. Going strings-free meant going truly strings-free, which meant taking a break from the long-term guy, even if he was a sweetie. As much as she knew she'd miss Parker, Eliza also knew that an exchange semester worth doing was an exchange semester worth doing right.

Eliza had been going to school with the same kids since preschool. She knew everyone and, frankly, they knew *her.* When the idea of studying abroad first came up, Eliza realized that this could be a chance not only to flex her independence, but also to reinvent herself. She could find some new friends and have some new experiences. And most important, she could do all that without being under the watchful eyes of the Washington elite.

Australia was *very* far from Washington and all those eyes. Australia was eyeless. Australia was, for all intents and purposes, blind.

Blind was good, in this case. In this case, blind was very, very good.

As for Parker, well, she was young, and she would be traveling halfway around the world. She told Parker that she wanted to take a break, and that if they were meant to be, they'd find themselves together again when she was back. Parker's response, a slightly puzzled "huh," wasn't exactly the enthusiastic agreement that Eliza had been hoping for, but at least she'd made it through a difficult conversation. She honestly didn't know what the future held for Parker and her. But in a way, that was just the point—suddenly, she honestly didn't know what the future held, period. For the first time, *ever,* her entire life wasn't carefully mapped out on a calendar, or committed to her mother or father's BlackBerry.

It was terrifying. But it was thrilling, too.

She checked her watch impatiently. Eight hours and forty-three minutes still to go. The fact that her father's executive assistant had scored her an upgrade to business class was only a small consolation. Eight hours was a *long* time no matter how much legroom you had.

Eliza yawned and glanced around the cabin, trying to figure out which passengers were Americans going to Australia and which were Australians going back home. She stood, shaking her legs out, and wandered up the aisle into the galley, all the while keeping her eyes peeled for signs of life.

Score! Standing in the galley was an unattended bowl of chocolate cookies—*that* was what she needed. Dumb romantic comedies and action movies always went better with snacks. Eliza quickly checked to make sure no one was watching, then ducked into the serving area and grabbed a handful of the cookies. She rationalized her rule bending by promising herself that she'd pass on the

cookies when the flight attendants brought them around the cabin later.

Home free, she backed out of the galley...only to collide with a somewhat impatient-looking flight attendant.

The flight attendant raised a questioning eyebrow in Eliza's direction. "Are you all set with your cookies, then?"

Eliza nodded, feeling slightly panicked. "I think I'm having a low-blood-sugar thing," she explained, wondering if she was pushing her luck with the fib.

Miraculously, the flight attendant seemed to buy it. Her expression softened. "In that case," she said, holding the bowl of cookies out for Eliza, "why don't you take another?"

Eliza shrugged. "Um, okay. If you insist," she said, now grinning for real. "I mean, better safe than sorry, right?"

She returned to her seat and placed her headphones on, settling back for a movie and munching away contentedly on her contraband snacks.

So far, this "independence" thing was working out kind of nicely...even if she *had* just been caught with her hands in the cookie jar.

Chapter Two

From: billiesurf@email.com

To: elizarit@email.com

Subject: G'Day!

That's Australian for "hello," of course! But I reckon you already know that if you've been studying your S.A.S.S. orientation packet. I'm happy that you wrote (it's always helpful to know a little bit about the person who's commandeered your bedroom when you've gone on walkabout, after all), and I can answer most of your questions.

First off, I do have two little brothers, twins. They're six

and very cute, if a bit hyper at times. Sam and Nick. If they give you any trouble, let 'em know I told them to lay off. As for the television, I should warn you that Mum usually dominates, and you shouldn't count on being able to wrestle away the remote. Especially 'round time for *Neighbours*.

You mentioned the beach, so I feel like I should warn you that, while we do have one about five kilometers outside of the city, I wouldn't break out your swimmers and sunnies just yet—nobody really "goes to the beach" (as you say) in Melbourne. If you can hang in there for a few weeks, I'm sure Mum and Dad will take you to their cottage in Sorrento. That's where everyone from Melbourne goes for some beachside barbies and to catch some surf.

I'd better be going, now. Write when you have a moment, and let me know how you're going with my family, etc.

Cheers,

Billie

"Aren't you eating those?"

"What's that?" Billie Echols looked up from her video iPod to find the seat mate on her right side bearing down on her affably.

Flight 181, Row 20 was cramped enough as it was without this man, a friendly but nonetheless undeniably...rotund American, invading Billie's personal space. Australians were known for being easygoing, Billie realized, but seeing as how this was about a twenty-two-hour flight (that was including the layover in Los Angeles, of course), Mr. Seat J really needed to learn some boundaries.

"Were you eating those? The chips?"

Right. No boundaries, then. Beautiful.

"Er, I guess not," Billie said, hesitant. While the chips themselves—some terrifying flavor hybrid of onions, cheddar, and a hint of ranch dressing—weren't all that appealing, she knew there wouldn't be any more food until breakfast service, and worried about midnight hunger pangs. Assuming her jet-lagged body would recognize midnight, that is.

"Would you—" she began tentatively.

Seat J needed no additional encouragement.

"Thanks!" he boomed, squeezing even farther onto Billie's seat—it was almost as though he was trying to meld his body into Billie's through the science of osmosis—and scooping up the sad, wrinkled foil bag. He tilted his head back and downed the last crumbs of potato chips as though he were a marathoner on his last leg and the bag was a bottle of designer sports water.

"Miss, if my husband is bothering you, just let me know. I can get him to back off."

That was the input of Seat L, or the woman directly to Billie's left. She and her husband, Billie noted, looked exactly alike: smooth, hairless faces and pink, smiling mouths. It was a little bit creepy.

Billie had offered, when they all first boarded the plane, to swap seats with the wife so that she and her husband could sit side by side, but for reasons that Billie truly could not fathom, they had demurred. Speaking of creepy.

"No worries," Billie lied, trying her hardest to keep her patience. She had specifically downloaded as many back episodes of *The West Wing* as she could fit on her iPod before heading off to the airport—"research," she reasoned, for her upcoming internship.

Internship. The word sounded exotic and glam, even inside of Belinda's head. S.A.S.S. was an incredibly competitive program, and she couldn't believe that she'd been accepted. She'd been a greenie ever since her mother first taught her to separate the plastics from the paper, but in her hometown, Melbourne, everyone had a pretty healthy attitude toward the outdoors and the environment.

In D.C., however—that was where she would have the chance to test her political passions, to stretch and flex and really *feel* the power of her convictions. She would be interning with Alan Ritter, a key player in the EPA. Ritter was most recently in charge of an effort to clean the Chesapeake Bay, specifically to eliminate pollution from a nearby sewage plant, and everyone in D.C. was waiting to see what his plan would be, and when and how it would go into effect.

The thought made Billie shiver. This trip to D.C. was the most grown-up thing she had ever done, and she couldn't wait to find herself in an honest-to-gosh office workspace.

Billie could just see it now: her, on the phone, screaming demands at a reluctant wonk. Her, tirelessly marching
in a (nonviolent) demonstration just outside of the White
House. Her, working into the wee hours of the night, grossly
overpriced designer coffee in one hand, as she entered
corrections to a fellow politico's speech. She was going to
save the environment—single-handedly, if she had to. And
she was traveling to America—America!—to do so.

Okay, she wasn't going to go to that Hollywood cliché of
America being a melting pot, a land of opportunity, where
the streets were paved with gold. That was a little too
Disney for someone who'd been raised in what had once
been a British penal colony, after all. But if programs like
Gossip Girl, *One Tree Hill*, or…yes, even *The West Wing*,
were to be believed, Americans were…interesting.

It was almost worth the sacrifice of trading in her trainers for fluorescent lighting for a whole entire semester. So
what if Billie, dedicated introvert and adventure enthusiast,
would be giving up the great outdoors? At the same time,
she'd be saving it. This was what they called one of those
tough decisions.

"He'd pick your whole tray clean, if you turned your
back on him," Seat L screeched, poking Billie in the rib.

Billie didn't doubt that for a moment, but she smiled
weakly, nevertheless.

Yeah. Interesting.

Chapter Three

The plane touched down on the runway in Melbourne ten minutes early. Eliza looked out the window for signs of anything "Australian," but the tarmac, at least, really looked a lot like landing at Dulles back home in Washington, save for the red and white kangaroo Qantas logo adorning most of the planes.

After taxiing to their gate, Eliza's personal flight attendant (thanks again to Dad's "can-do" assistant!) came to help gather her belongings, and they walked off the plane. There they hopped onto a golf cart to ride through the terminal. Eliza felt one part kind of special from all of the attention, but one part kind of babysat. She wasn't sure which sensation was stronger.

"Is this your first time down under?" the attendant asked, breaking Eliza from her post-flight daze.

"Um, yeah."

"Don't worry, you'll be right at home before long."

Eliza wondered whether the flight attendant mistook the exhaustion on her face for fear—not that they should look much alike.

As they zipped through the terminal, Eliza watched the posters on the wall going by. Many were for products she knew, but there were other ones for things she'd never heard of. Phone companies and candy bars. Even models of cars that they didn't have back home.

I guess a Subaru Outback has a different ring to it in a place that really has *an outback,* she thought.

Her little airport golf cart came to a sudden halt as they arrived in the immigration hall. Because Eliza was an "unaccompanied minor," the attendant was able to take her to the immigration line reserved for the crew. They waited behind several flight attendants and an older man in a wheelchair being pushed by another airport attendant. Eliza felt a little silly to be given the same preferential treatment as a disabled person, but this was the sort of thing that tended to happen when her father's team called in a favor. For better or for worse.

Soon they were next. Eliza slid her passport and

immigration form to the man in the booth. She beamed at him, half expecting some sort of acknowledgment that she had arrived—as though the continent of Australia had been waiting for her. Instead, he glanced at her, grunted, and stamped several documents before sliding them back across the counter to her and calling the next person up.

"Follow me," called the attendant as she pointed the way to the baggage claim.

This pampering is getting to be a bit embarrassing, Eliza thought, for the first time regretting her general status as favored daughter and pseudo-celebrity traveler.

They continued on to the baggage carousel and waited what felt like an eternity for her suitcases to come out. As person after person from her flight found their things and moved on, Eliza began to wonder what would happen if her bags weren't there. It dawned on her just how far from home she was.

Logically, she knew, it was unlikely that she would wind up wandering the streets of Melbourne without a toothbrush or a change of clothes. Still, the longer she waited, the more nervous she became that the Echolses, Billie's family, wouldn't be there when she finally claimed her luggage. Now her mind raced into lunatic-thinking mode: *What if they think I've missed my flight? Or that I got lost? What if I do get lost? How will I find them?*

Eliza realized she knew nothing about this place. For the first time since she'd decided to apply to the S.A.S.S.

program, it occurred to her that she might just be in way over her head.

Eliza was furtively checking her international cell phone, as if to reassure herself that she had some means of self-preservation, when suddenly, as if by magic, her two matching bags—bright red canvas suitcases that were impossible to miss—appeared on the conveyor belt. She and the airport attendant lugged them onto a cart and headed past the customs officials toward two big sliding doors made of frosted glass.

The doors parted, dumping passengers into the main terminal, where a horde of people was gathered, waiting for arriving passengers. Eliza scanned the crowd. She saw families reunite joyfully and business types make their way toward hired drivers holding hand-scrawled placards bearing their names. Men and women awaited their spouses with bouquets of fresh flowers in hand. She saw tons and tons of people…

She just didn't see anyone for *her*.

Then she spotted him: a tall, thin man with a bushy mustache and a big grin waving frantically in her direction. This had to be Mr. Echols. At his feet, two identical little boys waved a piece of paper with her name on it. She tentatively waved back, and they rushed toward her.

"Eliza?" the man asked.

"That's me." Eliza's voice was softer to her own ears than usual.

"Welcome to Oz!" Mr. Echols shoved his hand out enthusiastically. "I'm Frank Echols, and these two ankle biters are Nick and Sam," he said. He gestured to the twins, who were, by now, tugging at his pant legs.

Eliza knew that Billie had two younger brothers, but somehow the idea that she, Eliza, would now be living with two little boys hadn't quite connected. Looking at these twin balls of energy, who were by now grabbing at her bags, Eliza suddenly wondered if she was going to be wishing for her own very quiet house in D.C. before too long.

"And somewhere around here is Estelle. She went off to get us all something to drink," Mr. Echols continued.

He spoke with a charming Australian accent. He turned his *r*'s into *ah*'s, and everything had a singsongy lilt to it. Eliza liked him immediately; he seemed fun-loving and full of spirit. In a way, it reminded her of her own father. Fun-loving without the threat of public scrutiny sounded like a potentially ideal combination.

"It's very nice to meet you, Mr. Echols," Eliza said, "and you too, Nick…Sam." She had no idea which was which but figured that she could work that out later.

"It's Frank to you, Eliza," continued Mr. Echols. "Now, why don't you two be of some use and help Eliza with her bags instead of getting in the way?" he said, nudging Nick and Sam.

The two of them took Eliza's baggage cart and, with arms stretched over their heads, pushed it forward. They were too short to see over her bags, and soon the cart careened toward the crowds ahead with the twins pushing it at top speed and cackling to each other. People yelped and parted to make way for the trolley as Frank yelled after the boys to slow down.

Stepping through the sea of strangers, a woman wearing jeans and a knit sweater and sporting a cute blonde soccer-mom bob came rushing up to them with an arm full of sodas.

"There was a Maccas around the way there, but I had to go 'round to the vendy to find some cans!" she said, turning the cans over to Frank and extending an arm toward Eliza so as to encircle the girl in a half embrace.

Eliza looked toward where Mrs. Echols had come from and saw a McDonald's sign with an arrow pointing around the corner.

Mental Note: Maccas = McDonald's.

"Welcome! You must be stuffed after that trip from the States!"

"Um, well, they fed us well on the plane," Eliza said, thinking back to the cookies she had secreted out of the galley. She wondered if there was one still in her jacket pocket.

"No, no," explained Estelle, "you must be *exhausted*!"

"Oh…right, yeah, well, I guess. I sure am glad to be on the ground."

Mental note: stuffed = exhausted. I definitely need to get a notebook to keep track of all this.

"Well, let's get you home so you can get cleaned up and eat a proper meal," said Estelle. "We're very happy you're here, and we're going to have a great time!" She threw an enthusiastic arm across Eliza's shoulder again and squeezed. It was a change from Eliza's own mother, who as a general rule was more formal and subdued, but Eliza didn't mind this burst of affection.

It was sunny and a bit chilly as Eliza stepped outside and got her first breath of fresh air in what felt like decades. She inhaled deeply. She didn't know what exactly she was expecting, but it smelled just the same as the air at home. Weren't you supposed to be able to smell the eucalyptus trees when you stepped off the plane?

They made their way to the parking lot and wound through the parked cars, Nick and Sam narrowly missing slamming Eliza's bags into several of the parked vehicles until they stopped near a small blue sedan. It was obviously the Echolses' car, and Frank popped the trunk open. He manhandled Eliza's bags into place, slammed the trunk shut, and walked around to the passenger's side of the car, unlocking the doors. Eliza slipped into the backseat and was soon flanked on either side by Nick and Sam. Estelle climbed into the driver's side, and they pulled out of the parking lot.

As they made their way out of the airport, Estelle turned around in her seat to face Eliza.

"So, love, I hope you like steak because I got us some real beauts at the butcher shop this morning."

Eliza was momentarily confused about how Estelle was able to drive a car while turned completely around in her seat. But she breathed a sigh of relief as she remembered that here in Australia, they drove on the wrong side of the road and that Frank was actually in the driver's seat.

"Well, yes, that would be great," Eliza said. She meant it, she realized. Her mother was a bit of a nutrition fanatic, which meant that red meat was hard to come by in the Ritter household.

"You talk funny!" shouted Nick.

"Say that again!" Sam cried, giggling furiously.

"Say what again?" Eliza asked, confused.

The two boys began trying to imitate Eliza's American accent, exaggerating their *r*'s and flattening their vowels.

"You two…" Estelle scolded them, "leave her alone. Maybe it's the two of you who sound funny to her."

The boys appeared to consider this possibility. "Do you think we sound funny?" Sam (or was it Nick?) asked Eliza plaintively.

"Well, to be honest, you don't sound like my friends back home, but they all sound like me."

"That's silly," Sam decided, sitting back in his seat and folding his arms across his chest.

Eliza welcomed the twins' silence. She hated to admit

it, but the whole scene was getting to be a bit much. She had just spent nearly twenty-four hours flying around the world and now was crammed into the back of a car with a whole family of people she didn't know. She was on sensory overload.

She took the break in conversation as an opportunity to stare out the window at the city. She could see the small cluster of skyscrapers that made up the downtown area draw closer and closer as they passed through suburbs made up of small houses, then onto tree-lined boulevards with pretty two-story houses lined with balconies. There seemed to be a park on every other corner. Soon they were heading into the center of the city on what appeared to be a major boulevard with a trolley track running down the middle of it and some beautiful buildings on one side hidden behind tall ivy-covered stone walls.

"This is Royal Parade and that's the University of Melbourne there," Frank said, playing tour guide. "Those are the residential colleges where students stay."

Eliza thought back to Washington and how one of the great coups you could wrangle as a high school student was to get into a college party at one of the universities in the city. There was American University, and George Washington, and Georgetown. In the spring, Georgetown would have its annual reunion. If you could score a badge, you could get into the alumni parties claiming to be someone's kid. Eliza had *always* wanted to slip into one of those parties under the radar, but of course, as the dutiful D.C. daughter, never had. As she took in these colleges along Royal Parade she made a mental note that she was going to see the inside of one before she left town.

Eliza smiled to herself as she stared out the window while they followed the tram tracks. Occasionally they would come to a stop alongside one of the green-and-yellow tram cars. They seemed to span the city and were packed with students heading from campus into the city center. With everyone driving on the wrong side of the road and these trams edging through intersections, she was amazed that there weren't car accidents all the time, but nobody else seemed to be concerned, so she just sat back in her seat and took it all in.

The car passed through the downtown area with Frank calling out the sights.

"There's the Bourke Street Mall."

"That there's Flinders Station."

"Those trees over there are the Royal Botanic Gardens."

Much of the city felt far quainter than D.C. She once read that the people who designed the city of Washington had tried to copy the great old cities of Europe. They created the mall after looking at Versailles in Paris and the monuments of Rome. The goal was to build a city that impressed the visitor with its power and grandeur, but the consequence of that plan was a city that didn't

function very well. Traffic was confusing, and the government buildings seemed to get in the way more than anything. Melbourne was nothing like that.

The abundance of trees and small houses made everything feel very welcoming and manageable. Even the State of Victoria Parliament across from the Bourke Street Mall seemed approachable, with people sitting on the steps reading their papers and eating lunch. There was a charm that suggested that this was a city not meant to be visited but, rather, to be lived in.

After they passed the Botanic Gardens, the shops facing outward became much fancier. There were upscale clothing stores and fancy-looking restaurants.

I'll definitely have to come back and spend some time here, Eliza thought as she eyed the designer dresses in some of the windows.

"Nearly there now," said Estelle from the front seat. "This is Toorak Road, and we're in South Yarra, which is where our home is."

A short distance farther and Frank turned and pulled into the driveway of a low, ranch-style house.

"Welcome home!" Frank beamed, "This is our humble abode. We hope you'll make yourself right at home."

"It's very nice."

It wasn't as big as her parents' house, but it was, as she'd said, very nice. By now the lack of sleep on the plane had caught up with her and she was feeling a little groggy and overwhelmed by everything.

They pulled up the driveway alongside the house and parked the car in front of a small garage. Frank took her bags out of the trunk, and they passed through a little gate at the rear of the house that opened onto a back patio and pool area surrounded by an ivy-covered wall with large trees hanging over it.

A door off the patio opened into a kitchen with a big table for eating and older wooden cabinets at the far end over the cooking area. Nick and Sam raced past Eliza and down the hall.

"They're trying to be helpful. Your room's right here," Estelle explained, leading the way into a room off the side of the kitchen. "It's a bit private from the rest of the house— it even has its own little entrance off of the patio. It's Billie's room, and I made sure she cleaned it up for you."

"I'm sure it'll be lovely." Eliza stepped into the room. She scanned the walls, which were covered with posters of surfers and nearly every environmental group under the sun. At one end of the room was a desk with a corkboard over it, and at the other was a twin bed with a big comforter and some fluffy pillows. There was nothing "girlie" about the room at all. In fact, if she didn't know better, the room could just as well have belonged to a high school guy as to a girl. The decorations were all about surfing

and saving the trees, and the sheets and covers were all in earth tones.

Billie is in for such a surprise when she gets to my room, Eliza thought with a smile.

"Make yourself right at home," Estelle said as she patted a pile of presumably fresh towels that were stacked atop the bed. "There's space in the closet, and the top three drawers in the bureau are empty. Why don't you freshen up and come on out back, and we'll have a bite of supper in about half an hour or so?"

"I really should give my parents a call and let them know I've gotten here all right," Eliza said. She felt awkward around this new ersatz family.

"Oh heavens!" Estelle said with a laugh. "It's about two in the morning in America right now."

Eliza looked at her watch and realized that she hadn't yet set it for Melbourne time. She shook her head, trying to clear the cobwebs out.

"What time is it here?" she asked. If she couldn't handle the metric system, then she probably couldn't handle the time difference, either.

"About ten to six in the evening."

Eliza stared at the hour hand on her watch as she tried to figure out what time it actually *felt* like.

"Well, you get settled, and we'll see you in a few," Estelle said again, leaving Eliza to her unpacking.

Eliza hung up her dresses and blouses in the closet and laid her clothes in the drawers. She took out her laptop and put it on the desk, then dug out the plug adapter and plugged it in to charge.

Eliza flopped down on the edge of the bed and fell back into the covers. Staring up at the ceiling, she realized that she was a whole lot more exhausted from the ordeal of travel than she had thought. In fact, if she didn't get up and out of bed, she was going to fall asleep right then and there.

Not the best move to miss her first dinner, she knew. She picked herself up off the bed and stepped into the bathroom to wash up. Her reflection in the mirror was startling; her long journey sure showed on her face. Her hair had sprouted flyaways in every direction, her makeup had practically evaporated, and even her tracksuit some-how managed to look rumpled and wrinkled. She hastily finger-combed her hair and pulled it back into a ponytail. She splashed some water on her face and, feeling slightly refreshed, decided she was ready to face her host family and have some dinner.

Outside, Frank manned the grill with an enormous smile. As Eliza slipped into a chair at the table, Estelle approached with a tray full of the biggest, juiciest steaks she'd ever seen.

"I hope you're hungry!" she trilled. "Billie decided to become a vegetarian when she started high school, but the rest of us aren't, so we were glad to hear you're a bit of a carnivore yourself."

Despite being completely disoriented and turned around about time, Eliza was hungry. Dinner was delicious with steak, mashed potatoes, and string beans. The twins made a mess of their plates, dropping food left and right.

The Echolses had lots of questions for her, and she did her best to answer them. They wanted to know about the flight, about her family and her school. They were curious what Billie's classes would be like. The twins wanted to know about what movies were out in the States that hadn't come out yet in Australia. Before long she was stuffed—in the American sense of the word—and helped Estelle to clear the plates.

"Why don't you put those down next to the sink and go get some rest?" Estelle offered. "You look simply exhausted, and you have some big days ahead of you."

Gratefully, Eliza put the plates where Estelle indicated, said a thank-you and a good-night, and headed to her room. She closed the door behind her and flopped back in the bed. She settled herself on top of the covers, and before she knew it, she had drifted off to sleep, still sporting her tracksuit and smeared makeup. Anything else that needed taking care of would have to wait until tomorrow.

Chapter Four

Billie wasn't sure quite what she'd been expecting when her airplane finally touched down in D.C. Obviously she knew that, capital or no, it wasn't as though a marching band brandishing mini American flags was going to come stomping through the baggage claim area. Besides, after the horrifically endless flight to which she'd just been subjected, she wouldn't have had the energy for a marching band, anyhow.

Or would she? She stared dazedly, taking in as much of her surroundings as possible while she made her way toward the traveler pickup area.

After a moment she realized that one of the biggest clichés about America was apparently true. The country's fascination with McDonald's translated to two separate outposts that sprang up in the short distance from the arrival gate and the exit to ground transportation.

Billie was a vegetarian, and the thought of eating a Big Mac or Chicken McNuggets made her stomach churn. As she pressed toward the crush of family and friends who awaited her fellow travelers, Billie kept a sharp eye out for Mr. Ritter. S.A.S.S. had provided Billie with a recent Ritter family photo as reference, but she would have recognized Mr. Ritter without it. He was in the news often, crusading for the environment. The whole reason she'd been chosen for this exchange program was her proven dedication to eco-conservation, and Mr. Ritter was essentially Mr. Environment, as far as the U.S. government was concerned. Billie couldn't wait to meet him, and even—dare she dream it?—"talk shop" with him, as well.

Back at home, down under, Billie served on a bunch of different environmental groups, but they were a lot more hands-on; they held recycling drives, planted trees, and cleaned highway landscapes. It was gratifying, but Billie couldn't help but wonder whether it required a seat in-house with the government to really set change in motion.

"Belinda? Belinda Echols?"

Billie looked up. *Nobody* called her "Belinda." To her surprise, she found a woman, not a man, waving at her.

She quickly took in the twin set and pencil skirt, the sensible but clearly expensive pumps, and the sandy-blonde hair twisted into a stylish yet severe bun. She recognized those steely-blue eyes, she realized. But where from?

That's right. How thick could a girl be? She was obviously brain-dead from the plane, or she would have gotten it right away. This was *Mrs.* Ritter. She hoped her surprise didn't actually show on her face, but she suspected it probably did.

"That's me," she replied, trying to regain her composure and willing her cheeks to return to their natural, non-fire-engine color as quickly as possible. "Somewhat wrinkled, I'm afraid, but generally speaking, not too bad going. Oh, and you can call me Billie—everyone does."

"Going where?" Mrs. Ritter asked. Her eyebrows pulled together in a tiny "V" in the center of her forehead. "Never mind," she decided, before Billie had a chance to explain the Aussie slang. "Welcome, *Billie,*" she finished, sounding decidedly unenthusiastic about the nickname.

Vibes as subtle as a brick wall radiated off of Mrs. Ritter. She waved a hand toward Billie's bag as though she meant to pick it up and carry it, but instead she just gestured toward the large automatic double doors a few feet ahead. "The car's just this way," she said.

Billie fretted for a moment that she'd somehow, without even realizing it, done something to annoy Mrs. Ritter. But that was silly; she'd barely spoken two words to the

woman. She had heard that D.C. was a conservative town, and had been warned by those who'd been there that Americans were different from Aussies—less outgoing, and less friendly to strangers. So maybe Mrs. Ritter wasn't being aloof so much as she was just being American.

In which case, she could be in for an awfully long semester.

She followed the clipped, staccato sound of Mrs. Ritter's shoes against the asphalt, coming to a halt in front of…

No.

No way.

Billie was truly, utterly gobsmacked.

This was not the Ritters' car.

There was no way that the Ritters, family of a full-fledged greenie pundit, drove a gas-guzzling monster of an SUV. That just didn't make any sense at all.

Billie had, of course, assumed that the Ritters drove hybrids or, better yet, cycled to and fro when they needed. But not this. Between the carbon emissions and the miles-per-gallon rate of this car, driving it was the ecological equivalent of taking a ladder up to the top of the ozone layer and smashing a hole into it with a sledgehammer.

Billie realized her eyes were bugging out. This was not exactly subtle body language. She readjusted her expression as best as she could. *Be cool, she'll be 'right,* she told herself, hoping that if she thought it, it would automatically be true.

Mrs. Ritter must have seen her staring. "Of course, my husband drives a Prius," she offered, "but with Eliza getting her permit this year, I wanted something safe for the two of us to use." She had a high-pitched, nasal intonation to her speech that made her sound defensive. At least, Billie hoped that it was only the intonation, and not actual defensiveness, that made her sound that way.

It didn't matter; Mrs. Ritter was back to ignoring her again. She briskly pulled open the SUV's back door and waved her hand into the expanse. Clearly, the oldies in America weren't known for lots of warm fuzzy. Billie's own mother could suffocate you with an innocent hug, so this was bound to be an adjustment.

"You can put your luggage in here," Mrs. Ritter said. She did not offer to help with this, either, though in all fairness, she was so thin that she looked as though she'd keel over from the effort. Maybe her behavior was all just an elaborate form of self-preservation. Billie *really* wanted to give chilly Mrs. Ritter the benefit of the doubt. She knew that back home her brothers were bursting with anticipation for their visitor, and she fervently hoped that the same was true of her own host family.

Though to be perfectly frank, Mrs. Ritter didn't seem the type to burst with anticipation for *anything*.

Billie gritted her teeth and tried to ignore the tiny stabs of doubt reverberating inside her head. She hoisted her rolling suitcase up into the gaping expanse (really, didn't

the Ritters have only the one daughter? She wasn't trying to be sanctimonious, but what was the point of all of this *space*?), and tossed her backpack on top of it. When that was all taken care of, she slammed the door shut and brushed her fine blonde hair out of her eyes.

It certainly was going to be an interesting semester, she decided. For a whole lot of reasons.

If she'd expected an ear bashing from Mrs. Ritter, or some other sort of immediate female-bonding experience, Billie was flat out of luck. The drive from Dulles was quiet. Mrs. Ritter was no slouch with the small talk, but her friendliness felt rehearsed and masklike. Billie still had the distinct impression that she had somehow done something wrong, but since there were only a limited number of "things" that she had actually "done" since landing, she resolved to ignore the little gremlin of insecurity that had perched itself on her shoulder.

She was exhausted, too, she knew, which definitely lent itself to the disorientation. Back home, she had a pact with her brothers that she would be extra careful about her temper when she was short on sleep. That rule of thumb had to apply exponentially here, in this case.

She willed herself to focus on the scenery that whizzed by as they drove. Maryland was absolutely gorj, bright and colorful in a manner that was completely the opposite of Melbourne. Everything was crisp and tinged with gold and orange, where Melbourne was dominated by its cloudless blue sky. If she'd wanted a change, she had it now.

"This weather's a beaut, don't you think?" she said, gamely doing her best to keep her end of the conversation rolling.

"What's that?" Mrs. Ritter replied, her voice friendly in a stilted, party-hostess sort of way. All of her perfect—and perfectly hands-off—manners were suffocating the car ride.

"Right, er…the weather. Beautiful. Lovely day, right?"

Mrs. Ritter nodded swiftly. "Absolutely," she replied.

But she didn't say anything else.

After waiting several painful moments in vain for their scintillating dialogue to kick back up, Billie gave up and resigned herself to the silence. She crossed her arms over her chest, sat back in her seat, and resumed looking out the window as the landscape passed by.

Billie hadn't spent more than five minutes in Eliza's room before she realized that another cliché about America—that Americans watched too much TV—was apparently true as well. Billie loved her MTV reality programming as much as anyone—she'd watched the *Real World Sydney* devoutly—but telly *always* took a backseat to basking in the fresh air. Eliza, however, was a different story. Billie suspected that Eliza was in a category completely unto herself. Her bedroom was proof of that; the girl had her own TiVo system

set up, and a massive flat-screen television, too. Billie was gobsmacked—again—and jealous all at once. Back at the Echolses' household, TV was strictly for the family room. Eliza's room went way beyond a place for vegging out; if the girl wanted, she could transform herself into a right oversized chopped salad.

Eliza's room was astounding for other reasons as well. For starters, it was an explosion of lavender and lace. The walls were a soft mauve and the carpet was a deeper violet. The curtains, elaborate drapery with ornate ties, hung in sweeping purple hues. The bedspread was lace, and a purple chenille throw was tossed just so next to a mound of textured, sparkly throw pillows. The effect was…not understated. Billie was more of an earth-tones type herself, but she knew that going with the flow would be best. Besides, she'd come here for adventure, right? Maybe a scary-girlie purple room was adventure.

She slowly unpacked her belongings; judging from the size of Eliza's closet, she was more of a fashion plate than Billie. Billie was more "no muss, no fuss," clean and outdoorsy in her aesthetic. Sitting atop the vanity table was a snapshot of her alter ego: the photo revealed that Eliza was a striking brunette with a clever twinkle in her bright brown eyes. In the photo, Eliza leaned happily against a tall boy with dirty-blond hair. They had their arms slung around each other in a way that suggested that he was probably her boyfriend.

Billie wondered how Eliza's boyfriend felt about her spending the semester in Australia. Billie hadn't had too much experience with the opposite sex—she was a tomboy who mainly preferred her own company to that of anyone else's—but based on the experience of Val, her best mate from home, boyfriends could sometimes get clingy.

Suddenly Billie's unpacking felt very much like snooping. Guiltily, she faced the photo of Eliza and her mystery man away from her so that she wouldn't be tempted to do any inappropriate probing. She regarded a shelf full of stuffed animals that were appraising her sharply, sighed, and returned to making herself at home.

The house was deathly quiet, she realized. Back home, it was rare for her two little brothers not to be running and shrieking at top decibel through the house. Here, the only thing Billie could hear were the soft strains of classical music coming from the direction of the kitchen.

She was supposed to eat dinner with Mrs. Ritter, she remembered. Mr. Ritter was at an event and wouldn't be home until late. She decided that it was imperative that she bone up on her small talk. Unfortunately, her brain was complete mush. She flopped backward onto the bed and stared blankly at the ceiling, waiting for inspiration to strike.

Inspiration never came. (Billie could hardly blame it, though, if it was frightened and hiding away from all of the purple flash of the bedroom.) Before long, she was

downstairs having her so-quiet-it-was-actually-physically-painful dinner with Mrs. Ritter. In Melbourne, if Billie's family had company, they would happily treat the first night as a welcoming celebration—firing up the grill and eating some steaks (with a side of barbecued tofu for Billie, of course). The Ritters obviously handled this sort of situation much differently.

Mrs. Ritter had set the dining room table formally, with enough extra forks and side plates to confuse Billie. Billie's tactic was to keep her eye on her hostess for cues on good table manners.

Mrs. Ritter looked very much like someone who subsisted on water and lettuce vapors, so it wasn't too much of a surprise when dinner turned out to be grilled halibut, steamed vegetables, and brown rice. Billie may have been a vegetarian, but she wasn't a fitness nut or anything. In any event, she was going through the motions of eating the fish for the sake of Mrs. Ritter. It wasn't easy.

"Have you had halibut before?" Mrs. Ritter asked after she'd daintily swallowed a mouthful. Maybe she, too, felt worried by the blanket of silence that had fallen over the two of them.

"Actually, no," Billie replied. She wondered why she felt as though she needed to apologize for this fact. "My parents are firm carnivores, and they prefer red meat most of all. But I reckon it'll be cool to give it a go." She felt shy about telling Mrs. Ritter that she normally didn't eat meat.

She'd indicated on her S.A.S.S. application that she was a vegetarian, but maybe Mrs. Ritter thought for some reason that fish counted as vegetables. Whatever the reason, the slab of flaky white fish gleamed up at her from her plate. Maybe she'd expand her definition of vegetarianism to include seafood, at least for as long as she was in the States. Maybe.

"In that case, Eliza will really enjoy her time with your family," Mrs. Ritter said. She smiled a quiet little Mona Lisa smile to herself. "She hates that we don't eat red meat here at home."

Billie thought back to the photograph she'd found in her bedroom, and the glint in Eliza's eyes. She had a hard time believing that the fresh-faced, happy girl in the picture ever didn't get her way. But who knew? People were always full of surprises.

People like the Ritters were *especially* full of surprises. Billie discovered this as she and Mrs. Ritter cleared the dinner table and loaded the dishwasher. Even over the rush of tap water flowing from the kitchen sink faucet, Billie could hear a key turning in the front door of the house. Mrs. Ritter turned off the faucet, dried her hands on a dish towel, and walked out of the kitchen and toward the front hall, motioning for Billie to join her.

"Alan," she began, "Belinda is here, and she'd love to meet you."

Billie stepped forward and held out an enthusiastic hand to shake. "Most people call me Billie," she said, smiling.

"Great to meet you, Billie," Mr. Ritter said, smiling not only with his mouth but with his whole entire face. "Or should I say, G'day?" He affected an accent not unlike what it might sound like if Crocodile Dundee ran away to the Deep South. He winced as though he knew just how non-authentic he sounded, which made Billie giggle. She suspected she was in for a lot of that type of mugging, but she could rough it out.

"A for effort," she assured him, laughing. "That was ace." Already she felt closer to Mr. Ritter than to his distant, restrained wife. She could understand why he was so popular among the politicos—his enthusiasm was infectious, and he had heaps of charm.

Mr. and Mrs. Ritter offered to finish with the cleanup, and despite Billie's protests, she was relieved of kitchen duty and ordered upstairs to settle in.

Once back in her room, Billie realized how thoroughly grateful she was to have some downtime all to herself. She crawled under the covers of Eliza's bed, still wearing her clothing from dinner, and flipped open a trashy novel she'd bought at the airport in Melbourne. It wasn't the sort of book she normally read, but it had been slim pickings while she waited for her flight.

She'd made it through only three paragraphs, however, before sleep took over, and Billie lay prone, snoring lightly, her book splayed open across the front of her chest. When she awoke the next morning, she'd find herself in the same position, which she'd been in all night long.

Chapter Five

From: elizarit@email.com

To: billiesurf@email.com

Subject: the twins

So, uh, what time do they normally get up in the morning?

Booom!

Thud.

"Ahhhhhhhhhh!"

Thud.

Eliza awoke with a start.

What's going on? she thought to herself and—upon further reflection—*where am I?*

She sat straight up in bed and looked around. As she quickly took in the muted earth tones of Billie's bedroom, the events of the past day and a half flooded back to her. Light streamed through the windows. As Eliza slowly got her bearings, she was struck by a sudden fear that she'd slept all day.

She looked at her watch. Five A.M.! She flipped the covers off the bed, pulled on a pair of jeans and a T-shirt, and cautiously stepped out from the bedroom, down the hall, and into the kitchen.

"G'day, Eliza. I hope the boys didn't wake you."

Estelle smiled at her from where she stood at the range. She had an apron around her waist and a spatula in her hand, and whatever she was cooking smelled divine—greasy and salty and sweet and exactly what a person would want upon waking up in a foreign country after hearing strange and alarming noises. Not to mention, greasy goodness was the complete antithesis of everything her mom stood for. Nary a drop of cholesterol could be found in a typical Ritter family meal.

Eliza was about to ask what the twins were up to, but just then they came sprinting through the kitchen playing some form of tag.

At least that explained the thumping. And why no one else seemed at all concerned about the noise.

"I'm really sorry that I slept so late."

"It's Saturday morning and you had a big adventure yesterday. Saturday mornings are meant for catching up on rest," Estelle insisted. "Would you like some breakfast? Eggs will be up shortly, and there's toast, juice, and spreads on the table."

Eliza spied the clock over the stove. Eight A.M. She was slightly relieved to see that it was a much more reasonable hour to be getting up than she initially thought. How long had she slept? Eliza tried to do the math in her head, but it was slow going.

"Go on, sit down and dig in, love."

"Thank you." Eliza plopped down at the table and admired the array of spreads there were for the toast. She played with the dial on her watch until it was set at Melbourne time and prepared to dive into breakfast. Twelve hours of sleep was apparently just enough time to build up an appetite. She pulled a piece of toast out of a basket and laid on some butter and raspberry jelly.

"Frank is off down to Sorrento for the day, but you, me, and the twins are going to get you squared away and then show you around town while I run some errands."

"That sounds great."

Errands actually didn't sound all that great. She would have much preferred a shopping spree or a day trip to the beach. But she thought it was probably best just to go along with what was suggested. For now.

• • •

The next two days sped by in a flurry. Estelle and the twins took Eliza all over the city as they tried to give her a taste of what Melbourne had to offer—unfortunately, Eliza's taste and the Echolses' seemed to differ. A long Saturday afternoon walk through the Melbourne Botanical Gardens was pretty, but not what Eliza had in mind when she thought of freewheeling and fun-loving Australia. They had gardens in D.C., after all. Eliza wanted excitement! Adventure! Fun!

On Sunday, Ms. Echols had to do some shopping, and she decided to use that as an excuse to show Eliza the Victoria Market. It was a cavernous building that housed aisle after aisle of shops selling every type of food you could imagine. Eliza nearly lost her lunch in the butchery section at the sight of half carcasses of pigs hanging on hooks. If the Bot Gardens was a bit boring, this was downright terrifying.

She didn't get much of a look at any real "sights" as she knew them back home—things like the Air and Space Museum or the Washington Monument, but she was beginning to get the sense that Melbourne was the type of city that was made for living in and not so much for the tourists, as there were almost no "sights" to speak of.

That being said, Melbourne was a supremely inviting place with parks and shopping galore, and though she wouldn't be able to find her way back to a single location

on her own, Eliza suspected that she was going to be really psyched here—once she managed to shake her chaperones, escape the dead animals, and find some friends her own age. The Echolses were super-sweet, but she needed to have some fun with a capital *F-U-N*, stat.

"We are not here to be your friends, but to be your educators and, as such, we take our duties with great sincerity. This is a ladies' *preparatory* school and, regardless of what you are used to, you will be *prepared* for life according to our standards. Make no mistake, girls, here at St. Catherine's those standards are exceptionally high."

This could prove to be a serious *nightmare.* Eliza fought back the impulse to roll her eyes as she listened to Mrs. Connell, the headmistress of St. Catherine's school for girls, "welcome" the exchange students to orientation.

If by "welcome" you mean "terrify on pain of death."

As if this situation weren't bad enough as it was. Already this morning Eliza had been forced to submit to the indignity of dressing in a fugtastic uniform—a monstrous outfit consisting of a gray jacket with a crest, a pale blue shirt, and a gray, pleated wool skirt. It was like something her mother might wear, and a very far cry from the clothes she was used to wearing at her school back home. There, she was considered a conservative dresser since she didn't wear all black or 1980s throwbacks, which was the order of the day at her "artistically inclined" place of education.

Eliza's outfits tended to the Lacoste and Polo looks with pretty pastels, but this outfit was like someone had taken that idea and drained all the pretty from it.

A half dozen or so of her fellow exchange students sat in the room. The S.A.S.S. orientation at St. Catherine's was being held by Mrs. Connell, headmistress, and Mrs. Muldoon, the principal (though Eliza was unsure what the difference was between the two roles). Eliza knew that S.A.S.S. was a global exchange program, but it appeared that she was the only American here. The others were two girls from England—frumpy and frumpier—one from France, who refused to talk to Eliza during the break, and one from Japan, who, though sitting very attentively, seemed not to speak a word of English, as she responded to every question with a curt nod of her head and a quick "yes."

"You will all learn your class assignments from your teachers, and we expect that each of you will fulfill all the requirements just as you would at your schools at home. We will be reporting back your grades, along with any other information that may be appropriate—including behavior problems, ladies. Furthermore, you will each have to participate two days a week in your assigned internships, information about which is in your welcome packets."

Eliza knew a bit about what she was supposed to be working on down here, since it was a match to the work

Billie was doing back home. Her father specialized in marine environment and wetlands protection, and thanks to some string pulling on his part, Eliza was going to be working for a group in Melbourne that specialized in coastal ecology conservation. When she'd first read about the S.A.S.S. exchange, the idea of working outside, on the coast, had struck her immediately as a fantastic way to spend a semester. Sunshine, ocean waves, and complete freedom from her parents. At the time, it had sounded divine.

Right now, though? She was starting to have some serious doubts.

In particular, what she did not like as she scanned the welcome packet internship description was the use of the phrases "fieldwork" and "appropriate attire for inclement weather." After all, the only work her father did in the "field" back home was the occasional lunch at Ruth's Chris Steak House on Capitol Hill.

She certainly hadn't accounted for inclement weather.

But then, this was Australia, land of beach bums and surf gods. "Inclement" was probably a relative term.

Right?

"There are many wonderful activities for you to participate in, and you will have advisers to help you find your way and answer your questions," Mrs. Connell continued. "You should look forward to a fulfilling and educational time, but remember that you represent the long history of

St. Catherine's in all that you do. So equip yourself accordingly in your behavior. We do not stand for your acting as anything other than the ladies you are. No smoking, no cursing, no tardiness, no roughhousing; and for those of you staying on campus, absolutely no alcohol and no boys. Let me be clear, St. Catherine's is an educational institution for women, and gentlemen callers are not allowed on the premises."

Mrs. Connell's rules for keeping up appearances are actually not all that different from Mom and Dad's, Eliza mused to herself with a wry smile. She thought back to sneaking quick smooches with Parker by her locker and realized that even despite similarly lengthy rule books, an all-girls' school was going to take some big-time acclimation.

I know all about keeping up appearances, Eliza thought, *but right now it's time to shake things up.*

The following day was the first day back at classes after the midwinter break. Yes, the *midwinter* break. Eliza had followed the packing list that S.A.S.S. had sent her, and she had brought sweaters and jeans but, frankly, had really focused on the sundress and sandal component of her wardrobe. As much as she understood the way hemispheres worked, her brain was struggling with the idea that August was a winter month and that it would get warmer as they got near Christmas and New Year's. She

hoped the spring weather came soon because she was woefully short on cold-weather clothing.

Eliza made her way to her first class, math, without much difficulty. She had been given a school tour as part of the S.A.S.S. orientation, so she had a sense of which way was which, but it was a good deal more complicated when the halls were full of students. She stood outside the door to the math room for a moment to gather herself. She was surprised to find herself genuinely nervous.

What's going on? Come on, girl, you're going to rock this place, so pull yourself together and let's go.

Eliza took a deep breath and then, after combing her hair with her hand one last time, opened the door and entered the classroom.

The room was filled with a dozen or so girls. Row after row of neatly ironed blue shirts and snug gray blazers greeted her. The girls were gathered into a couple of small groups, with the exception of two or three wallflowers who were sitting at desks by themselves. A number of the girls sized Eliza up as she looked for an empty seat, but then returned to conversations about what they had done over the break.

Eliza decided the best course of action was to present an air of calm, cool, collected self until she deciphered the social system here. She threw her shoulders back and made her way to a chair near the windows.

Eliza may not have been the queen bee back home, but she had a comfortable, large circle of friends, and it was awkward suddenly to feel like she was the odd man out.

Well, this is a change in perspective, she thought to herself as she made her way to an empty seat.

"Oi! You the American?"

Eliza glanced over to see a tall, dark-haired girl looking at her from the next aisle over. She was backed by another girl leaning in from the chair on the far side. Both had their gray blazers tied around their waists, and the sidekick had a shock of blue hair framing the right side of her face, fading back into a brown razor cut.

It was slightly intimidating. Not that Eliza was going to let them know it.

"Um…yeah…that's me." She coughed, trying to psych herself up to sound more assured about it. "That's me."

"How you goin'?" the tall girl said. For all that her looks were kind of edgy and "bad-girl," she seemed pretty friendly.

"Excuse me?"

"How you goin'?"

"Just to the chair here. Is it taken?" Why were they looking at her so strangely?

Now both of the girls laughed in unison.

"Nah…Go on, take it," the tall girl continued, moving closer to Eliza so that she wasn't shouting across the room.

"I'm Jess, and this's Nomes." She jerked her thumb at her backup dancer.

"Hey. I'm Eliza."

"So, have you ever been to Melbourne before?"

"No, never been to Australia. I've never been west of California before."

"This is your first time out of the U.S.?" Jess asked with surprise. "A country bumpkin?"

"Oh no, not at all. I've been to South America and the Caribbean, and last year my dad took us to Paris for my mom's birthday." The words came out in a rush, and Eliza realized that after a few days with Estelle and the twins, she was sort of starved for company from girls her own age.

"No way! I totally want to go to Paris! What was it like?" Jess asked with wide eyes.

"It was totally great. I've got pics on my laptop I can show you sometime."

"That'd be cool." Jess smiled.

"I like your hair," piped up Nomes.

"What?" Eliza asked, reaching for her head. She remembered that she had twisted her hair into a bun in the back and had two ebony chopsticks with sparkles holding it in place. "Oh, this?"

"Yeah, it's cool. How do you do that?" Nomes asked.

"It's not hard, I'll show you." Eliza took out the chopsticks, shook down her hair, and with a deft flip, twist, roll, and skewer, had redone her hair perfectly.

"Right on, that's excellent. Welcome to St. Cat's."

"Thanks!" Eliza smiled. "So, this is pre-calculus, with"—Eliza checked her schedule sheet—"Mrs. Carroll?"

Jess nodded. "Carroll's cranky, but she grades easy and she doesn't like throwing too many exams."

"And then I have"—Eliza checked her sheet again—"world history."

Nomes perked up again. "Oh, I'm in that one, I'll get you there. After math I'll show you the way."

Nomes and Jess were a lot different from Eliza's friends back home, she could tell just from their brief exchange. For starters, even in a school as liberal as hers, the children of politicos were not the type to dye their hair Day-Glo colors. That mere detail made these new girls seem the tiniest bit dangerous.

Which, for Eliza, sounded just about perfect.

For the next four hours Eliza played perpetual catch-up. It was strange joining things in the middle of a year. Back home, she was friends with nearly everyone in her class. Here, nobody was rude to her or anything, but most were too consumed with finding out what each other had done over vacation to pay much mind to the new girl.

Despite some aggressive-looking piercings (one nose, three in her right ear), the blue streak in her hair, and a tiny scar above her eyebrow, Nomes turned out to be really nice, and she took Eliza under her wing for the morning.

The teachers each made a point of welcoming her, and Eliza got no end of amusement from hearing all of their Australian accents. It was hard not to like someone who spoke in that singsong. Her classes seemed pretty similar to her classes back home, and she didn't see that she would have a lot of trouble getting up to speed on the work. Eliza was a good student and always had been, much to her parents' delight.

At lunchtime, Nomes guided her through the halls to the cafeteria. They spotted Jess sitting with a couple others at a table and made their way over.

"So, how you going?" Jess smiled.

"Just here. Can we join you?"

"No," Jess said, startling Eliza. "I mean, yeah, sit down, but when someone says 'How you going?' they're not asking, 'Where are you going?'—it means 'What's up?'"

"Oh…that makes more sense." Eliza paused for a moment as all of the conversations she'd had so far that day came rushing back to her. She felt her cheeks flood with color. "I was wondering why everyone was asking me that. I told one person I was going by foot…." She rolled her eyes at her own lameness.

Jess laughed and turned to Nomes. "And you let her just humiliate herself?"

Nomes shrugged. "It was dead priceless."

Jess laughed again. "No worries," she chirped, clapping Eliza on the back, "you'll catch on."

"So you're trading with Billie Echols, right?"

"Yeah, I'm staying with her family here."

"They're in Toorak, right?" Nomes asked.

"Nah, South Yarra, I think," Jess replied.

Eliza honestly couldn't remember, and just shrugged her shoulders as she ate a slice of apple.

"I don't know for sure, but they're nice enough, and Billie and I traded a couple e-mails as well," she said.

"Yeah, they're good people." Jess nodded. "We all went to middle school together, but Billie's kind of into the whole eco-warrior thing—she's always off at rallies or getting people to sign petitions for the 'Save the Wombat' or whatever. It's good stuff, just gets to be a bit much sometimes, I guess. That's her best mate Val over there." Jess pointed to a girl sitting a couple tables away who was wearing her uniform with Crocs. With socks underneath.

Dad's going to love Billie, Eliza realized. *They'll be able to talk "Save the Whales" for hours.* While Billie definitely wasn't part of Jess's group, Eliza also realized that St. Catherine's was a pretty small school, and everyone seemed to know everyone else pretty well.

"Billie's dad is a riot, isn't he?" asked Nomes. "He's a bit of a bogan turned city boy."

"What's a bogan?" asked Eliza.

"Someone from the country."

Eliza nodded, trying to commit the new slang term to memory.

The rest of lunch was spent talking about boys and shopping—two subjects Eliza felt very at home with, even if she didn't know the boys in question. It seemed that there were several boys' schools in Melbourne and that the girls had a pretty elaborate ranking system of where the cutest guys were.

It also turned out that the Echolses lived in a great location, near one of the best shopping areas, and the girls all made a plan to spend some time over the weekend exploring the finer points of Chapel Street's stores.

Eliza decided that, as first days went, this one had been pretty successful.

Over the course of her first week, Eliza slowly began to feel more at home with her schedule and her surroundings. She learned how to take the tram to and from school each morning and would meet up with Jess each day a couple of stops from her own so that they could chat the whole way to school. Eliza found that she had some precious information about what was happening on upcoming seasons of TV shows like *Gossip Girl* and *Lost* because they hadn't aired down under yet. By the end of the week, she felt really comfortable with Jess and Nomes.

At lunch on Friday, Eliza was hoping she'd be invited to do something fun with them over the weekend when she remembered that she was going to have to start her internship on Saturday.

"This totally sucks," Eliza moaned as she bit into her tuna fish sandwich. "I can't believe that I have to spend my whole Saturday at this stupid internship."

"Well, the orientation is this Saturday, but usually it won't be, right?" asked Nomes, who was eyeing her tray of cafeteria food with great suspicion.

"Not sure. Some of it's going to be after school on Wednesdays, but we'll have to do a couple of full days over the weekend here and there," Eliza replied dejectedly. "I have to do the environmental internship because of my dad, but I guess it could be worse—after all, it's a day down at the beach, right?"

Jess and Nomes chuckled.

"What?" Eliza implored.

"Nothing, nothing at all. You'll have a rippa' at the beach!" Jess said with a toothy grin.

When Eliza had pictured Australian beaches, she'd imagined a tropical paradise lined with gently swaying palm trees and possibly an Australian lifeguard hottie to play Frisbee with or to help her apply her suntan lotion.

But what Eliza got instead was a rocky coastline in the port of Melbourne backlit by factories with not a palm tree in sight.

And the lifeguard? Oh no, there was no such hottie. Instead, there was Mr. Winstone, a thin man in his fifties with a bushy mustache, hairy earlobes, and a

very questionable enthusiasm for unpleasant work and unpleasant weather.

The other problem was that since she'd been in Melbourne, the weather had not climbed above about 10 degrees Celsius. Ten degrees Celsius itself didn't mean much to Eliza, but a little Googling determined that, in fact, it was 50 degrees Fahrenheit that day at the "beach." So therefore it was more like a sandy, surfy tundra. A sandy, surfy, *rainy* tundra. It was the middle of winter, after all.

But interning waited for no exchange student, and thus Eliza found herself standing on a cold, windswept rocky beach under gray clouds, wearing rubber waders and a rain slicker and holding a plastic collection jar in one hand.

This stinks. Eliza was shivering down to her waders.

"Four seasons in a day we get 'round here," Mr. Winstone said with a wink.

"Really...that's amazing. All four?" It was amazing. In a bad way.

She glared at her collection jar. Apparently part of her responsibilities included taking soil samples and testing them for mineral levels, which would determine the rate of potential erosion. In all honesty, it was a nice counterpoint to the work Eliza's father was doing at the EPA, which, while all *about* the environment, didn't seem to involve much time spent in the environment.

"Now make sure you try to get at least one jar of each

of the types of soils listed on your sample sheet, okay?"
Mr. Winstone reminded Eliza and the four other students.
"You'll be collecting from different areas of the shoreline
so that we can compare and contrast. I'll then take all the
samples back to the lab, and we'll get a better picture of
how pollution is affecting the erosion of our ocean ecosys-
tem—including the creatures that live all through the tidal
zones of the bay."

Eliza spent her day scraping grains of sand into glass
jars, trying her best to muster up the enthusiasm the other
interns seemed to have. But eco-warrior she was not, and
by the time it was over, she was soaked through with rain
and seawater and chilled to the bone.

It wasn't the worst day of her life, but one thing was for
sure: there was *no way* she was going to get a tan of any
sort if this kept up.

At least the weather was only going to get better as the
semester went along. All she had to do was look at the
palm trees that lined the edge of the bay and think warm
thoughts.

"Oh, you poor dear. Let me get you a cuppa and some
bickies while you get changed into some warm clothes,"
Estelle cooed when she saw Eliza standing in the kitchen
sopping wet.

After she'd changed into fresh clothes and warmed
herself over a cup of mint tea, Eliza started to feel a bit

more like a human being. Her fingers were less numb, though they still looked like prunes.

She decided to ask Estelle about something that had been on her mind all day. "Who planted those palm trees by the boardwalk that we passed in the car?" she asked.

Those were lying palm trees. Trees that made you think a beach was a place of sun, warmth, cute boys, and volleyballs. Those palm trees were an insidious form of false advertising by very sick people—that was for sure.

"You mean in St. Kilda?"

"Yes, I think so. That was a joke, right? I mean, palm trees aren't really native to the area, are they? They were planted by the tourist office or something to convince the world that it's warm and sunny all the time, right?" Call her paranoid, but Eliza suspected a conspiracy at work. How else would she have ended up doing her impression of a drowned wombat with the rest of the environmental crusaders?

Estelle laughed. "I suppose it's possible. Rose-colored glasses and the like. But just you wait until things warm up and we head down to Sorrento; it's magnificent. Hang in there, and the winter will be over soon."

Eliza drew another sip of her tea, quiet and thoughtful. *Not soon enough,* she decided. *Not at all.*

Chapter Six

It was bright and early on Saturday morning when Billie cautiously peeled open her eyes. She allowed herself a suspicious glance at the digital alarm clock on the nightstand: 9:30. That meant it was…hmm…around eleven at night back home. No wonder she felt like she'd been hit by a train.

At first, she had no idea why she was even awake—clearly, her internal clock had gone completely screwy from her journey. Then she realized what had roused her: it was the static-y murmur of talk radio floating up into the bedroom from the kitchen.

The Ritters were up. And apparently, eager-beaver early birds. Mrs. Ritter was almost like a caricature of herself. Even her morning radio was no-nonsense.

Groaning, Billie reluctantly sat up and swung her legs around onto the floor. On a scale of one to ten, her desire to be up was something like a two. She knew it was smarter to pull herself out of bed now, though. The harder she was on herself, the faster the jet lag would be over.

She dressed quickly in her track pants, trainers, and a hooded sweatshirt, hoping to head out for a run. From what she'd been able to tell the night before, D.C. was a bit more humid than she was used to. Thank goodness she wasn't the type to fuss all that much about her appearance; a swipe of lippie and a finger-comb of the hair, and she was good to go.

Downstairs, she was pleased to find Mr. Ritter manning a frying pan. Frying pans were usually good news.

"I figured you might be homesick," he said, seeing Billie come into the room, "so I thought I'd scramble you some bangers and mash."

"Thanks heaps, Mr. Ritter," Billie said appreciatively, "but…actually…aren't bangers and mash English?"

"Could be," Mr. Ritter responded cheerily. "To be totally honest, I'm not even really sure what they are. So I was just going to give you some scrambled eggs and toast and keep my fingers crossed."

Billie giggled. "Scrambled eggs sounds perfect. A proper American brekkie." She took her seat at the table and glanced across it to where Mrs. Ritter was drinking from a mug almost as large as a dinner plate. It looked as though the mug was brimming with black coffee, and she didn't appear to be eating anything.

"Aren't you going to have some?" Billie asked, spearing up a healthy portion of the eggs that Mr. Ritter slid in front of her.

Mrs. Ritter shook her head quickly, making a face that suggested that eating breakfast was a sin on the scale of baby snatching, jaywalking, or indulging in full-fat frozen yogurt. "I'm off to yoga in a minute. Can't work out on a full stomach."

"Yup," Mr. Ritter chimed in. "It's a regular old Saturday here at the homestead. The missus has yoga, and I've got to head in to work."

Wow. Billie was amazed. Mr. Ritter really was every bit as hardworking and idealistic as she had assumed. She was so thrilled to have the chance to work in his organiza-tion—and possibly even alongside of him—this summer!

"Is there anything that I can do?" Billie asked brightly. "I mean, I know that the internship doesn't start properly until Monday, but if you'd like a shadow in the office today, I'd love to be of help."

"Nonsense," Mr. Ritter proclaimed. "After the intern-ship starts in earnest, you're going to miss having your

weekends. You should enjoy yourself while you still can."

Billie nodded. "There were a few things I was hoping to see." She blushed, thinking of her guidebook stashed away in a desk drawer upstairs. The thing had so many highlights and colored stickies it looked more like a maths textbook.

Okay, so maybe she was a little bit gung ho about this program. She was a nerd in crunchy clothing. What was wrong with that?

"Well, why not start at the top and work your way down?" Mr. Ritter suggested. "My office is on the Hill, so I can give you a lift."

Billie knew that "the Hill" was short for Capitol Hill, which was where many of the important government buildings were located. It was definitely the number one stop on her self-guided tour of the area.

She grinned broadly at Mr. Ritter. "Ace," she said. "As long as there's time for me to take a quick run beforehand, you've got a deal."

After Billie and Mr. Ritter parted company, she gave some thought to where she might like to visit this afternoon. It was yet another crisp fall day, and so her love of the outdoors won out. Therefore, a stroll across the mall was called for.

She glanced at her dog-eared guidebook, embarrassed at looking like a gawking tourist. She read that the Mall had been officially established in 1965, which was funny to think, since in her mind, the image of the vast expanse of grass was synonymous with Washington, D.C., itself. It was hard to imagine that there'd ever been a time without it.

Billie smiled and took in the cloudless blue sky and the crisp snap in the fall air. She was so excited she thought she might jump up and down, but realized how silly she'd look if she did. She felt lame. Totally and completely lame.

She had good reason to feel that way; at the moment, in addition to the goofy smile she had plastered across her face, she was being twenty different types of conspicuous, the way she kept glancing at her guidebook, and squinting across the lush lawn. She had a sudden urge to peel off her socks and shoes and run across it barefoot, but she had a feeling that that would really make her stick out like the proverbial sore thumb. Not to mention, it was possibly illegal.

I'm practically begging to be pickpocketed, she decided at last, coming to her senses and remembering that she'd read D.C. could be dangerous. She stashed her guidebook back into her messenger bag before something was nicked, and resolved to find her way around through sheer determination. The Washington Monument reared up in the distance on the far end of the Mall, framed in Billie's view like an image from a postcard. She headed across the Mall and toward it. That much, at least, she could handle without a guidebook.

• • •

At first, Billie thought that the most exciting thing she'd seen in D.C. was the exterior of the White House (apparently you needed to book a tour of the interior in advance, which she planned to do as soon as she could). Then she visited the Smithsonian National Museum of American History, and laid her eyes on the original ruby slippers that Judy Garland had worn in the movie *The Wizard of Oz*. So for a while, that was number one on her list of amazing sights. Then she wandered through the International Spy Museum, where she had a chance to develop her own spy "alias" and cover story, which immediately bumped the ruby slippers out of the running.

Eventually, Billie had to admit to herself that, all in all, her first weekend in D.C. had been fairly fantastic and there was no use in putting absolutes on the experience when it'd all been great, anyway.

Also great was a run-of-the-mill Starbucks in Dupont Circle, which proved very useful in combating Billie's incredibly persistent jet lag. She'd been jogging to Starbucks on two consecutive mornings now before the sun rose too high in the sky, relishing the alone time, the fresh air—and the java fix.

Now it was Monday, and Billie's first day at Fairlawn Academy. She had no idea what to expect. Back in Melbourne, Billie attended St. Catherine's. St. Cat's was all-girls, and had a required uniform. Billie longed for that uniform right about now. She had tried on three separate outfits this morning, worrying about her fashion sense, and becoming extra sensitive when she realized she was now trying to impress both the girls *and* the guys.

She finally settled on a denim skirt, boots, and a long-sleeved polo shirt. It was a uniform of sorts itself in that it looked like something any other American girl might wear. Or so Billie thought. She supposed she'd just have to wait and see.

She arrived at school early; she was laid-back like the typical Aussie, but she was responsible, as well, and she didn't want to miss her S.A.S.S. orientation conference, which was scheduled for eight-thirty sharp.

She congratulated herself on her punctuality as she made her way to the guidance counselor's office on the first floor, only to discover that the guidance counselor in question looked as though he'd been in his seat, at his desk, waiting on her, for at least the last ten years. Although of course that couldn't possibly have been the case, something about his pallor and his heavy-lidded gaze suggested he, in fact, spent most of his time in his office.

"Ah, you must be Belinda." A slight man, he pushed his horn-rimmed glasses farther up the bridge of his nose as he peered at her over a sheet of paper. She knew the paper was some sort of background information on her, and she

wondered what else, aside from her name, it might say.

"That's me," she said. "G'day. But everyone back home calls me Billie."

Her accent, which she'd never noticed much before, now sounded thick and exaggerated, like a record played at the wrong speed.

"Well, welcome to Fairlawn, Billie," he amended affably. "I'm Eric Roger, and I'm the guidance counselor here at school. I also oversee our S.A.S.S. Goes Green program.

"I've prepared a handbook to help you acclimate," he continued, passing Billie an immense sheaf of paper.

Handbook? It looked more like a telephone book, it was so thick. Billie didn't want to be ungrateful, but she already had a binder full of papers from S.A.S.S. Were they trying to smother her with a crush of flyers?

"The one thing that I'd like to stress to you is that Fairlawn may be very different from what you're used to back home. We're a progressive liberal arts school, which means that many of our students are artists of one form or another. We have a strong interdisciplinary program featuring dance, creative writing, music, and drama, in addition to the general education requirements of the state."

Billie took a moment or two to zone out. She knew all about Fairlawn. In fact, half the reason that she'd applied was that their curriculum was challenging, but "self-designed." "Self-designed" was apparently code

for "spend all day working on whatever you so choose."
Hence, her internship.

Eric wasn't finished. "Students here are free to express
themselves creatively, in almost any way that they choose.
In fact, we have no dress code here; as long as you're not
undressed, you're fine. So you may see that kids take certain, ah…fashion risks that maybe you didn't find at your
school back home."

He meant that they all wore black, pierced their noses,
and dyed their hair green. She'd visited the school Web
site before coming, after all. Just as long as no one held
her down and tattooed her against her will, she reckoned
she'd be fine. After all, prim and proper Eliza Ritter went
to Fairlawn, didn't she? And she hardly seemed to be the
piercing type, unless you were talking about ears. Actually,
Fairlawn had a reputation for being one of the very best
schools in the area, which Billie suspected had a lot to do
with why Eliza was enrolled there. And Eliza couldn't have
been the only student to attend Fairlawn for the education
as much as for the arts appreciation.

"Classes are small, and many of the students have
known each other since as early as nursery school. It's not
uncommon for exchange students to feel edged out. But I
assure you that if you're patient, and you make the effort,
you will develop some rich and rewarding bonds during
your time here this semester."

Okay, so in summation, Eric had just basically warned her that kids dressed like weirdos, that classes were, well, fluid in their execution, and that nobody exactly embraced outsiders into the fold.

This semester was suddenly sounding much more inauspicious than Billie had at first thought.

Well, there was no point in whining about it, she decided. She was a friendly, outgoing girl, and she'd do her best to meet people in this new school. She knew from experience—*recent* experience, in particular, if the plane ride over was to be counted—that Americans were suckers for an accent, so at least she had that on her side.

Or so she hoped.

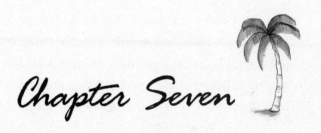

Chapter Seven

From: elizarit@email.com

To: billiesurf@email.com

Subject: Fairlawn

Hi Billie!

About Fairlawn, your first impressions are hilarious—and correct. It's true, people there are definitely "creative." I always thought it was funny to watch. Obviously, I'm a little more conservative...and most of my friends are, too. Which, so far, has been the complete opposite of the girls I've met down here! Do you know Jess and Nomes? They

told me they know who you are, but that you mostly hang with the outdoorsy crowd. Craziness! For me, outdoors is the place you go when you're walking from the Gap to Banana Republic....

Talk soon.

Eliza

Monday came around and Eliza found herself surprisingly eager to get back to the girls at school. Between the ill-fated beachcombing for her internship and the never-ending mayhem of the twins, she was ready to spend time with people her own age in a dry and warm room—even if that room was a classroom. The Monday morning pre-calculus classroom, to be precise.

First-thing-in-the-morning math should be illegal, Eliza thought as she made her way to class.

"Oi! Zazza," someone yelled as she entered.

It took Eliza's brain a second to process her newly appointed nickname. She had quickly discovered that everyone, and that meant *everyone,* down here had nick-names. It made it very confusing when it came to introductions. Naomi was Nomes, Belinda was Billie, and now Eliza was Zazza. Everyone would introduce themselves with their proper name but refer to one another by nicknames, and for a while it felt to Eliza like there were twice as many people everywhere she went.

Eliza whipped her head up to see Jess and Nomes

waving from the back corner. She wound her way over to them, pleased to have made friends in her new school.

"How was the weekend?" Jess asked as Eliza settled into her seat.

"Cold," Eliza admitted. "This internship at the beach isn't what I had in mind."

"Oh mate, nobody goes to the beach this time of year." Jess snorted to indicate just how lame a person would have to be to consider otherwise. "Unless," she relented, considering, "you're going to the Espy."

"Espy?" Eliza asked.

"The Esplanade," Nomes said. "The best place to see bands in Melbourne and a good spot for tuning."

"I see," said Eliza, though she didn't. She made a mental note to ask Billie about "tuning" in her next e-mail.

"We're going to check out some shops up on Brunswick Street tomorrow arvo if you're interested," Jess said, interrupting Eliza's train of thought.

Being invited to go shopping was way more exciting than having a seat saved in class. It was like a whole different level in the friendship hierarchy. Eliza perked up, then deflated when she realized that this was probably out of the question.

"That'd be great," she began, "but I think my host family is expecting me home after school to help out with the twins. I've got the internship two days a week and am responsible for babysitting two other days. That just leaves

Friday evenings." It killed her to say those words out loud, but she thought she should try to stay out of trouble while she was abroad—for the first couple weeks, at least. Even if that meant putting a pin in her whole "newfound independence" campaign.

"That will never do; we've got to get you out of this," Jess said, clucking her tongue thoughtfully. She drummed her fingers against her desk in contemplation. "What about if you say you're doing house activities or something?"

"I don't know, I guess I hadn't thought about that." Eliza didn't want to admit that the reason that she hadn't thought of "house activities" was that she was relatively unclear on what they were. *Probably the same thing as "extracurriculars" back home,* she decided.

"You don't have to be living in the campus dorms to be in house activities?" Eliza asked.

"No," Nomes chimed in, "so why don't you tell them you're joining a sport?"

Eliza mulled it over in her mind for a minute—probably a minute longer than she should—but finally felt common sense taking hold.

"I don't know, guys. I think I should probably just stick with the plan for the moment. If my dad found out I was ditching school, he'd go through the roof. Can we do it Friday after school? Then I'm totally free and I really want to hit the shops."

"All right, ya piker," Jess said. "No worries, but we're taking you around on Friday, no excuses."

"Definitely," Eliza said with a grin.

Definitely.

Eliza couldn't wait for Friday to arrive and, when it did, she was bursting at the seams to get out and see the city. The last four days had consisted of going to school, mucking around in the bay (she had become strangely efficient at prying mollusks off rocks), and trying to keep the twins from tearing the house to shreds while Estelle took classes for a master's degree two evenings a week.

But now the weekend had come. The three o'clock bell had rung and she, Nomes, and Jess had made their way to a shopping center on Chapel Street a few minutes from school.

You have got to be kidding me.

I have traveled a hundred bajillion miles, spent two days sitting on planes, and have moved into another family's home, and after all that, I am now standing in front of a…

T.G.I. Friday's?

Eliza was utterly surprised to find herself in the much-hyped Jam Factory shopping center, where in front of her was the afore-mentioned T.G.I. Friday's, and flanking it was a Virgin Megastore and a Borders.

It was almost like being back home. Unfortunately.

"Really, you brought me to see this?" she asked Jess. Next they were probably going to eat at McDonald's. "You do know we have shopping malls back home, right? Heck, I think they were actually *invented* by us—and these stores, they're all American, too."

"Actually, I do believe that Virgin is British," Jess said with panache, rolling her *R* to emphasize the British accent she used. "Nomes wanted a CD, then we're going up to Brunswick Street, and you can stop your bellyaching."

"Okay. But I'm pretty sure T.G.I. Friday's is American." She smirked.

"Shut up and just come on."

"Aye aye, *mate*."

After Nomes had found her CD, they walked back to Toorak Road and waited at the tram stop.

Eliza had come to love the trams even in the short time she had been in Australia. The Metro in D.C. was deep underground, and the long escalators creeped her out. The trams, on the other hand, cruised on tracks down just about every major avenue with arms that reached up to grab the power lines overhead. Riding them meant you got to see the city going by but, unlike with a bus, there was never any traffic to hold you up.

The three girls boarded one of the old-fashioned trams with the wooden interiors that ran on some of the lines, found seats at the back, and gossiped their way across the city. Eliza tried to take in as much of the landscape as she could while chatting with the girls. She recognized the Royal Botanic Gardens, and the view of the Yarra River as they crossed over near Flinders Station was beautiful. The late-afternoon light sparkled on the water as the tram sped across the bridge and then *whooshed* up the avenue in front of Parliament.

Twenty minutes later they exited the tram at Elgin Street in an area that looked a lot like some of what she'd seen on her way in from the airport.

"Is that the university there?"

"Yeah, that's uni, and those fancy-looking buildings are the residential colleges. You want to take a look? There's the footy pitch inside there."

"Can we?" Eliza was curious. She thought "footy" probably meant soccer, and "pitch" meant "field," but she decided to wait until she had a visual for confirmation.

Jess checked her watch. "Yeah, but then we should hoof it if we want to get some time at Brunswick Street and still get you home for dinner."

They crossed the street and cut down a little access road and onto the university grounds. Soon they came to a wide-open area rimmed on one side by the industrial buildings of the university and on the other three by a sweeping oval bounded by the residential colleges. They stood on a small rise in the center and looked around.

Eliza could see a bunch of guys in matching sleeveless

sports jerseys, shorts, and knee-high socks running back and forth on a large oval field with stands on one side. She was impressed that they were willing to be out in 45-degree weather without sleeves. She, by contrast, was pleasantly bundled up, including a very cute wool-cap-and-scarf ensemble she was proud to be sporting.

Every so often one guy on the field would break from the pack and sprint down the lawn, bouncing what looked like an American football on the ground every few paces, before finally kicking it down the field. There, another group of guys would leap into the air and start grabbing and punching for the ball. It all seemed to be little more than controlled chaos.

"What're they playing?" she finally asked.

"It's Aussie Rules," said Nomes. "Greatest game on the planet."

"Don't get her started." Jess snorted. "I can't stand the game. Don't see what everyone sees in it."

"Bloody oath! What's not to like? Cute boys getting all sweaty…"

Eliza had to admit, there were some good-looking guys on the field. They spent a few more minutes appreciating the view until Jess broke in.

"Come on, guys, put your tongues back in your mouths and let's get moving." She led them off back toward Elgin Street. "We'll find Eliza a good bloke soon enough," she said, her eyes twinkling with promise. "That is, if you're over Mr. Parker yet...but for now, it's shopping."

Eliza was fine with that. The shopping...*and the bloke hunting.* Melbourne was *way* too interesting to be worried about people back home.

Jess said it was about a kilometer walk, and Eliza furrowed her brow as she tried to figure out what that meant from an effort perspective.

What's a kilometer?

She knew what a kilometer was, of course—it was distance. But...how *much* distance? Suddenly she realized why Ms. Isaacs, her eighth-grade science teacher, had insisted they would one day need to know what the metric system was. Sadly, Eliza had used that opportunity to learn to text message underneath her desk.

A quick ten-minute walk from the uni landed them on Brunswick Street (it turned out a kilometer was definitely less than a mile). Both sides of the street were lined with low, two-story buildings, and in the ground floor of each one was a funky boutique, a bar, or a restaurant. Down the middle of the road ran a tramway. This was kind of what Eliza imagined Sunset Strip in Los Angeles to be like—but more, well, *Australian.*

She wasn't quite sure how to define "Australian," but she could just sense it. Back in D.C., people were loud,

brash, aggressive. Here, it was more laid-back, with people strolling casually and even making eye contact on the street!

You did *not* make eye contact on the street in Washington. And people didn't stroll—more like strode, with purpose. People in the Northeast were usually in some kind of big, important hurry.

They traipsed along as Eliza eyed the shops. She wanted to try on every single thing they had for sale. Washington had Adams Morgan as its cool, funky neighborhood, but even that was getting super-trendy and yuppified. And it wasn't just the Aussie clothes that Eliza loved. The staff was all friendly and smiling, crowing "G'day" every time they walked in. Back in D.C. everyone took themselves so seriously. In Melbourne, it seemed, no one took *anything* too seriously.

The girls went from shop to shop investigating the wares on offer. They browsed the racks at a vintage clothing store where Jess tried on a pair of flared jeans that hung perfectly on her hips. Eliza found a very cute blousy top to wear over jeans when the weather turned a bit warmer. They picked through the offerings in a funky little jewelry shop where Nomes grabbed a pair of dangly earrings with some sort of purple stones in them.

Too quickly, however, evening was approaching, and the girls had to find their way back home. Eliza stuffed her new shirt in her school bag, and they hopped a tram through downtown, back over the bridge just after dark, and on into South Yarra and Toorak, where they parted.

Eliza found herself alone on the tram for the last few stops. As she looked at the people walking along Toorak Road, heading into restaurants for dinner, she thought back on what a great day she had had. It hadn't taken long for her to make great friends, she loved Melbourne already, and she didn't miss suffocating D.C. one bit.

The following week passed quickly for Eliza. After spending a day of her internship up to her thighs in the muck of the bay collecting enough specimen jars to start her own museum, she had caught a pretty good head cold.

But she'd recovered quickly and now was looking forward to spending a Saturday afternoon with her new friends.

She met Jess at the tram stop, and the two rode all the way down to the beach at St. Kilda. There, they walked to the Espy—the famous Esplanade Hotel—to listen to some bands. It was a gray afternoon, and there was a strong wind blowing from the sea. As they strolled easily along the boardwalk, Eliza noted the palm trees she had complained about to Estelle. They waved so...*tropically*...mocking her. The imposters.

"Stupid palm trees."

"What's that?" Jess asked.

"Nothing..." Eliza shivered, but she tried not to let it

show. "I'm just glad I'm by the bay this Saturday and not in it."

They crossed the street and hopped up the steps of a big, old Victorian building. They opened the front door to a blast of music and voices from the inside. It was warm and inviting, the music sounded rocking, and in they went.

The place was crowded. Jess led the way toward a back room with a small stage and some old velvet couches lining the walls. The music from the band in the front room faded, and they found an empty couch with a couple chairs across from it and sat down. Jess pulled out her cell phone and rang Nomes.

"We're in the back room. It's crowded as all get out, but we'll save some seats for you. When are you getting here?" She paused and then rolled her eyes and made a hand-puppet yapping symbol with her free hand, smiling to Eliza.

"Right, see you in a few." She snapped the phone shut.

"Oi, the girl can yammer on something fierce. So, you stay put, and I'll get us some drinks." Jess tucked her cell phone back into her handbag.

At the mention of "drinks," Eliza suddenly realized that there was one small problem with Jess's plan: she didn't think her friend was talking about lemonade or iced tea. The drinking age in Australia was eighteen, and though Eliza had tried on various occasions to procure ID, she'd never been able to get her hands on one. Thus, drinking was, regrettably, off the table for her this evening. She sadly shared that fact with Jess, who promptly threw back her head and laughed.

"That won't be a problem, mate. Nobody has fake ID here. We don't need it. You Americans are so prudish about some things. Just sit tight and guard our seats, okay?" She grinned.

Eliza nodded and spread out their coats to cover as much of the empty seating as possible. She sat back and picked an invisible piece of lint off of her jeans. This afternoon's wardrobe had required careful consideration. She had told the Echolses that she was spending the day with the girls, but she hadn't said they were going to a club; thus, she had needed something that could be covered up when she left the house, so as not to arouse suspicion, but would be suitably flattering should they encounter any members of the male of the species. She wasn't sure that they would be mad, necessarily, but she felt like perhaps a sin of omission was the best policy. In the end, she'd settled on jeans, which looked nondescript enough underneath her jacket, and a fitted black sweater, which, once her jacket was removed, made the outfit a bit sexier.

Frankly, she realized that it was pretty similar to what she would have picked had they just been going shopping, but maybe with a little extra dollop of "oomph."

"Oomph" turned out to be a good thing. It wasn't long before someone approached.

"Are these seats taken?"

Eliza had been lost in thought. She jumped a little, startled, and recomposed herself, slightly embarrassed. She looked up to see the very vision of an Australian guy—which was to say, a mess of rumpled, dirty-blond curls, his eyes a sparkling shade of deep brown.

"Um, yes, I'm sorry, but I think they are," Eliza said, really meaning it. At that moment she would have gladly sacrificed her friendship with Jess for a chance to sit next to Mr. Aussie-bloke.

"You *think* they are?" He seemed amused by her uncertainty.

"No, well, yes, they are taken. My friends and I are sitting here."

He looked to her left, and then her right, raising a quizzical eyebrow. Clearly he thought her friends were of the imaginary variety. "It looks like it's just you sitting here."

Eliza blushed. "Well, they're coming. One's at the bar and the other will be here any minute."

She was flattered by the attention, and a little flustered as well, which didn't happen often. She didn't want to chase him off, and thankfully was saved the decision as Jess returned.

"Hamish Bloody MacGreggor! Get your good-for-nuthin' mitts off my mate there!"

He's Jess's friend? And also—his name's Hamish?

"Hey, Jess. I didn't know you guys were together. She

kept saying that she had all of these mates, but I thought she was just playing hard to get."

"Yes, we are, she was, and keep your paws off." Jess smiled.

He held his arms up in a "Who, me?" pose. "I was just looking for an empty seat," he protested. "No paws, I swear," and he winked at Eliza. She had to hide a smile.

"Hamish, meet Eliza. She's from America on exchange." Jess gestured from Hamish to Eliza by way of introduction.

He stuck his hand out. "I'm Hamish, but everyone calls me Macca."

Macca? It was almost as bad as Hamish. He was lucky he was such a hottie.

"Macca? Like McDonald's?" Eliza tried not to giggle as their palms made contact and they shook hands. Jeez, one cute guy and she was totally dorking out.

Macca tilted his head back and drained the rest of his beer. "No, ma'am. It's Macca as in MacGreggor—and no self-respecting MacGreggor would be caught dead near a louse like a McDonald. You got that?"

"Okay, Braveheart." Eliza gave her most winning sunny grin and folded her arms across her chest. *Check and mate.*

"Fair enough, but this William Wallace is out of grog and is heading to the bar." He smiled right back at her and gave a wink.

And that's the game.

She'd never met a guy like this back home. Of course, most of that was because Hamish was clearly so über-Australian, in addition to being a hugely cocky flirt. But it was more than that. He was rugged and outgoing in a way that the boys back at Fairlawn weren't. In a way that Parker wasn't, for sure. Most of the Fairlawnians thought black was the new black and listened only to Emo bands with male lead singers in eyeliner. And even though Parker was more like Eliza and her group—in other words, practically a walking Gap ad—that only made the contrast between him and Macca all the sharper.

And Parker was on hold for now, anyway.

Upon mutual agreement, they squished their seats together and dragged some more chairs over so there'd be room for them all. Macca and a couple of his friends sat with them while they waited for Nomes to show up. Jess gave Eliza a little wink as Macca slid in next to her.

They tried to keep up the conversation despite the music blaring in the background. It turned out that Macca was a senior at Geelong Grammar, a school in a city a little south of Melbourne, but his parents lived in Toorak, pretty near the Echolses. In fact, he even knew Billie—they'd surfed together as kids, he said.

Oh man, he's a surfer. Eliza thought back to a brief obsession with surfers based on the TV show *Laguna*

Beach. Now there was absolutely zero chance that she'd escape a big-time crush. She was a total goner.

The musicians had, by now, taken the stage and were starting their set. As the band launched into its first song, Eliza sat back, happy to be holed up in the Espy next to an Australian surfer demi god. She smiled to herself.

This semester is getting better by the minute....

Chapter Eight

Although many of the clichés about America were obviously true, Billie had found that at least one—that all Americans were completely high-strung and neurotic—didn't seem to be. The Americans whom Billie encountered at Fairlawn that first morning were decidedly *un*-neurotic. In fact, they were so thoroughly chilled out that she thought some of them might even be asleep. It almost made her chuckle; Australians were always known for their "no worries" attitude, but this school was so hippie-dippie that the mood in the air went way beyond "no worries." This was more like "no pulse."

She found her way to her "homeroom" without any trouble. Homeroom was apparently what Americans called the first class of the day. You didn't learn anything in homeroom, though—it was just the place where teachers took attendance and made any sort of school-wide announcements. Billie decided that she would remember the meaning of homeroom by thinking of it more as "home base." To her, that made much more sense.

Billie was the only S.A.S.S. student at Fairlawn, which might have made her feel self-conscious, but even though she was an introvert by nature, she actually wasn't shy in the least (awkward conversations with Mrs. Ritter notwithstanding). As if to prove her point, she smiled at the girl who slid into the seat beside her.

"G'day," she said, grinning. "I'm Billie Echols."

"You must be our exchange student," the girl replied. "Whose house are you staying at?"

"I'm with the Ritters," Billie said proudly. She still couldn't quite believe that she'd been assigned to work for the number one eco-warrior in the world. Or, at the very least, in the American government.

"Nice," the girl said to her, nodding approvingly. "Although I think Mrs. Ritter is sort of like the diet police."

Billie shrugged, thinking back to the brown rice and bland fish. "I can be sneaky. Especially when it comes to something as urgent as biscuits." At the girl's blank look, she explained, "You know, bickies. Biscuits…cookies!"

"Right." The girl smiled. "Your accent's awesome."

What is it with Americans and accents? Billie smiled.

"I'm Heather, by the way," the girl continued. "Heather Small. I'm going to intern next semester. But I don't know where yet."

"Gotcha," Billie said. "So everyone at this school has to intern?"

"For at least one semester of high school," Heather confirmed. "It's sorta one of the only real rules this place has."

"It does seem very…touchy-feely." Billie laughed, hoping that she wasn't offending her maybe, sort-of new friend. But Heather just grinned in agreement. Billie felt even warmer toward her.

"What can you tell me about Eliza?" she asked boldly. "The only things I've been able to suss, based on her bedroom, are that she likes purple, and that she likes cable TV. Oh!" Her eyes widened as she remembered one other juicy detail. "And there was a bloke in one of her pictures. Someone she was pashing with?"

"If 'pashing' is Australian for 'smooching,' then yes, the *bloke* was probably her boyfriend, Parker," Heather explained. "Parker Green. He's great—really a friendly, nice guy. Everyone here at school likes him."

"Sounds perfect," Billie mused. Her experience with boys thus far had been minimal. She had lots of guy friends, and even a few crushes here or there, but nothing major. Nothing official. In fact, maybe that should have been one of her goals for her time in the United States: to pine after a boy (and vice versa)? "Pining" sounded incredibly romantic.

"Yeah, I guess. Though I'm not sure how thrilled he is that Eliza suggested they take a break while she's away. I mean, he still puts on his merry sunshine front. But it's, like, I think he doth protest too much. And, he'd never admit it, but he has been a little bit cranky about newspaper deadlines since Eliza left." Heather rolled her eyes to show what she thought of this sort of behavior. "We're on the paper together," she explained. "So I try to keep him in check. Boys can be so dramatic, you know?"

Billie just nodded vaguely. She actually *didn't* know, and she didn't really want to go advertising that fact. Like pining, drama was something else that could be romantic, even if it was a little bit annoying.

"Oh!" Heather exclaimed, as though just remembering something. "You'll meet Parker. He's doing the Ritter internship, too." She lowered her voice. "Also a scandal—he and Eliza were set to do it together, until she decided to skip town, instead."

Billie's eyes widened. That *did* sound scandalous. Was it wrong that she found it kind of intriguing as well?

Of course, now that she had some more background on Parker, she was all the more eager to meet him. The idea that she had in her head of Eliza was a strange one; it was almost like they were long-lost twins, in the way that

91

they were literally exchanging lifestyles with each other for the term. But the composite of Eliza's self that Billie had cobbled together was based on only a few flimsy context clues. Eliza's American persona was a mystery that Billie was excited to learn more about.

In the end, it turned out that Billie and Parker were actually in chemistry class together. Science was Billie's weakest subject, and therefore she couldn't give too much attention to Parker and his relative state of being. But from first impressions, he seemed to be much the way Heather had described him. He was one of the few students clad more like a refugee from an Abercrombie advert than a Marilyn Manson acolyte, but his cheery demeanor seemed almost aggressively upbeat. Billie tried to keep her gaping to a minimum, and she decided she'd wait until she had better found her feet before she got too chatty with him. She was definitely curious to hear more about this newspaper thing. Writing was something that had always fascinated her.

Or at least, if she couldn't stop herself from gaping for the foreseeable future, she'd wait to approach him until she'd kicked her jet lag, which didn't seem to be going anywhere anytime soon. Wasn't the equation something like, one day per hour of time difference? That meant she'd be spacey just about forever.

That would never do. She didn't have forever. All she

had was this one semester in D.C. And she was determined to make the most of it.

Luckily, Billie's enthusiasm for her internship that afternoon perked her up. While she'd spent the morning of
classes wandering the halls of Fairlawn in a semi-fugue
state, now she was buzzing like she'd mainlined ten shots
of espresso in a row. All of her eco-conscious activities in
Australia had been leading up to this moment. She was
going to Take Charge, Be Heard, and Do Something.

Actually, to be more specific, she was also going to
Jump Out of Her Skin if they couldn't get to work sooner
rather than later.

Billie and her fellow interns had arrived at Mr. Ritter's
office at two P.M., all itching to jump in and get involved.
There was a certain amount of terror over suddenly having what felt suspiciously like a real job, but it was, for the
most part, overridden by a pervasive enthusiasm unique to
volunteer-type people.

Any moment now, Billie knew, she and her co-interns
would be handed their clipboards and canteens and sent
out to survey land, collect samples, or mash up paper from
recyclables using only their bare hands.

Any. Moment. Now.

She jiggled her foot in her seat impatiently, trying not to
make too much noise in the process. She sighed under her
breath. She chewed on her fingernails. She contemplated

helping herself to another cup of coffee but rejected the idea for a host of reasons. She was already half mad from adrenaline as it was.

She was trapped. Trapped in a dimly lit conference room on the fifteenth floor of an office building.

She surveyed her fellow interns briefly. Of course there was Parker, who'd offered her a smile of recognition and a nod when they'd first arrived. She assumed that he knew she was the one staying with Eliza's parents for the semester, but they hadn't had a chance to discuss that just yet. Instead, the two of them had spent the last few minutes shifting uncomfortably in their seats and generally avoiding eye contact with the other two members of their little group: thin girls with pale skin and brownish-blonde hair who were dressed in nearly identical jeans and pastel cable-knit sweaters.

As if aware of Billie's eyes on her, one of the two girls (the one in the lime-green sweater, as opposed to the one in Pepto-Bismol pink) glanced up.

"I'm Fiona, and this is Annabelle," she offered. "We're freshmen at Fairlawn. We had to apply special to be accepted into this program with upperclassmen." She sounded extremely proud of this fact. She also seemed to be the designated spokesperson for the two of them. It was odd, but Fiona was clearly doing her best to be friendly, and as far as Billie was concerned, her overture was welcome.

Less welcome was the ages-long orientation speech to which she and her colleagues were soon to be subjected. The door to the conference room opened with a creak, revealing a crisp, no-nonsense type woman in sensible shoes, black pants, and a baby-blue sweater set.

More pastels? What was it with Americans dressed like Easter eggs? Billie wondered.

"I'm Iris Meyer," Easter Egg began, clearing her throat. "I'm your internship coordinator. I'm just going to quickly take attendance, and then we'll go through the ground rules." She settled herself in a seat at the front of the room and quickly referred to the clipboard she'd been carrying, reading off names to confirm that all of the interns were, indeed, present. Billie couldn't help but notice that Fiona and Annabelle both responded to each of their names.

"Bathrooms are located in the front of the hall, on either side of the elevator banks," Iris droned. "You'll need a key for that, so check in with the receptionist when you need to go."

Billie frowned. Why were they sitting around talking about toilets when there were rain forests to replant? She'd been doing almost nothing since she arrived but flit in and out of getting-to-know-you sessions. She knew that it was very important to be properly acclimated to new situations and stuff, but it was getting to be a bit much. When were they going to get up and actually Do Something?

Oh—now. Now they were getting up.

In her personal pity party, she'd almost missed it. Parker sort of nudged her on the shoulder as he brushed past her seat, teasing her for zoning out.

"The conference room where we were just sitting is where most of the office meetings will take place. If for some reason we need more space, then we meet on the seventeenth floor," Iris said. "In that case, you'd be informed by e-mail." Her low-heeled pumps whispered softly as she strode forward, in full-on tour-guide mode.

She led them past an *extremely* miniature kitchen. The fridge was so teeny that Billie wasn't sure it would even fit a jar of Marmite.

"This is the break room," Iris continued. "If you bring food from home, you can keep it in the refrigerator. But be sure to label what's yours," she warned, "so that it doesn't go missing."

Billie's eyes widened. Since when did activists nick one another's tuck boxes? Then she remembered that Americans weren't too keen on Marmite, and she realized that theft probably wouldn't be an issue.

Iris came to a stop in front of an enormous room filled with copy machines. Honestly, it looked like every single copier in the entire world had been shoved into the same space. The dull industrial lighting bounced weakly off of the machines' shinier surfaces.

"Are you guys ready for your first task?" Iris asked,

sounding, in all truth, rather subdued. Her tone of voice was not exactly what Billie would call inspiring.

Nevertheless, it was all that she could do to avoid leaping into the air and pumping her fist. Who cared if Iris was running on low batteries? *She* was ready for her first task, definitely. She'd been—what did the Americans say again?—*born* ready. She rubbed her hands together like a cartoon villain.

Apparently it was meant to be a rhetorical question, because Iris plunged right onward with her spiel.

"You are all familiar with Proposition Seven, yes?" Another rhetorical question, but of course the answer was yes. Proposition Seven was Ritter's bill to de-pollute the Chesapeake Bay, which had been deemed dirty water. The EPA had announced a proposed cleanup initiative to start at the end of the calendar year.

She nodded at Iris, as did the other interns.

Iris pressed her lips together. Her expression was inscrutable...not a smile, but not a grimace, either. More of a non-expression.

"We've recently been made aware of some new developments regarding the EPA's proposed cleanup. This"—she slid a sheaf of papers out from the mass of her clipboard—"is the press release, which should tell you all you need to know about the new information." She passed the papers to Fiona. "Fiona, you and—"

"Annabelle," Annabelle chimed in helpfully.

"Annabelle," Iris repeated mechanically, "can collaborate on our e-mailing list of potential volunteers. We need to update them on the news."

"E-mailing list?" Annabelle asked. She sounded disappointed.

"Yes," Iris said. She smiled. "You two can put together the e-mail addresses, while you"—she pointed at Billie and Parker—"can work on the body of the e-mail itself." She narrowed her eyes. "Nothing too flashy. Just stick to the facts."

"Of course," Billie replied warily. She eyed her cohorts, none of whom seemed wildly impressed with the level of responsibility they were being given.

"Anything else?" Iris chirped, practically daring the group to come up with another query.

The room was silent.

Iris clapped her hands together briskly. "In that case, you know where to find me."

And with that, she was gone.

It wasn't until Iris was long out of earshot that Billie had a moment to peruse the press release their coordinator had left with them. And when she did, a dawning horror crept over her.

There were some changes planned for Proposition Seven and anti-pollution funding, to be sure. Some *big* changes. Namely? The cleanup was being postponed. Indefinitely.

Chapter Nine

From: billiesurf@email.com
To: elizarit@email.com
Subject: first days

G'day, mate, and how are you going? I trust by now you've started to get into the swing of things down under. Myself, I had my first day at the internship yesterday, and it was definitely...interesting.

I met your friend Parker, too, since he's interning with me—but I guess you knew that? We didn't have too much time to talk on our first day, though, since we were

handling PR for Proposition Seven and the new changes to the regulation funding. Did you know about any of that? Seems sort of...drastic.

Anyway, I don't mean to be critical, of course—it's so exciting working for the EPA, and I'm sure that everyone involved knows what they're doing. I guess I was just surprised, is all.

But nothing wrong with a good surprise every now and then, right? Here's hoping you're having a few—pleasant surprises, that is—of your own!

Billie

"Miss Ritter, might you come to the front of the class and share with everyone your solution to question number six from last night's homework?"

Eliza froze in her seat, her brain in overdrive.

"Excuse me?" It was as though the teacher had spoken in Swahili. Eliza had completely blanked out.

"Miss Ritter, I don't believe I'm stuttering or mumbling. Am I?" Mrs. Lambert stared over her glasses at Eliza.

"No, ma'am." That much, at least, Eliza knew to say.

"Then please stand up and favor the class with your insights into the effects of the *Mabo* decision."

Though she was generally a good student, Eliza had a real block on remembering names, dates, and places. It was no surprise, then, that history was not her forte. By extension, then, *Australian* history was not accorded much

room in her mind (especially not when there were concerts, shopping, and cute Ozzie boys to keep track of). It
was not ideal that she was now being asked to recall it for
an audience. Fortunately, though, an idea struck her.

Well, less of an "idea" and more of a whisper and a
nudge from Nomes.

"Was it…something about…the Aboriginaries?"

A titter of laughter ran through the room. Eliza looked
down to see Nomes biting the sleeve of her sweater to
keep from erupting in hysterics.

"How about you have a seat, Miss Ritter? And I suggest
you spend a little more time at your studies and a little less
with some of the reprobates in your peer group."

"Yes, ma'am." Eliza sat down, her face flaming with
embarrassment. She turned to Nomes. "What did I say?"

"It's *Aborigines*." Jess snickered again, not unkindly.

"Really? I thought they were Aborigin*aries*…you know,
like canaries." Eliza flushed.

"Ladies, there will be time enough for your idle prattle
when you are not intruding on your fellow students' learning. Yes?" And with that, Mrs. Lambert gave them a curt
nod of the head that indicated any more shenanigans
would be met with some draconian disciplinary action.

"Yes, ma'am," Nomes and Eliza replied in unison.

Slowly, Nomes's laugher died down to an occasional
muffled choking sound, and Eliza's face returned to its
original flesh-colored hue.

Still, Eliza was flustered. She had always been one to cross her *t*'s and dot her *i*'s. But without the constant pressure of her parents hanging over her, she had admittedly slacked off. In fact, since she'd been in Melbourne, she'd developed quite the skill at using her foreign-ness to maximum advantage. It seemed that as much as people back home were suckers for a good Australian or Irish accent, the people down here got no end of amusement out of her flattened vowels. It was particularly funny to hear them imitate her accent using voices that sounded like John Wayne in one of her dad's old Western movies.

That all being said, it had become harder to play the lost foreign student with each passing day, and her teachers appeared to have tired of it. Though she really had thought it was pronounced *Aboriginaries.* Unfortunately.

Eliza hopped off the tram and headed up the hill toward the Echolses' house. After school, she, Jess, and Nomes had spent the afternoon listening to some incredible live music at a pub on Brunswick Street. It was a pair of guitar players who jammed every Thursday afternoon. She and the girls sat on the floor and listened as they strummed fantastic covers of classic songs from the 1970s and '80s.

Eliza was pretty happy with the way things were going in Melbourne, all in all. She had found a good group of friends who were into the same kinds of things that she was into. She still had to deal with the oppressive internship, which was less swimsuits, sun, and beach, and more waders, gloves, and mud. But she generally had Friday evening and a good bit of the weekend free—which she made the most of. The Echolses were cool enough about her free time, and they gave her the space to do what she wanted. It was a huge change from her life back in D.C., which was, of course, the whole reason she'd gone abroad to begin with. She even was coming to like Nick and Sam— at least when they weren't bumping about the house at the crack-of-holy-heck in the morning. They somehow never quite got over how funny her accent sounded, and their favorite pastime when she was watching them was coming up with words for her to say in an American accent.

Eliza's whole life had turned upside down in the last month. It boggled her mind: if she'd stayed at home, she'd still be floating around Fairlawn, playing the perfect student. She'd still be with Parker, too…which was fine, but not nearly as exciting as a fledgling flirtation with an adorable Australian. There would be no footy; no Victoria Bitter (VB, as it was known, was Jess's drink of choice); no words like snog (kiss), tune (pick up), and pash (also kiss; there were a lot of words for kissing here—hopefully that meant that there was lots of kissing, as well); and none of the horrors of the sludgelike Vegemite that people put on their morning toast. Even the icky parts of Australian life were a treat to be savored (though, in the case of Vegemite, not literally).

"I'm home," she sang, making her way into the kitchen, where Estelle was getting dinner ready, as usual.

"Good evening, Eliza. How was your day?"

"Great, thanks." Why worry Estelle with the story of her humiliation in history class?

"That's lovely. Why don't you drop your things in your room and come have a seat in the kitchen? Frank and I would like to have a chat with you about something."

"Um, sure....I'll be right out."

Oh no.

Frank had come home early so that both he and Estelle could talk to her. This did not bode well. Eliza knew she had fibbed to them a few times, but what had they caught on to? Was it the trips to the pub? Blanking on her homework?

Eliza dropped her schoolbag on her bed and then came back into the kitchen, seating herself primly at the table. Frank and Estelle had positioned themselves directly across the table from her. They looked very serious.

Eliza wondered if she was about to find herself on a very long plane ride home. They wouldn't send her home for blowing off a few homework assignments, would they?

"Eliza," Frank started, "something has come to our attention that has us concerned."

Suddenly Eliza felt like a derelict. It was an unfamiliar sensation. She was not exactly known for being a wild and crazy rebel, after all.

"I was up last night getting myself a glass of water, and

I overheard you on your mobile," Frank began, solemn. "It appears that you've been using it to speak to some of your school friends well past eleven. As you remember, eleven is lights-out in this house."

They were upset with her for speaking on the phone after eleven at night? Even on a local call? Eliza was so stunned that her mouth actually dropped open into a startled little O. She quickly closed it.

"Yes, dear," continued Estelle. "You really have no business being on the phone at eleven in the evening...or even later, as it would appear."

This was unreal. She had a phone curfew? Who had a phone curfew? She'd been the perfect dutiful daughter since the moment she was born, and now, here, in Australia, she'd engaged in the most minor form of rule breaking....And yet the Echolses looked deadly serious about the situation. She absolutely could not believe this. Back home, her parents couldn't have cared less about Eliza's phone habits, provided she wasn't blabbing delicate information to the political bloggers she knew.

Frank nodded gravely. "Now, we will spare you the embarrassment of our speaking to some of your classmates' parents about this, but we must insist on curbing this behavior. Therefore, we have decided that we'll be collecting your mobile at eleven and returning it to you at breakfast every morning."

They *were* serious. Serious as a busy signal. Jeez. Eliza

couldn't believe she was getting called out for something as petty as this. Then again, handing the phone over to them at eleven was *far* preferable to the idea that they would call her friends' parents and inform them of their bizarre and overly protective rule.

The Echolses proved difficult to figure out sometimes. On the one hand, they were very casual and open, but on the other, they had strict rules that seemed more appropriate for a family thirty years ago. Or maybe even thirty centuries. It wasn't exactly modern, that was for sure.

"I'm sorry it had to come to this, but we must insist that while you're in our home you obey our rules." To his credit, Frank did look truly sorry. Not that it made a difference.

Estelle chimed back in. "Your parents have entrusted us with your well-being, and that includes making sure you are focused on your studies. I hope you understand."

Eliza was dumbstruck. *Poor Billie,* she thought.

Although, when you think about it—Billie's the one living it up at my house, chatting without any consequence well into the witching hour. Poor Billie, my foot. Poor Eliza, she decided.

"Oh, I understand. I'm really sorry; I guess I just got carried away. You know, being new here, and so excited about making friends." Eliza hung her head. The sad truth was that although she definitely thought that the Echolses were overreacting, she hated ever to be chastised or to feel like she was letting anyone down. And so the guilt that radiated off of her was actually 120 percent genuine.

"Well, that's all right, love. Let's not mention another word about it." Estelle patted Eliza's hand reassuringly.

"She'll be 'right, mate. Don't worry about this anymore, and let's eat." Frank rose from the table to help round up the twins.

Eliza watched as he headed off into the house. She hadn't meant to disappoint them, but losing late-night phone privileges wasn't the worst thing in the world, by a long shot.

Still, she most definitely wanted to avoid having another of these awkward conversations. So if she was going to bend the rules from time to time, she was just going to have to be careful to keep it from them. Very careful.

The first Echols-approved phone call Eliza made on her phone was to Macca the next morning. Apparently he'd gotten her number from Jess (and Eliza couldn't *believe* her friend had managed to keep that fact a secret), and had called her the night before, but alas, not before 11:07.

"Are you serious?" Macca asked in disbelief when Eliza told him about the Echolses' new rule.

"Yep, no cell phone after eleven." She sighed, but her glee to be talking on the phone with Macca overrode any lingering annoyance about the curfew situation.

"All right. Is this a home stay or some sort of detention camp?"

"Shut up, you." She grinned despite herself.

"So when can you meet me for a coffee? How's tomorrow?" She imagined she could hear Macca's own grin over the phone.

"I'd love to, but I have my internship down at Port Phillip Bay. How about Friday or over the weekend?" Eliza asked, hoping for a yes.

"No good, some mates and I are going up to their family's house at Mount Buller for some snowboarding before the end of the season. You can't get out of the internship, just this once?"

"I'm really not supposed to." Skipping school—any form of it—was several notches above late-night phone calls, as far as infractions went. Eliza wasn't so sure she was ready to take the next step with her Aussie rebellion.

"How are they going to find out? Just call in sick, tell him you'll be there at the next one."

Eliza thought it over. She knew she shouldn't, but she really didn't want to have to wait forever before she got to see Macca again.

"Come on, you know you don't want to be mucking about in the bay. Didn't you come to Australia to have fun?"

Appealing to her sense of adventure was exactly the right angle for Macca to work in order to get Eliza to see things his way.

He was right. Eliza knew it. Macca obviously knew it. She hated the thought of sneaking around, but she was going to have to find a way to get out of the internship for Saturday.

Mr. Winstone had fallen for it—hook, line, and sinker. Everyone being a little more trusting down here made some things almost too easy. As if Eliza weren't feeling guilty enough about her little ruse as it was.

For Mr. Winstone, all Eliza had to do was put on her best "sick voice"—accomplished by pinching one nostril with her finger, coughing generously, and sounding particularly pathetic—and he bought every word. She had told him that she had caught another cold after the last afternoon session and thus, it was felt, she should not spend this afternoon traipsing about the shallows of Port Phillip Bay.

It was cold and drizzly as Eliza tucked herself in at a cozy café the next day. She had heard so much about the good weather that would come as spring drew closer, but she was now suitably suspicious after weeks of people smiling knowingly at her as they reminded her for the umpteenth time about Melbourne's four seasons in a day. She was still confused by the "spring" of October, when back home leaves would just be falling from the trees.

A tap on the glass pulled Eliza out of her reverie. She tried to contain her smile as Macca looked in at her. She

waved and gestured for him to come inside. He grinned, and a few moments later shook the water off his jacket as he plopped down on the couch beside Eliza.

"How you goin', Zazza?"

By now she knew how to answer that question.

"I'm okay. How about you?" She blushed at his adorable use of her new nickname.

"Not so bad. We have a day off for some teacher conferences down at Geelong, and I figured I'd come up to the city to catch up with my new mate." He prodded her flirtatiously.

Eliza hoped she could be more of a "crush" than a "mate" to Macca, but either way, she loved hearing him speak. When he talked, he grinned from ear to ear like he was in on some great joke.

I wouldn't mind being in on that punch line, too, she thought to herself.

"So tell me. What's the deal with your real name? Hamish MacGreggor? Who gets named Hamish?"

"Don't laugh, there's three of us Hamishes in my class, and we're mighty proud. There's me—Macca, there's Misha, and there's Floyd."

"Floyd? From *Hamish* to *Floyd*? Admit it—now you're just messing with me." Eliza burst out laughing.

"No, really. I mean, his real name is Hamish Follender, but everyone just calls him Floyd."

Eliza shook her head, still smiling. Macca and his easy

charm were wonderfully relaxing. For the bajillionth time since she'd gotten to Melbourne, she was extra glad that she and Parker had decided to put things on hold.

"So, are you getting the full Aussie experience?"

"I think so. I've been to Brunswick Street, and, you know, the Espy."

"Right, where we met." Macca winked. "What about the MCG? Have you caught a footy match yet? You really haven't experienced Melbourne until you've eaten a steaming meat pie while barracking for your team."

"Oh yeah?" Eliza raised her eyebrows. "And who do you 'barrack' for?"

"No question in my mind. I'm loyal to Geelong." Macca threw both arms into the air and yelled, "GO CATS!"

Before Eliza could even think of being embarrassed by his outcry, a stranger from the other side of the café called back.

"Oi! Oi!"

"You see," said Macca, "we're a loyal bunch down here."

Clearly, Eliza thought.

Aloud she simply said, "Aha. Well, I haven't had the pleasure yet, but maybe *someone* will take me so I can have a look." She cocked an eyebrow at him.

He didn't miss a beat. "Tell you what. I'll make you a deal. I will do you the favor of taking you to a game at the MCG if you do a favor for me."

111

Eliza was intrigued. "And what would that be?"

"Well, my brother is in his second year at uni, and they have a formal coming up at his college. We can't go to the dinner, which is fine because they're boring, but he can get us into the after-party. Technically, the invites are for students at other residential colleges, but if we act like we belong, no one will give us a hard time."

Eliza was floored, and momentarily rendered speechless. She looked down to make sure that her heart, which was beating a mile a minute, wasn't actually bursting out of her chest. She took a little breath and tried to play as cool as she could, all things considered.

"Well, I guess that sounds like a pretty fair deal," Eliza said with a grin. "I accept, but only because you're doing a nice favor for me," she said, reminding him playfully.

"Great, it's the week after next on Friday night. It'll be a ripper!"

Eliza had no idea what a "ripper" was. But she had a feeling she was going to like it. A lot.

Chapter Ten

From: elizarit@email.com
To: billiesurf@email.com
Subject: Re: first days

Hey there—

How're you going? (And how's that for "cultural acclimation," huh?) Things are great down here—other than the weather, that is. People keep telling me it's going to get warmer, but so far, no dice. Which makes it all the more difficult to get motivated to spend time collecting soil specimens on the cold, windy beach.

But I shouldn't complain about my internship when it sounds like you've got your hands full. I spoke to my dad the other day, and he mentioned the new roll-out schedule for Proposition Seven. I can't believe funding is getting pushed forward by two years! I mean, I'm not, like, some kind of environmental crusader or anything, but I know about the EPA—how could I not, given my dad's job, and all of the preparation that I had to do for S.A.S.S. Goes Green? He says it's because other projects are taking priority, but given what a hot issue Chesapeake Bay pollution has become in D.C., I'm still shocked. No wonder he's got you guys running point on damage control.

Hang in there!

Eliza

Things just weren't clicking for Billie.

She was discouraged to have learned that her primary reason for wanting to be in the United States—the chance to work with Mr. Ritter on Proposition Seven—amounted to little more than pushing papers. Today, an e-mail blast. Tomorrow, a snail mailing. All for the sake of letting the public know that money to clean the bay wasn't going to be available for another two years at the earliest.

She should have known. His wife *did* drive an SUV. How could Ritter be anything *but* a farce?

From what Billie had read, ever since the Chesapeake

Bay had been officially declared dirty water, one of the EPA's announced objectives had been to fund a massive cleanup. There wasn't a single classroom in Washington that hadn't heard about Proposition Seven and the plans to finally clean the bay. But apparently the EPA's budget for programming had come in lower than expected, and—as Eliza mentioned in her e-mail—other projects were suddenly bumped ahead on the priority scale. Cleaning the bay would have to wait. Which would have been awful enough news on its own, even if it hadn't meant that Billie's job now consisted of finding ways to spread the news about the proposition in a positive and enthusiastic light. She felt like a fraud, like a typical government spin doctor.

At any rate, she would have much preferred to spend her days collecting soil samples, or testing water for contamination. Even if Proposition Seven were progressing full steam ahead, she wanted to get her hands dirty—like Eliza was doing. The girls' work was meant to be opposite sides of the same educational coin. The two schools had arranged it that way. At the end of the semester, they'd exchange reports on their internship experiences, as well.

It was almost as though she and Eliza had switched places, and the American was the one who was all hands-on. Not that Eliza begrudged her academic doppelganger a worthy cause; instead, she wished they could somehow

be sharing that cause. Couldn't they be twins instead of shadow sisters? Firing off impassioned e-mails every five minutes wasn't going to change the world.

And also, it was pretty clear that Iris was growing weary of Billie's constant barrage of questions. Her expression darkened every time Billie either raised her hand or started with a timid "excuse me." It was apparent that Billie was most definitely not excused.

To her surprise, she hadn't made any real, close friends since she'd been here, either. Fiona-belle mostly stuck to themselves, which was just as well; they were kind of creepy. Heather seemed to like Billie well enough, but Billie's internship kept her so busy that they didn't get as much time together as she would have liked. And Parker, while outgoing, was, to a certain way of thinking, Eliza's. Even if Billie didn't know what was going on with the two of them this semester, she felt a bit awkward trying to get to know him better, given his relationship to the girl with whom she'd swapped places.

The rest of the American students were all friendly enough (and incredibly taken by Billie's accent), but they had clearly settled into their own little bubble of high school existence ages ago and weren't necessarily looking to take any new stragglers into their cliques.

She wondered how Eliza was faring at St. Cat's. People there were generally more outgoing. Or was it just that it *felt* that way to Billie when she was home, surrounded by everything familiar? Eliza had mentioned talking to Jess and Nomes, so she'd have to ask if they'd become better friends.

Monday morning proved to be more of the same. D.C. was rainy—she'd had to skip her before-school run, which meant that she was doubly stir-crazy—and Billie's sandy hair was frizzy from the humidity, clinging to her forehead in unruly waves. D.C. was *always* humid, no matter what else the weather was doing. It wasn't the sort of thing that Billie would whine about in general, but each day her hairstyle became increasingly mad, until she wasn't surprised that she wasn't being mobbed by American fans on a daily basis. Thank goodness for hairpins. She'd be relieved to get home to the Australian climate—even if it was reliably unreliable.

At least the topic of discussion in her social studies class seemed interesting. Ms. Franklin was just getting the class's attention.

"Proposition Seven looks to reduce pollution in the Chesapeake Bay by thirty percent over the next five years," she began.

In an alternate reality, Ms. Franklin must have been Billie's kindred spirit. She was the only person whom Billie had met in D.C. who was as interested in Proposition Seven (as opposed to, say, interested in *sending out five million e-mails about* why *Proposition Seven would have to be postponed*) as Billie herself was.

"Does anyone know how they plan to do so?"

Poor Ms. Franklin. Billie suspected she was the only one really paying any attention to the teacher.

Or was she? From the front row of the classroom, Parker hesitantly inched his arm forward. Ms. Franklin nodded at him.

He sat up straight in his seat. "The EPA wants a cleaner and healthier bay, and is committed to holding polluters accountable and to working with all of our partners to speed up the cleanup. That means using innovative and sustainable tools and focusing on environmental coopera-tion."

Was it Billie's imagination, or did he turn to her and actually wink?

She wasn't seeing things. Parker was grinning at her from across the room. And no wonder. She was the only person in class likely to know that he was quoting directly from the press release that Ritter had sent out the week before. Printing and collating five hundred copies of it tended to leave an imprint on one's memory.

Before she could stop herself, she snickered aloud.

"He's actually right, Billie," Ms. Franklin said. "But did you have something that you wanted to share?"

"Oh, no, of course not…" Billie replied, embarrassed. She hadn't meant to speak—or, for that matter, snort—out loud. How humiliating. If only she could meld to her plastic seat like a human chameleon. Unfortunately, the seat was a misguided shade of banana yellow, and Billie's peaches-and-cream complexion stood out all too starkly against it. Between that and the snorting, she figured there was no way to get out of answering Ms. Franklin.

"It's just…" she hedged, trailing off uncertainly. She had to be very careful how she answered this question, after all. The last thing she wanted was to go on record slamming Mr. Ritter, so instead she just jabbered on endlessly like an enormous prat.

"I guess I just feel like there are some other, more, um, urgent steps that we maybe should be taking right now?" Her voice went up at the end of her suggestion, making it sound like more of a wild guess. Now, in addition to looking like a lunatic, everyone would think for sure that she was a bit mental. "I mean, that sentiment is nice and all, but without funding, the bay doesn't get clean."

Ms. Franklin readjusted her glasses and peered over their lenses at Billie. "True enough, but surely the money has been set aside for equally worthy programs. In which case, what would you have the EPA do?"

Billie swallowed. "Well, funding is crucial, of course. I certainly don't mean to imply otherwise. But we can also solicit volunteers for actual fieldwork to help clean the water, until the money to bring in professional teams is available," she said, trying to project more confidence.

Eeep! Had she actually said that out loud—that she was starting to see things from the *non*-Ritter point of view?

The classroom was stonily still except for Parker, who'd taken to rubbing his hands together with an almost cartoonish glee. At least she had *one* ally in the room, Billie thought. Since the look on her teacher's face was utterly inscrutable at best.

Ms. Franklin mashed her lips together, her expression still impassive. "Hmm," she said, finally. "I see."

But that was all.

"Hmm" could have meant many things, but apparently, in this case, "hmm" meant, "Billie, please stay after class."

If Billie had been embarrassed before, now she was fairly desperate with panic. She hoped she wasn't getting into trouble, or getting sent home, and even though neither outcome seemed especially likely, by the time the bell rang signaling the end of class, her palms were slick with sweat and her heartbeat was fluttery inside her rib cage. What if they'd called Mr. Ritter in just to have him feed her a nice kick in the butt for speaking ill of his program? Could you be fired from an unpaid internship that wasn't even, technically, a job?

"You wanted to see me, Ms. Franklin?" Billie asked, clutching her heavy stack of notebooks close to her chest defensively.

"Yes." The teacher looked up from her grade book. "I was interested in what you were saying earlier in class about Proposition Seven."

Billie flushed and ran a hand through her fringe to move it out of her eyes. "It was just…you know, a suggestion. I mean…everybody knows how essential clean water is."

"I don't think everybody *does* know, Billie," Ms. Franklin replied pointedly. "If they did, I think we'd see funding going toward cleaning the bay right away rather than two years from now." At this, Billie could only shrug. True or not, she wasn't sure what Ms. Franklin was getting at.

"I know that, through S.A.S.S., you're working for Ritter," the teacher went on, leaning forward as though she were sharing a secret, instead of just telling Billie something she already knew. "It sounds to me like maybe you're getting a little bit frustrated?"

Billie cast her eyes down onto the floor, toward an invisible point several inches in front of her feet. She didn't respond. If she made too much of a fuss, or threw too much of a wobbler, would they send her back to Melbourne? She certainly wasn't ready for her semester to end.

Sensing her reluctance to spill any details, Ms. Franklin continued. "I can tell that you're trying to be diplomatic. That's a good thing. That's the professional way to be. You obviously know better than to be too squeaky of a wheel at work."

If only Ms. Franklin actually knew.

"To be honest, I think I might already be too much of a squeaker as it is," Billie confessed. Maybe she really had been starved for a new BFF; she was so appreciating

talking freely with Ms. Franklin. "It might be time for me to tone it down at the internship, and decide to just make peace with sending useless e-mails on a daily basis."

To Billie's surprise, Ms. Franklin actually burst out laughing. Now her teacher, the last vestige of her support system, was openly having a laugh at her expense?

"There are lots of other ways to get your voice heard, you know," Ms. Franklin said gently as her laughter died down. "Ways that might be more subtle, but also more effective."

"Like what?" Billie asked, curious.

"You could write a piece for the school paper here, maybe an editorial or a human interest piece about conservation. Take a hard look at some of the states that have imposed a clean-water tax and compare it to the budget problems here in D.C. and Virginia."

Billie nodded, considering the suggestion. It wasn't a bad idea at all. "But…this being the capital and all…even the school paper must get heaps of submissions about things like the environment, or politics, or…" She trailed off. "The environment" and "politics" were all she'd taken in of D.C. since she'd arrived. Those, and museums. Did people write about museums?

"You'd be surprised," Ms. Franklin said. "I think, precisely *because* we're an arts-based school in a political city, the newspaper tends to shy away from 'issues' and lean more toward coverage of the arts—and specifically, student or school projects and exhibitions. Your viewpoint could bring a breath of fresh air to the paper."

Billie grinned. "No pun intended."

Ms. Franklin smiled right back. "How can you be sure of that?"

Ms. Franklin's suggestion was such a good one that, at lunchtime, Billie went straight to the student activities office. She found it on the third floor of the building, just next to the faculty lounge. It was a dingy room that some kind—and optimistic—souls had obviously seen fit to try to decorate with a smattering of inspirational posters (HANG IN THERE!) and teen magazine pullouts.

The room was empty save for two people. One was Heather, hunched over in her seat with her back to the door. She appeared to be focused intently on a notepad she held in her hand.

The other was Parker.

What were the odds? Billie wondered. Two of the only people she really knew in D.C., and they both worked on the newspaper for which she now wanted to write. This had to be one of those "karmic" moments that people on daytime talk shows always went on about.

Billie cleared her throat, and Heather whirled around in her seat. Her eyes widened when she saw Billie, and she tapped Parker's shoulder. The two of them seemed awfully surprised—though not unhappily so—to see Billie in the

newspaper office. She took the fact that they were both offering quizzical smiles to be a good sign, and forged ahead.

"Hi," she said, waving a tentative hand. "Sorry, I didn't mean to startle you guys."

"You didn't," Parker insisted. Then he took a breath and smiled even more broadly. "Duh. Obviously you did. Don't worry about it."

"What are you doing here?" Heather asked, grinning. "Did you want to get your write on?" She tilted back in her rickety chair and ran her fingers through her mass of curly brown hair.

"It's just…Ms. Franklin told me that this was where I should go to sign up for the newspaper?" Billie scanned the room, seeing nothing by way of a sign-up sheet and, in fact, no real signs of life other than Parker and Heather.

"Yup," Heather replied brightly. "But you don't have to literally sign up. I mean, there's no, like, sheet, or roster, or anything. You just get an article assigned to you."

"Okay," Billie said. "Easy enough. Who does the assigning?"

"That would be me," Parker said, standing up. "I'm the editor in chief of the paper. And you"—he added, eyes twinkling—"are suddenly, what, my stalker or something?"

Billie couldn't help herself, she giggled. "You wish," she quipped, then bit her lip nervously. Was she *flirting* with Parker? Was this what actual flirting was? If so, it left her feeling slightly weird. It was like she was…*spying* on Eliza, somehow. The fact that she and Parker seemed to have so much in common made it only odder still.

"Right," Parker said, making a goofy face. "Tell me the truth—did Eliza put you up to it? Following me around, I mean?"

"It was dead simple," Billie teased. "I recognized you straightaway from the pictures in her room," she blurted without thinking.

At this, a slight blush crept up Parker's neck, spreading across his cheeks until he was fully flushed. "Yeah? She still has those up?"

"Oh, yeah," Billie said, waving her hand in an "of course" sort of gesture. She felt a flush creeping up her own neck, though she wasn't sure exactly why it was happening.

Suddenly the air in the room had taken on a charge, like electricity. It was as though the mention of Eliza's pictures, however innocent, had suddenly set everyone on edge.

"I've been e-mailing her," Parker continued, "but I haven't heard back yet. I guess she must be busy."

Uh-oh. Have I walked into some relationship drama? Billie worried to herself. If she didn't even have a relationship of her own, the last thing she needed was someone else's complications. Eliza hadn't mentioned much about Parker in her last e-mail to Billie, but then again, it wasn't like the girls were so close that they'd exchange all manner of boy-friendly secrets. *Now what?* Billie wondered. The

room had grown awkwardly quiet. Even Heather was looking like she'd rather be buried in quicksand than caught
in conversation with Billie and Parker.

Billie knew she had to say something. Purely on instinct,
she tripped over herself agreeing with Parker enthusiastically.

"Yeah, the S.A.S.S. programs...they're murder on your
social life." Not that she knew this from experience, of
course. The whole reason she wanted to write for the
paper, after all, was because of her complete and total
lack of social life.

"I'm sure you'll hear from her soon," she added, briefly
wondering if that was true. Or why she cared, for that matter. She'd never even met Eliza, and up until now, Parker
had only been a bloke at her internship.

Heather shook her head softly, just outside of Parker's
view. Then she rolled her eyes.

"Yeah," Parker said shortly. "She just needs space, you
know, to adjust over there...." He abruptly trailed off, as
though afraid of having revealed too much. "Anyway," he
said, sighing and changing the subject, "you wanted to
write?"

"Well, yeah, Ms. Franklin suggested it," she said, wondering why she was suddenly feeling so shy. "Just, you
know, as a more creative platform..."

"So, you want to do, like an op-ed piece?"

"Right." Billie nodded. "About conservation. You know,

what we can do, and how much, literally, of a difference each of our decisions makes every day."

"Are you going to mention Proposition Seven?" Parker asked.

"Um, I think so," Billie replied. "I was going to maybe look at a side-by-side analysis of other states that have enacted clean-water programs, and talk about the benefits of federal funding versus volunteer efforts." Parker shrugged. "Works for me."

Aces, Billie thought. From where she still sat, Heather nodded, echoing her agreement.

He shook her hand, making their agreement that much more official. "Five hundred words. By Thursday, five P.M., if possible."

"Too right!" Billie smiled. "No worries."

Chapter Eleven

From: park@email.com
To: elizarit@email.com
Subject: busy bee!

Hey there—

I'm assuming they've got you running in circles down there in the outback, based on your radio silence! Don't worry—we're all managing here without you—just barely. ☺

I don't know how much you've been e-mailing with the exchange student, Billie, but she and I and have been interning together, and yesterday she came by the newspaper wanting to write. She seems pretty cool. She's really into the environment—I know, duh—but, like, even more so than a lot of the students here at Fairlawn. She's doing a piece on the benefits of an all-volunteer clean-water act here in D.C., assuming there is one. For her sake, I kind of hope there is one—who knows what your father will think if she keeps going on about how bummed she is that the Chesapeake Bay cleanup has been postponed. That could be awkward.

If you get a chance, shoot me a line. I want to hear how you're doing. But in the meantime, as they say where you are: "No worries."

Parker

It felt like Eliza had merely blinked, and before she knew it the two weeks since Macca invited her to the college party had flown by. She had traded e-mails with Parker in that time, and was glad to hear that he seemed to be having fun back home, but their exchange really served only to underscore how excited and eager she was to be spending more time in Australia with Macca.

One thing she wasn't excited about, though, was the tight rein that the Echolses still held over her. It wasn't that they were mean, per se, but Eliza knew by this point that the Echolses did not look favorably on her being anywhere they couldn't find her after sunset—the incident with her cell phone had only reinforced that belief. She couldn't

help but reflect on the fact that her own parents were, as a rule, much more lenient. Of course, she also had to admit to herself that, back in D.C., it was rare that she ever did anything after sunset that would give a parent pause. So there was that.

Regardless, Eliza was certain that sneaking into college parties with strange boys was probably on the Echolses' "forbidden" list. But bowing out was not an option. Therefore, she had, with Jess's help, come up with a plan that involved equal parts cunning, conniving, and conspiracy. Now the day had come, and Eliza was in the midst of nervously executing her scheme.

The girls had gone shopping the previous week. Eliza dipped into her spending money for a fabulous, funky black cocktail dress they'd uncovered at a thrift shop. She stashed it in Jess's closet so as not to arouse suspicion. Eliza had gotten the Echolses' permission to sleep over at Jess's house that night. She had called Mr. Winstone late that afternoon and, in strained tones, had told him that she would be unable to make the morning sample collection on Saturday as she was laid up with a terribly sprained ankle from a sports accident.

Now the pieces were all lined up in place, and all Eliza had to concentrate on was getting gorgeous for her Australian formal debut. Fortunately, Jess was in on those machinations, as well.

"Here, you have to try these." Jess held a pair of diamond studs up to her ears. Eliza was focused on adjusting the hemline of her dress, turning to one side and then the other and squinting at herself in the mirror, making sure it looked good from every angle. Finally, satisfied that she was absolutely, every bit as cute as she could be, she glanced up at Jess.

"They're gorgeous. Are you sure it's all right for me to borrow them?"

"Absolutely. They'll look great on you; just don't lose them, okay?"

"Come on. You know me better than that." She winked and held her right hand over her heart. "I do solemnly swear that I shall guard these earrings with my life."

"Yeah, yeah." Jess rolled her eyes. "Just get a move on 'cause you're running late and you don't want to keep Hugh Jackman waiting."

Eliza fastened the earrings, spritzed her hair with shine spray, and stealthily made her way downstairs and through the back door of Jess's house with Jess in tow. They walked out to the main road, where the cab they'd called earlier was waiting. Eliza opened the passenger door and turned back to Jess.

"How do I look?"

"Fab. Now get out of here and have a corker of a night. Okay?"

"Wish me luck." Eliza gave Jess a hug and hopped into the cab.

"Where to, miss?" asked the driver from the front seat.

"Trinity College, please? Royal Parade."

"Going to a formal tonight?"

"Yeah, I guess, I am. It's my first."

"Good on ya'. You're going to have a great night."

That's the plan.

The cab made it through the city in no time, and soon they were dodging trams as they headed up the tree-lined avenue she had first come down with the Echolses on the way in from the airport. They swerved out of the center lane and came to a stop outside the main gate to Trinity College.

An ivy-covered stone wall surrounded the grounds, and the main gate was a large wrought-iron fence, like something out of a Tim Burton movie. The gate was open, and inside she could make out a lawn and some sprawling, Gothic-style buildings.

Eliza paid the taxi driver, thinking again how glad she was that she'd been fairly frugal with her spending money, and stepped out of the car. There were a number of young people arriving at the same time—some walking from the other colleges, others in taxis and cars. Everyone looked so glamorous. The guys were all in tuxedos and the girls were in an assortment of cocktail dresses ranging from modest to extravagant. It was like being at the Oscars, if the

Oscars were held at an Australian university. And attended only by actors twenty-two or under.

Eliza had been to plenty of black-tie fund-raisers with her dad, but they were always boring functions in some banquet hall filled with government workers and, well, old people. She'd still never been to an American prom, so the idea of getting dressed up and going to a gala with people closer to her age made her feel very adult. Seeing everyone all glammed up, but with Macca nowhere in sight, Eliza was suddenly struck by a moment's anxiety.

What if this is a joke? Maybe he thought twice about inviting me, and brought another date? Or worse, maybe he stood me up. Maybe he isn't here at all. Are they going to notice that I'm still just a high school student? Eliza remembered Macca's advice from before and tried to act as if she belonged.

Before she could let her thoughts completely get the best of her, she spotted Macca. He was standing off to one side of the front gate where they had planned to meet, leaning against the high stone wall of the college. He had one foot up against the wall, and his hands were thrust into the pockets of his tuxedo pants. He looked like an old photo of James Dean or something—gorgeous, and cool, and completely disaffected. As Eliza came up he spotted her and broke into a broad smile.

"Well, don't you look spunky?"

"Excuse me?" Eliza asked. "Spunky" sounded more Orphan Annie than Academy Awards.

"You look good. I mean…r-really good."

Was it possible that a boy as ruggedly cool as Macca could be nervous? How else to explain the stammering? Eliza allowed herself a moment to tick off a mental victory for herself.

"Oh. Thank you. You look…nice."

It was an understatement, of course—but a girl had to keep some of her tricks to herself, didn't she?

"Come on. Things are getting started, and this night is fixing to go off!" Macca took her hand, looped it under his elbow, and began walking away from the gate.

"We're not going in?" Eliza asked.

"No, we are, we just don't have the proper invite, so my brother's meeting us at a side gate to let us in."

Eliza's stomach did a small flip of nervousness at the idea of even more subterfuge, but she pushed it aside, deciding not to be too bothered by this. Once they were inside, everything would be fine, she told herself.

She and Macca walked along the outside of the wall to a parking lot, which they cut through until they'd found their way to the back of what looked like a dorm. Macca let her hand go, walked up to one of the ground-level windows, and pounded on it. A moment later the door opened.

"Hamish!" came a yell from inside.

"Oi!" Macca took Eliza by the hand, and they ducked inside. Holding the door open was a guy who looked like an older version of Macca. He gave young Macca a big hug and then turned to Eliza.

"And you must be the Yank."

"Yes, I guess I must be." *Yank.* It was better than *spunky.*

"How you going? Good to meet ya'. I'm Piers, and this is Kate." He gestured behind him at a striking girl with jet-black hair and bright green eyes, who in turn smiled at Eliza.

"It's very nice to meet you. Macca's told me a lot about you," Eliza said. Even if that wasn't strictly true, she felt like it was the right thing to say.

"Oh, yeah?" Piers looked dubious, but amused. "Well, first off, everything he said is a lie, and second, around here, he's not Macca. He's either Hamish or Little Mack." Piers gave Eliza a big, toothy grin.

"Well, I guess that makes you Big Mack?" She raised an eyebrow.

"Exactly." Piers smirked. He turned to Hamish. "I like her."

"Well, hands off," Macca countered. "She's my date."

Flattered, Eliza smiled to herself. This night was going to be a *total corker*, for sure.

As Big Mack and Kate led the way across the grounds to the party, Eliza got a good look at the college for the first time. It was a large quad with a broad green in the

middle. On three sides were a series of large Gothic dorms like something out of Ye Olde England. The fourth side of the lawn was dominated by a large cathedral that was all graceful, soaring arches.

Twinkling votives lined a path across the lawn and toward a building with a tall, ivy-shrouded tower and vibrant stained-glass windows that appeared to be the main building of the residential college.

"It's beautiful," said Eliza as she took the whole scene in. She felt like Cinderella making her grand appearance at Prince Charming's ball.

"This is the bulpadock," Big Mack explained. "We're heading over to Bishops, the party is in the JCR."

"Bulpadock? JCR? I'm lost."

"This is the bulpadock." Big Mack gestured to the large lawn. "It was where they kept the college cows in the old days. Hence 'bull' 'paddock.'"

"Aha." Eliza decided it would be better just to go with things rather than spending the entire evening with her jaw hanging open. No overthinking was necessary in this case. She smiled at Macca, and he pulled her hand a little tighter against his side.

They walked through the bulpadock to a long, low adjacent building with cloisters running on the lawn side. There were lights and music coming out of a large room at one end.

Inside was a DJ on one side of the room and a fire-place and bar on the other. The students were gathered in clumps talking, joking, and dancing. Eliza looked around, expecting people to be staring at her, the American high school student, but in fact, no one seemed to take much notice one way or the other.

The whole room had the feel of the dining hall at Hogwarts, if on a bit of a smaller scale. At the far end of the room was a dais where the senior faculty sat. A very old man, who appeared to be asleep, was perched in the middle of the table.

"Who's that guy?" Eliza asked Piers. "And why is he sleeping?"

"He's Dr. Stanley, the warden of Trinity. And I'm assuming he's sleeping because he's tired."

"The warden? Like at a prison?" Eliza blinked. That was just plain weird.

"Well, yes, I suppose. But the real discipline is handled by the angry-looking guy next to him. That's Mr. Cunningham, and he can make your life very unpleasant. But don't worry, they clear out before long and usually don't give us a hard time during the parties." Eliza looked at the man and decided that he was someone she would prefer not to encounter under any circumstances.

As Eliza was taking in the rest of the scene, a tall guy with blond hair, a broad smile, and a glass of red wine in

one hand came up and smacked Macca on the back.

"You wanker! I thought they wouldn't let you in this place."

"I'm surprised they let you in, too," Macca replied as the two guys gave each other a little bro hug. "Will, this is Eliza."

"Good to meet you! I thought this loser was making you up, but you are a far sight prettier than I imagined. What are you doing with a yobbo like this?" Will asked, jokingly poking Macca in the shoulder.

"Buzz off. If you don't have anything nice to say, you can get stuffed, mate!" Macca replied, taking an openhanded swipe at Will's head. Will ducked out of the way and gave Eliza a wink.

"It's nice to meet you," Eliza said. Feeling bold, she added, "But one might ask what Macca is doing with *you*!"

"Ahh," Will said with a smile. "Now I see why he likes you."

Piers had gone to Geelong Grammar and was only a year ahead of Macca. Because of their closeness in age, Macca seemed to be good friends with a lot of his brother's friends, and they were all surprisingly nice. It didn't take long for Eliza to relax into the scene, and eventually, her lingering anxieties about all of the white lies she'd had to tell to get to the party in the first place completely evaporated from her mind.

Everyone was interested in hearing about what living in Washington was like. She almost began to feel like she was taking a quiz, what with all of their questioning, but she didn't mind so much; there was plenty of champagne going around, and after a few sips she had warmed to the gentle barrage.

"Have you been to the White House?" (yes)

"Have you met the president?" (no)

"Have you been to the Australian Embassy?" (yes, for her student visa)

Finally Macca came to her rescue. The music changed to a slow song, and he grabbed her by the hand.

"May I have this dance?" he asked.

"But of course," Eliza replied, trying to stifle her smile. Macca pulled her close and spun around so they were now on the dance floor.

He wasn't the greatest dancer, but what he lacked in grace he made up for in charm. His arms were strong, and he made a grand show of spinning and dipping her. Somehow, his excess energy seemed to fit in with the spirit of the evening, as everyone was becoming more and more boisterous. Before she knew it, hours had passed, and the crowd was beginning to thin out. She and Macca had been dancing for a while, and the room had become hot and stuffy from the evening's festivities.

"You want to go outside and get a breath of fresh air?" Macca asked, reading Eliza's mind.

"Sure."

"Come on." Macca took her by the hand and, grabbing a bottle of wine and a couple of glasses, led her out the door.

They walked around a corner and behind the building with the Gothic tower. Soon the narrow gravel path they were on opened into a garden of neatly ordered hedges and a variety of flowering plants that were not quite in bloom.

Eliza was in heaven. It was crisp, but not cold, and Macca's hand was warm around hers. The moon was out, and the air was sweet with early spring flowers. The night couldn't have been more perfect if she'd planned it herself.

Macca dropped her hand, poured a glass of wine, and held it out to her.

"I don't need any more," Eliza said. She was having enough fun without it and wanted to be clearheaded so as to take in the whole evening in crystal-clear detail.

"Just to toast," Macca prompted. "It's bad luck to toast empty-handed." He poured her a tiny glass and then held up his fuller glass.

"To a wonderful evening with the finest Yankee bird I've ever met." He clinked his glass gently against hers.

Eliza took a tiny sip, in accordance with the Hamish MacGreggor Laws of Toasting. "Have you met a lot of Yankee birds?"

"No. You caught me." He grinned. "But you're still my favorite, hands down."

"Glad I could beat out all of those other imaginary Americans that you've been seeing," she teased. "Well, here's to a wonderful evening with new friends and the finest Aussie bloke I've ever met." This time she didn't drink. Her toast, her rules.

Macca gently pried her glass from her hands and placed it on the ground next to his own.

"What is it?" Eliza asked, though she thought she might know.

Macca didn't say anything, he only pulled her closer with his hand, leaned in, and kissed her. His lips were soft and warm. Eliza snuggled against him.

"Ahem!" came a voice from the entrance of the garden. They broke their embrace quickly and turned to see the dreaded Mr. Cunningham standing in the garden.

"The Vatican Lawn is not open at this hour, and I must insist that you leave. The party has concluded for this evening, and it is time for you to make your way home. Have I made myself clear?"

"Yes, sir," they each said in unison, and they filed out of the garden after him.

Eliza didn't need to stay any longer, anyhow. The night had already been completely and totally perfect.

Chapter Twelve

"If you're like most of us, you're busy as a bee! Between school, homework, sports, activities, and after-school jobs, the last thing that you want to do is take on yet another responsibility. But the environment needs us, and if you're willing to make a few small changes in your daily routine, you can make BIG changes for the Earth—and our future."

Billie watched helplessly as Parker scanned the computer screen on which he'd called up her article, and now read it, half aloud and half to himself in such a way that made her feel extremely self-conscious.

"You said to bring it by this arvo," she pointed out

needlessly, feeling compelled to fill the awkward space between them. "I know you said before five, but I had it ready, so…" She trailed off awkwardly.

"What?" Parker turned away from the computer, clearly having heard none of Billie's jabbering.

Heather, sitting at his side as she'd been the other day, poked him in the ribs. "Zombie. The girl wants reassurance." To Billie, she sighed and said, "He goes spacey when he's in editor mode."

"No worries," Billie replied, immediately feeling more at ease. She was liking Heather even more.

"Sure, yeah, five, sorry," Parker said, snapping back into the here and now. He abruptly fixed her with a pointed stare. "The article's good," he said. "I can run it on Friday."

"But?" Billie prompted, sensing Parker had more to say.

"Well, weren't you going to do a piece encouraging people to spearhead volunteer efforts for cleaning the bay? This is well written, but it's much more…general."

Billie's shoulders slumped. "I know. I caved. At the last minute, I couldn't bring myself to write something that could potentially go against Mr. Ritter. The hand that feeds you and all that, you know?"

"So, you do support a volunteer movement while the EPA focuses funding on other programs?" Heather waggled an eyebrow knowingly.

"Could be." Billie wasn't going to say any more about it. Not just yet. Maybe not ever.

"No big deal," Parker said. "We can run this. I like it. But don't be shocked if kids don't immediately start driving solar-powered cars and stuff," he warned her.

"Yeah, it's weird," Billie said. "Back home, my friends are big greenies—um, I think you call them 'crunchies' up here. I thought for sure, with the internship, and Mr. Ritter, that I'd be in for some real action in D.C."

Parker laughed shortly. "Yeah, you're going to have to lower your idealism flag to half-mast. Almost everyone at Fairlawn is the daughter or son of some urgent left-winger. Which, of course, makes us all want to rebel against our parents and throw ourselves into something angsty and emotional like art. So, you know, it's not that we don't care about politics, but more like..." He paused, fishing for exactly the right word.

"You've got other things on the agenda for right now," Billie supplied.

"Exactly," Parker said.

"So you're telling me my article won't even get read?" Billie asked. "Should I be feeling like writing it wasn't worth my time?"

"Well, you believe in what you wrote about, right?" Parker's eyes glittered with intensity again.

"'Course." Billie shrugged.

"Then it wasn't a waste. Besides, Prop Seven is a really

hot issue right now. You can't be the only person who's been thinking about this."

"That's very comforting," Billie teased. She did think it was nice of Parker to try to make her feel better, but that didn't make the situation any less frustrating.

"I'm sure," Parker said, picking up on her not-so-subtle emotional vibes.

For a brief flash, Billie felt that there was maybe some connection forming between the two of them. He was still focused on her with all kinds of eye contact, and suddenly it seemed his Abercrombie-polo'd self was crying out for, if not a hug, then at least a clap on the back.

He was sweet. And he wanted to help her. That was also sweet.

"Are you doing anything after school?"

"What?" Billie had been so preoccupied thinking about what may or may not have passed as chemistry between the two of them that she'd completely missed what he was saying.

"After school? Do you have plans?"

"Oh, er..." Was he asking her out? On a date? Eliza's boyfriend? *Was* he even Eliza's boyfriend, for that matter?

"A bunch of us are going to get coffee in Adams Morgan," he continued. He jerked his head in Heather's direction. "Heather'll be there."

Heather nodded. "True story. Good times."

A bunch of people. Right, so—not a date, then. Bunches

of people were not usually dates. At least, not especially romantic dates.

Not-a-date was good, though. Not-a-date was less confusing than the alternative. And this way, maybe she'd also get to know some of her other classmates.

"I'm in," she said. "What the heck? I need to celebrate the fact that I'm now officially a fair dinkum journo." She decided that she wasn't going to let anything rain on the parade of having written her first article for the school paper.

Parker shook his head. "Meet us at the front entrance to the school at three-thirty. And…bring your Australian-to-American dictionary. The abridged version."

Adams Morgan was officially considered to be the "funky" D.C. neighborhood. It was located only two miles from the White House, and easily accessible via the Metro. As Billie and the others stepped out and into the sunny afternoon, she immediately noticed the bright, colorful cafés dotting the streets, and took in the sea of ethnic restaurants. It reminded her a great deal of Brunswick Street back home.

"Tell me we're not going to Starbucks," Billie pleaded. There *had* to be more interesting places to get coffee in this part of town.

"Give me at least a little credit," Parker replied, rolling

his eyes. He pointed to an awning halfway up the street. "That's it," he said.

"Okay, enough playing tour guide. We have to get there ASAP, or there won't be any couches left!" Heather winked at Billie to show that she was kidding...sort of.

Heather, Parker, and another news-writer friend of theirs, Kenneth, apparently took their "coffeehousing" (they'd even somehow managed to create their own verb) very seriously. As Parker explained, they met once a week after school to head to Adams Morgan to write, drink fancy coffee drinks that didn't taste much of caffeine, and tap away at their laptops or scribble ideas into tiny spiral-bound notebooks. It sounded very literary, and Billie was all for hanging out. Today she brought a book with her to read, since she'd come to school with neither a special writing journal nor a computer. Talk about unprepared.

"Does it get very crowded at the shop?" she asked.

Parker nodded. "Georgetown students love to camp out on the couches and pretend like they're slumming."

Billie laughed. "Really? That's so bogan. Er, I guess you'd say, 'trashy,'" she amended, seeing Parker's confused expression. It wasn't a perfect translation, but it was the best she could do.

Ahead, Heather quickened her pace, and ducked into the café that Parker had pointed out. Parker, Kenneth, and Billie followed shortly after her.

Parker held the door for Billie, bowing at the waist with a flourish. "After you," he insisted.

Billie quickly discovered that she was delighted by the extremely indie coffee shop. It was nothing like a Starbucks at all. For starters, it was twice the size of any chain coffeehouse, and despite Heather's concerns, it looked like there was ample seating. The floor was cluttered with so many overstuffed chairs and sofas that walking became a bit of a maze challenge.

Heather immediately flopped down onto a love seat in a quiet corner, tossing her books onto the couch that sat kitty-corner. "I'll guard the seats," she said. "If someone will be kind enough to grab me a café mocha. Extra large, extra chocolatey, please." She smiled, flashing white, even teeth.

"That sounds good," Billie chimed in. Normally she was a black-coffee sort of girl, but when in Adams Morgan… Anyway, what could it hurt her to branch out a little bit now and then? "I'll have the same. Stay put," she insisted, waving at Heather. "I'll fetch them for us."

"No, Billie, this is your maiden coffeehousing voyage," Parker protested. "You have to sit and take in the atmosphere. I'll get the coffees."

Billie could see there was no point in arguing with Parker. Chivalry was apparently alive and kicking. "Good on you," she said. "I'll get the next round."

As Parker went off to forage for sustenance, Billie

allowed herself to sink back into the squishy, smooshy couch cushions. "I like it here," she decided aloud. "Sort of social, but quiet at the same time." It was a place where she could be alone with her thoughts—and still be with other people, she realized. Normally, when she was alone with her thoughts she was just that: alone. It was a lot to be offered by one small coffeehouse. She was a little bit impressed.

"Yeah, welcome to the club," Heather replied. "I'm serious," she continued, when Billie did little more than to smile by way of response. "I was welcoming you."

"I got that," Billie assured her.

"Oh, good. I can be really sarcastic sometimes, and then people don't take me seriously when I'm being sincere. Or so I'm told." She rolled her eyes—sarcastically, of course.

"We're good," Billie insisted. "So, are you guys the only regulars from Fairlawn here? What about the other newspaper people?"

"We are the other newspaper people," Kenneth said. "Or, I mean, we're kind of the *only* newspaper people. Not that we mind, but we're kind of a skeleton crew."

"What about Eliza?" Billie asked. "Did she ever come here with you guys? Um, you know—like, seeing as how she and Parker were together?"

If she'd been trying to hit a casual and breezy tone, Billie realized, she'd missed it by a few dozen kilometers. She wasn't sure what about the subject made her most

uncomfortable: feeling like she was snooping around for dirt on Eliza, who, even if only a pen pal, was someone she was growing closer to every day; the gossipy nature of her query in general; or—and this was the possibility that really threw her insides for a loop—the strange little fluttery feeling she got at the back of her throat every time that Parker smiled in her direction. But uncomfortable or not, there was no turning back now.

"You mean 'are' together," Heather corrected her. "Don't let Parker hear you suggesting otherwise. It's sort of a sore topic."

Billie made a face as her suspicions were confirmed. That at least ought to help with her inner flutters. The plot thickened. "Ugh. How come?"

"Well, there was a whole drama. Eliza told him she wanted to take the semester off, so that she could be in Australia with no strings attached."

"But Parker liked strings," Billie guessed.

"Well, Parker *liked* Eliza. In the end, I think she agreed to 'try' to stay together. Parker is pretending like that means that nothing's changed."

"You don't trust Eliza?" Billie filled in.

Heather shrugged. "I don't really know her well enough to say. Don't get me wrong—I do think she cares about Parker. I mean, he wouldn't have ever been with her to begin with if there weren't something there. But Eliza spends so much of her time in the public eye that sometimes I think what she likes most about Parker is how good he looks in the spotlight. He's the kind of boy you *can* bring home to Mama."

Billie nodded as knowingly as she could.

"But, you know, I'm just speculating. It's not like I really have any inside information. And I'd never tell Parker my suspicions about what Eliza is *really* up to over in Australia—it's not my place."

"Well, it's certainly not mine, either," Billie said, mentally promising herself that she'd avoid the topic of Eliza entirely, going forward. Her last e-mail from Eliza had waxed enthusiastic about attending a uni formal with a cute bloke she'd met, information that Billie was fairly certain Eliza had kept from Parker. But that was for Parker to deal with, not Billie.

Their conversation trailed off just in the nick of time. Parker wove his way from the counter and back to the crew, barely managing to balance four mugs in his hands.

"Should we toast?" Heather asked, lifting her mug to her lips, but not actually sipping just yet.

"Too right!" Billie replied, raising her mug enthusiastically. "To...er..." She thought for a moment. *To book nerds who love to write? To awkwardly defined relationships? To international exchange programs?* None of those sounded quite right, even inside her head. Then she smiled. "To coffeehousing!"

"To coffeehousing!" her new friends echoed, clinking their mugs together and taking long sips.

"Today, you four will be archiving."

Iris seemed particularly pleased to be passing along this news to the interns. Her smile was tight and smug.

Billie nearly tossed her notebook across the room. Unfortunately, as she was in the Ritter campaign conference room, the walls were very widely set apart, and hurling a notebook would probably not have the desired effect. Not to mention, doing so would likely result in a scolding and subsequent embarrassment. Instead, she rammed her hands under her legs so as to ensure that she didn't accidentally go ripping her hair out at the root, she was so frustrated.

Archiving. As in, going through old press mentions and coverage of the EPA's activity under Ritter, and cataloging the material. Literally, filing it all away. And worse than the tediousness of the task (in fact, Billie wouldn't have minded so much if her whole job had to do with reading and researching the EPA) was the fact that they were dealing in hard copy. *Hard copy.* In the information age, no less. Whereas Billie truly would have thought that the EPA would opt for digital files—so much more green.

Then again, Ritter's wife did drive an SUV. So clearly Billie's instincts and impulses were 116 percent off base.

And if filing weren't soul crushing enough, there was

the fact that when Billie had applied to the S.A.S.S. program, she hadn't bargained on feeling so...cooped up,
spending all of her time in an office, bathed in artificial
light. She wondered fleetingly how long it would take for a
vitamin-D deficiency to kick in.

"We'd like to have all this filing taken care of by the end
of the day," Iris continued.

"What's the rush?" Parker chimed in. Billie bit her lip to
keep from grinning at the question—really, it bordered on
cheekiness. Despite what Heather had said about Parker's
lingering funk of missing Eliza, he'd been letting little
snatches of real personality shine through the thunder-
clouds of late. It had been days since their visit to Adams
Morgan, but Billie still felt wired, as though an entire
carafe of coffee coursed through her veins and she was
humming on a frequency only Parker could tune in to.

She wasn't sure what that meant, but she sure did like
the feeling.

"The *rush*, as you say, Parker, is that we need to clear
out space in our storage room. The EPA is hosting a dinner in two weeks, and we'll be assembling gift baskets
and other things for the event; we'll need somewhere to
put it all." Iris raised a sharp eyebrow, as if daring Parker
to retort.

"What's the dinner for?" Billie asked, almost without
thinking.

"It's a fund-raiser," Iris said, waving her hand as though

she couldn't be bothered spending any more time on explanations. "Five hundred dollars a plate."

Fiona-belle gasped at the figure, but Billie would have preferred to gag over it. She couldn't believe that Ritter's organization was going to throw a party and raise oodles of money that was then not going to be used for Proposition Seven. Not to mention the cost of the party itself, and the waste it would generate. If there was no money for Proposition Seven, wouldn't it make more sense to forgo the party and solicit donations to clean the Chesapeake Bay? Or were they all just drowning in a sticky web of red tape?

Since arriving in the United States, Billie had begun to rethink her attitude about the way that the government allocated funding for environmental issues. People paid a lot of lip service to ecological programming, but nothing ever *happened*, near as she could tell. Maybe she needed to start up a Proposition Seven newsletter, or a blog— something really to get her point across. Since that had worked so well at Fairlawn...

"Does anyone have any questions?" Iris asked. It could have been Billie's imagination, but it certainly felt as though Iris was boring down directly on her, daring her to have a question, comment, or issue with the whole situation.

Of course Billie had an issue with the situation. But she was too smart to say anything about it now.

She smiled sweetly at Iris. "Will the interns be attending the party?" She was sure that they wouldn't be, seeing as how the whole shebang was costing mucho bikkies.

Surprisingly, Iris raised her eyebrows and smiled at Billie. "Of course!" she trilled enthusiastically.

Billie's mouth opened into a little O of surprise. She quickly closed it, though she remained as gobsmacked as ever.

Iris grinned. "We'll need your help ushering the event." She slapped her palm on the table for good measure, and turned and left the room.

That'd be right, Billie thought. She sighed. *It's going to be a screamer of a bash.*

Chapter Thirteen

From: billiesurf@email.com

To: elizarit@email.com

Subject: G'day again!

How're you going?

Things are good here, if a little bit rainy. I'm not used to spending this much time indoors. You must be in heaven, out doing fieldwork all the time instead of hunched over some computer.

Not that I'm complaining—I love working in your father's

office! Right now we interns are helping to organize a benefit dinner. I'm sure you're accustomed to these glam political functions, but the whole thing sounds seriously swank to me! I guess my only thought is whether it would be possible to be raising money for Proposition Seven, you know? I still can't believe it's been pushed aside for two years.

Hmm...but what was that I said about not complaining? I do think the party will be fun. Even if we're working it, rather than attending as guests, I'm getting excited.

I also had a chance to spend some time with Parker and the other folks from the newspaper the other day. We did some major "coffeehousing." Parker is great, and it's cool that he does something as important as running the school newspaper. He tells me you're not a writer, but maybe you'll have more to say now that you've spent some time down under, getting your hands dirty!

But now for the real scoop...how was the uni formal?

Billie

As she sat in the taxi back to Jess's house from the formal, Eliza was grinning so widely her cheeks hurt. Her night could not have been better if she had scripted it herself. She had gone to a fabulous college party with a sweet, sexy bloke (it made her giggle to think of a guy as a "bloke"), and they had kissed under the moonlight. She

didn't care if it was cheesy, romance-novel material. It was also perfect. Australia was shaping up to be better than she could have hoped. Way better.

One of the most surprising things about kissing Macca was how much she didn't think about Parker when the kissing was going on. In fact, if she was totally honest with herself, she hadn't been thinking much about Parker on this trip at all. Since their quick e-mail exchange a few weeks before, they'd mostly fallen out of contact, and Billie's note about hanging out with him was the closest she'd come to a proper update in a while. She was surprised that she felt a little guilty about this. In her heart of hearts, she knew that she and Parker had had different ideas about what "taking space" truly meant. But she couldn't help herself. Australia was her own personal buffet, and Macca was the dessert table.

Besides, Parker was cool, and independent, and not the kind of guy to pine away wistfully. His last e-mail was pretty upbeat, and obviously he and Billie were getting along. Maybe all he'd really needed was a new friend and a new focus for his energies in order to put their romance on hiatus the way she had…

Eliza had almost managed to convince herself of this fact as she got out of the taxi and headed for the back door that led to Jess's kitchen. Jess had said she would leave the door open so Eliza could sneak into the house and into Jess's room. The lights were on in the kitchen.

She slid the door and blinds open, slipped inside…and let out a small yelp of surprise.

There, at the kitchen table, sat a very tired and anxious-looking Jess, her father, and Frank.

Perfect, Eliza thought as she screwed up her face into an awkward smile, which she hoped conveyed the appropriate mixture of innocence and shame—something akin to a dog tucking its tail between its legs. It was clear immediately that it had little effect on her audience.

"Eliza, please come sit down," Frank said sternly. Eliza slid into the empty fourth seat at the table. "You'll never guess what happened tonight."

"Um…what?" Eliza didn't really want to know. She didn't like guessing games. Not one bit.

"Estelle and I were sitting down to dinner with the boys when we received a call. Do you know who that call might have been from?"

"No?" Eliza drummed her fingernails against the table, refusing to meet anyone's gaze. How could she possibly escape this situation? If only a trapdoor in the floor would hinge open and suck her down.

"It was Mr. Winstone. He was calling to say that if you couldn't work in the water because of your ankle injury, he could still use a hand cataloging the samples, and so you should come down anyway." He cleared his throat. "That, of course, begged the question of what sort of ankle injury you had and why it was something bad enough to skip

out on your internship but not so bad as to prevent you from hanging out with Jess for the evening." He arched his eyebrows suspiciously.

"So Estelle and I were very concerned about your welfare, and we decided we should find out what happened, but you weren't answering your mobile. Naturally, we grew concerned, and I rushed to the place you told us you would be. After I got here and waited for you and Jess to return, how curious it was that only one of you came through the door."

Eliza suddenly realized that she hadn't even thought about the fact that Mr. Winstone might call the house. Her excuse for the night was built on a very weak foundation, and someone had just kicked out one of her structure's legs. It was clear, based on Frank's expression, that he was not at all pleased with her, and that her entire life outside of class was about to change rather abruptly. A sense of impending doom crept up her spine, making her skin break out in goosebumps. But Frank wasn't finished.

"We are very disappointed in you, young lady."

Somehow, being called "young lady" felt more scathing than being called "brat," or maybe even a choice four-letter word. How was that even possible? Eliza wasn't the sort of girl who normally disappointed people. She was unhappy to learn that the experience left a hollow feeling at the base of her stomach.

"I think your parents would be most upset if they knew

you had snuck out to a college party in the middle of the night. Furthermore, you have abused the trust and respect that Jess's father, Estelle, and I have extended to you. You have lied to us, and more importantly, you have let us down."

Eliza felt a pang of genuine remorse. As much as she was different from the Echolses, with their 1950s *Ozzie and Harriet* sensibilities, she had grown to like them. She also wasn't used to going behind people's backs, or breaking rules. She realized that if word got back to anyone in D.C. about this, it could reflect poorly—very poorly—on her father.

Maybe if the Echolses knew what she'd snuck out for—how imperative it had been that she go to an Australian university formal—maybe then they'd be more sympathetic. They were kind, reasonable people. It could work.

"I'm sorry, I really am. I just got all caught up in everything. I really wanted to go to the formal, but I didn't know how to tell you about it. I just didn't want to miss out on such a culturally rich experience." She risked a searching glance at her host father.

Alas, no one was buying her mea culpa. Jess was doing everything she could not to look anyone in the eye. Her dad had busied himself preparing another cup of coffee and was now leaning against the kitchen counter, stirring his mug and staring off at an undefined point in the distance.

Frank leaped in again. "You cannot, I repeat, cannot go off and do something like this without talking to us. We are responsible for looking after you on behalf of your parents and if, heaven forbid, something were to happen to you, how would we know? How would we feel? How would your parents feel? Some things are about more than you."

Eliza flushed, guilt creeping up her spine like an actual, physical creature. She knew that some things were about more than her, of course, but couldn't this one thing—her semester abroad—be hers and only hers? Who was she really hurting, anyway, by going to a party with a boy whom she liked?

"I'm really sorry," she repeated, having run out of other appropriate words for the occasion.

Frank frowned at her. "Well, 'sorry' isn't going to cut it. Things are going to change now that you've shown you can't handle the level of personal responsibility we offered you. But for now, go gather your things, say good night to Jess, and apologize to her father. Then we'll be going."

As Eliza grabbed her stuff from Jess's bedroom, Jess came in to help.

"Ouch, that was rough," Jess said with a sympathetic smile.

"You're telling me." Eliza shook her head in disbelief.

Jess laid a hand on Eliza's forearm. "Listen, just lay low a little bit and let them cool off. I'm sure things will work themselves out."

"I hope you're right," Eliza said doubtfully. "I can't help but wonder if maybe I should have just been honest with them from the get-go. No matter what, you can bet I'll be on a short leash from now on." It was too awful to contemplate. And here she'd thought the Echolses were overprotective even before any of this mess had transpired.

Jess gave Eliza a hug and another sympathetic smile before they turned and headed back to the kitchen, where their parents were waiting.

Following some cursory good-byes and an apology to Jess's father, they were in the car cruising back home. Frank didn't speak a word to her. She felt like a villain in a comic book, *The Evil American*. She'd been exposed as the embodiment of every negative image people had of Americans—brash and arrogant, self-centered and obnoxious. And manipulative. She couldn't leave out manipulative. Not only had she let the Echolses down, but now Jess's family was onto her, as well. She wasn't used to being thought of as a troublemaker.

This was a disaster, an absolute disaster. The rest of the semester suddenly seemed like an endless expanse, indeed.

Eliza's life became considerably less free over the next few weeks. She was under a strict curfew, which the Echolses enforced stringently by insisting on driving her to, and picking her up from, her various activities. When they

couldn't be there themselves, they asked that the teacher or supervisor in charge call them to make sure Eliza had shown. It was humiliating. She was being treated like a prisoner out on parole.

For her own part, Estelle was determined to get Eliza back on track with her internship. She drove Eliza down to the site an hour early the following Saturday to meet with Mr. Winstone to discuss how Eliza could make up for her behavior with some extra-credit work. They arrived at the cramped warehouse office where the lab kits and equipment were kept to find Mr. Winstone awaiting them grimly. He gestured to two rickety folding chairs that faced his desk, indicating that they should sit, and so they did.

Eliza nervously picked at a cuticle and tried to avoid looking at either of the adults as the "sick day" excuse she had used a couple weeks earlier also came to light.

"Eliza, I have to say I'm very disappointed about this whole affair." Mr. Winstone looked genuinely angry. "I had trusted you, and to be honest, a stunt like this could jeopardize your eligibility to continue on as a S.A.S.S. student."

Eliza gulped. It hadn't occurred to her that she could be booted from the program. How would she ever live that down? And what would it mean for her father? A scandal like that was the sort of thing on which snarky bloggers thrived. There'd be no way to keep something like that under wraps.

Mr. Winstone sighed and continued. "However, we

do believe in second chances here. So rather than get S.A.S.S., the school, and your parents involved at this point, we are willing to explore make up options with you."

Eliza felt a rush of relief so strong that she wanted to jump across the desk and kiss Mr. Winstone. She managed to restrain herself as he went on.

"Believe me when I say that this will be your last chance. I must underline what I'm saying: this program was competitive, and you are here in place of many other qualified students who wanted to be here, and who I do suspect would take this program a good deal more seriously."

"I know, and I'm sorry," Eliza said, hoping he could hear the sincerity in her voice. "I really appreciate being given a chance to show you how much this opportunity means to me." And it was true; as much as the internship wasn't what she had expected, she wasn't ready to give it up. "I know I've really messed up, but I promise that I'll do better. I think I just got carried away with all the excitement of meeting new people and trying new things. You know, it's my first time away from home and all."

"Mr. Winstone, about the make up options: is there some sort of extra credit that Eliza might be able to do that would get her back into the swing of things?" Estelle asked.

"It's not something I've had to deal with before, but I'm sure that I can come up with something, and we can see how things go. Perhaps you can do some work during the

spring break?" Mr. Winstone looked thoughtful. "Some sort of special project?"

"That would be fine. Whatever you want," Eliza said quickly. The idea of working over her break wasn't perfect, but at least she wouldn't be sent home.

Mr. Winstone turned to Estelle. "I understand from Eliza that you will be spending the break down on the Mornington Peninsula. I have a friend who is a ranger on Prince Phillip Island, and I am certain he could use a hand counting and tagging the fairy penguins for a couple of days. He and his crew are responsible for monitoring the penguin population down there. It's important work but also, I should think, fun. Perhaps Eliza could help him out and write a report for me about it afterward? It would be a nice extension of the studies we have been doing on aquatic life in the bay here, and the interconnected eco-systems. Besides, Eliza—I'm told the young penguins are rather adorable."

"Why, yes! That sounds like an excellent idea for a project," Estelle enthused. "The twins have never been to Prince Phillip Island, so it will give us a good excuse to take them."

Eliza was pleasantly surprised. She smiled and accepted that this was the best possible outcome of being caught on her little personal walkabout. The weather would be warming up, and she could spend some time with cute and cuddly penguins—it had to be a step up from the mollusks, right?

Right.

Penguins: cute, Eliza thought to herself with determination. *Macca: even cuter.*

I can do this.

Of course, Jess and Nomes had been amused by what had happened. It seemed that her clandestine partying was seen by them as a rite of passage, and Eliza had passed with flying colors.

"So when are you going to be free to come out again? I'm sure Macca would love to see you," Jess prodded as they walked to the cafeteria on Monday.

Eliza blushed. "I don't have a clue. Spring break is coming up, and the Echolses have a house down by the sea and some sort of shop..."

"FISHY WISHY!" the other two girls chorused, startling Eliza enough that she nearly walked right into another student.

"What?"

"Fishy Wishy," Jess repeated, grinning. "I can't believe you're going to work there."

"It's a fish-and-chips place down in Sorrento," Nomes added. "Everybody knows it. Everybody goes down to the Mornington Peninsula since we were kids. You're going

to love the uniforms. And you thought the St. Cat's outfit was bad!"

Jess must have noticed the look of panic spreading across Eliza's face. "Don't worry," she consoled her. "It won't be so bad. You'll be there for two weeks. I know you'll get some time to hit the beach."

"I appreciate the thought. Hopefully they'll start easing up on me soon. I've been playing everything very by the book, and they seem to appreciate that, so maybe they'll give me a bit of a break once we get there." She sighed, feeling extremely sorry for herself. She knew she'd made her own bed, but that didn't make lying in it any less irksome....

"Listen, who knows? Once you're down there, things might turn out differently than you expect. Maybe the Echolses will loosen up. Just be sure to be on your best behavior for a bit." Jess tried her best smile of encouragement, but it wasn't quite enough in the face of this sad situation.

"I have been," Eliza said. "It's just, I'm not the kind of girl who usually has to be *told* to be on her best behavior." She shrugged. "Never mind. So what are you guys up to later?"

"The weather is supposed to finally turn, and if it's warm, we're going to spend the evening at Luna Park checking out the rides." Nomes looked hopefully at Eliza.

"Lucky you. With my curfew I'm *definitely* not allowed

out to go to Luna Park. Besides, I think we're going to see some old steam train so the twins can ride around on it for a while. Do you know anything about that?"

"Oh, man. Puffing Billy? I haven't been there since I was a kid." Jess rolled her eyes. "The thing runs around this track for no reason at all, and after a couple hours you're back where you started. It's not so bad, I guess; the scenery is nice. I'm sure it'll keep the twins happy."

The girls fell silent, and Eliza stared at the ground as they walked into the cafeteria. The twins had their whole lives to explore Australia. Eliza had only this one semester.

"Hey," Jess said as she put her arm around Eliza. "You buck up, all right? Remember, there's a reason we say 'no worries' down here. We're going to find a way to make your time a good one, I promise." She jerked her head meaningfully at Nomes.

"Yeah, we promise," and Nomes put her arm around Eliza's opposite shoulder.

Sandwiched between her two friends, Eliza couldn't help but laugh. "Well, okay," she conceded, "but only since you both *promise.*" She lifted her chin and threw her shoulders back like she was in the military, causing Jess and Nomes to giggle. "No worries!" she said brightly.

She only hoped it turned out to be true.

Chapter Fourteen

From: elizarit@email.com
To: billiesurf@email.com
Subject: squeaky wheel

G'day, mate! (Sorry, I couldn't resist. Are you sick of hearing that yet?)

Thanks for your last e-mail—it sounds like you're having a good time, and settling in nicely.

I'm sorry to hear that things are a little weird over at your internship, though. I hadn't really ever thought about all of the red tape that my father and his group have to deal with. I guess I sort of always took for granted that the bureaucracy was just the way things are. But if you're used to being outdoors and actually working in the environment, I can see where watching funds get funneled away from things you care about—like Proposition Seven—would be really frustrating. But maybe try not to feel bad or guilty about the weirdness, if you can help it—maybe they need a squeaky wheel over there to shake things up?

The funny thing is that I've never been the squeaky type, myself. I always just assumed that everything my father and his various groups did made perfect sense. And yet, since I've been down here, I've done nothing but make trouble. Not intentionally, but that doesn't seem to change the outcome. Your parents must be losing their minds.

I don't understand it myself. There must be something about travel that helps me to tap into my rebellious spirit. Which is hilarious, considering I never even knew that I had one....

Oh—and I'm glad to hear that you and Parker have been having fun. Tell him I say hi and I will write back to his last e-mail soon!

Eliza

The thing about busywork, Billie was learning, was that it could be so very...*busy*. Stuffing envelopes, making copies, and occasionally even—gasp...collating!—didn't sound like very hard work, and really, it wasn't. But it was soul-

crushingly dull, mind-numbingly boring, and completely and utterly *not* inspirational. Not one bit.

Billie wasn't above paying her dues with a little administrative work, but none of this made her feel like an environmental crusader. Rather, as time passed and she grew old and wrinkly under the dull glow of fluorescent lighting, Billie only felt increasingly smoggy. Her brain, that was. Her brain was as black and dusty as the inside of a vacuum cleaner. Or as soggy and polluted as a compost heap. She'd been keeping up with her habit of daily jogs at sunrise, mainly because it was the only time of day she got to take in fresh air, but it wasn't the same as being back home, out on the surf. She was starting to feel like a landlocked mermaid, or a goldfish that had tripped from the bowl.

She sighed heavily and almost completely subconsciously, her entire upper body shuddering with the weight of it, and was startled when Parker, her partner in said busywork (today it was gluing dozens and dozens of address labels to big, fat first-class mailers—would the paper trail never end?) responded to her with a chuckle.

"It's not that bad," he said. He slapped a mailing label onto an envelope with gusto, sticky-side down, just for emphasis.

"Maybe not," Billie said, "but I sure wouldn't want to see it get much worse."

"It could be cold calls." Parker waggled his eyebrows.

"You could be phoning people for surveys. And phoning, and phoning, and phoning—"

"I get it," Billie interrupted, rolling her eyes. "Yes, I reckon that could be a crack more painful. Ugh." One thing that Billie had learned about herself during her U.S. stay was that, despite the fact that her native language was English, people often had no idea what the heck she was saying. Something about the accent really threw them, even as they giggled and launched into their own Crocodile Hunter impressions. It was completely baffling. So phone calls would have been a particularly unique form of torture.

She straightened up in her seat at the thought, rolling her shoulders backward as though to shrug off the jinx of Parker's supposition. "Let's change the subject," she suggested. "I'd hate to see our deepest, darkest worries accidentally come true."

"Fair enough," Parker said. He drummed his fingers against the top of his desk. "I think the problem is that it's too quiet here today."

He was right. Fiona-belle had been put on poster duty for the morning, and were off slapping flyers on every community bulletin board between Ritter's office and Capitol Hill. Though posters were just as egregiously unecological as oversized first-class mailers, Billie was actually a little bit jealous of them for being out in the sunshine and actual fresh air.

Feeling the first tinges of a rumbling in her stomach,

Billie glanced at her watch: 12:43. No wonder she was grouchy. It was feeding time. She looked longingly toward the windows on the far side of the cube farm where she and Parker were camped out. She didn't really have time for a proper tuck in the honest-to-outdoors for the lunch hour. But.

A pick-me-up might be just the thing to get me through the rest of the afternoon, she thought to herself. It certainly couldn't make her any *less* motivated than she was already feeling, that was for sure.

"Do you fancy nipping out for sarni?" she asked Parker, swiveling her chair in his direction.

He knit his eyebrows together and pretended to consider her offer. "I'm assuming you're asking me to lunch," he said, grinning.

Billie nodded. "I keep forgetting to draw you up that glossary you so desperately need."

"Yeah, well, Australian English, American English—no matter how you say it, I'm kind of starving," he admitted. He smacked one more label onto an envelope, then pushed back from his desk and out of his chair.

"You realize that if we go out to eat, we're going to have to work double-time just to finish up this crazy stack of letters before six."

Billie nodded and pointed again toward the windows, this time specifically to the cloudless blue sky.

"That's a chance I'm willing to take."

• • •

"This day's a beaut," Billie said, breathing in the crisp fall air. "The only thing that would make this"—she gestured to the verdant lawn of the Capitol Mall—"absolutely perfect would be if the street vendors carried Marmite." She dunked a chunk of soft pretzel into a small container of mustard resting on the park bench beside her for good measure.

She swung her legs out in front of her happily. For the thirty minutes that she and Parker had managed to escape the cube farm, Billie felt energized and alive. And she obviously wasn't the only one. Couples strolled hand in hand along the sidewalk; business types managed to keep their mobiles tucked securely in their pockets, at least for the duration of lunch; and birds twittered in chorus with a nearby guitarist. The whole scene was like something out of an advert for Washington, D.C. For once. Color, drama, bustle, energy. Billie loved it.

She'd love it even more if she had some Marmite. But that was not to be.

Parker shuddered. "I don't know what Marmite is, but from the sound of it, it's bad news."

Billie laughed through a mouthful of pretzel. "It's yeast spread." She paused for a moment, contemplating. "I suppose 'yeast spread' does sound pretty disgusting when you put it baldly like that." She smiled. "I think you're just going to have to trust me on this one."

175

Parker arched a dubious eyebrow in her direction. "Trust you? Maybe. Try it? Pass."

Billie shrugged and took another bite of her pretzel. Swallowing, she said, "Isn't that the whole point of a cultural exchange? We introduce each other to our countries' customs and habits?"

"Consider me sufficiently introduced. I would prefer not to get any more chummy with Marmite," Parker said, laughing.

"Fair enough," Billie said, shaking her head. "Eliza said the same thing in her last e-mail—that my parents have been pushing Marmite on her every morning with her brekkie…" She trailed off as she realized that Parker's face had gone still at the mention of his maybe-ex-girlfriend.

Dumb, dumb, dumb, she thought. She couldn't believe she'd been so thoughtless as to bring up Eliza's name. Especially when she and Parker were having such a fun time just enjoying some sunshine on their lunch break.

But as quickly as Parker's expression had darkened, it cleared again. He blinked as though determinedly wiping away unpleasant thoughts. "I didn't realize you guys talked," he said, finally.

"We e-mail," Billie admitted. "It sounds like she's been keeping busy. But she told me to say hi." She winced as she passed the message along to Parker, who no doubt would have preferred to hear from Eliza himself. There was a funny feeling stirring in her chest, too, as she watched a mix of emotions pass over her new friend's face. Could it be...was it actually...

Was she *jealous*? Of Parker's relationship with Eliza?

Of course not. That would be silly. She and Parker were just friends. And even if they weren't, what was going on with him and Eliza was clearly complicated at best.

Whatever Parker was thinking, he didn't let on. His mouth had settled into an impassive line. After another beat he said, "Tell her I say hi back."

"I will," Billie said, wishing the subject would change itself.

No such luck, though. "How is she liking her internship?" Parker asked lightly.

"I think the great outdoors have taken some getting used to," Billie said.

At this, Parker finally smiled. "I'm sure."

Billie felt emboldened by his grin. "We talked a little bit about how frustrated I've been at *our* internship. She was pretty understanding." Billie wasn't sure why she was so surprised about that fact, but she was—after all, she and Eliza were still practically strangers, when all was said and done.

"Really," Parker mused. "That's interesting. You must be rubbing off on her."

He paused. "You know, someone at school mentioned

this group to me. They call themselves the Green Gorillas. They do guerrilla marketing and stuff for the environment. They're a high school offshoot of a group that first sprung up on college campuses. They meet once a week. I can't remember where, but some Internet café near Georgetown. New members always welcome. You should swing by one of their meetings. Check it out. You never know. I'm sure you can find them online."

"Guerrilla marketing," Billie repeated. "That sounds serious."

"Well, it's gotta be more serious than scanning and photocopying all day, right?"

"You've got me there," Billie conceded. "Will you come with me?"

Parker nodded. "I will. Even though I really shouldn't—not if I want to keep my grade-point average up," he said. "Physics is killing me." He glanced at her. "But for you, anything."

Billie knew he was only teasing, but her stomach did a backflip at the lilt in his voice just the same. "I understand," she said, tossing her now-empty mustard cup into the paper bag her snack had come in and crumpling the whole thing into a wrinkled ball.

"Speaking of killing"—her eyes twinkled—"aren't you just dying to get back to work?"

Parker shook his head. "You have no idea."

Chapter Fifteen

Eliza was sitting in Billie's bedroom at the beach house staring at a nearly life-sized purple, stuffed dolphin. If the bedroom in Melbourne was a seven out of ten in terms of eco- and surfing-obsessed, this was an eleven. There were posters of surfers on preposterously large waves, dolphins and whales in the wild, and sunsets over exotic beaches in places like Tahiti. There were even some photos tacked up to the small vanity mirror by the closet showing Billie and a freckle-faced friend mugging for the camera. Eliza recognized her as Val, another crunchy-type from school.

Val seemed nice enough, though she definitely didn't run with Jess and Nomes.

It was shocking to Eliza how different she and Billie were. Their S.A.S.S. program was an exchange program, and yet it was hardly as though the two girls could be dropped into each other's life seamlessly. She wondered how much of who they each were was innate and how much was a product of circumstance, of environment. It was a strange thought—if she had been born in Australia, to the Echolses, she might have turned out like Billie.

Or would she? Would she have loved shopping, shoes, and sipping lattes, and hated mud, marshes, and malls of the non-shopping variety no matter what?

Eliza wasn't thrilled with the direction her semester had taken, but there wasn't a lot she could do about it now. She was going to make the best of the situation and see how things would roll out. That apparently included culti-vating a newfound appreciation for surf photography and friendly stuffed animals.

She flopped down on the bed and pulled out her mobile to call Jess.

"Eliza! What's going on? How's Sorrento?"

"Musty." She sniffed the bedding, which clearly had not had a thorough airing out all winter. "How's Noosa?" Jess and her family had a vacation home in Queensland, near the barrier reef, where she was spending the vacation.

"It's good. Sunny and warm, which hits the spot."

"I can't believe everyone else gets to have a fabulous break, and I'm stuck here."

"I'm telling you, Sorrento can be awesome, and we'll be home soon to hang. You're going to have a ripper if you just roll with it. Remember, no worries, right?"

"Yeah, no worries," Eliza said without conviction. The Aussie catchphrase held little appeal to her at the moment. "I should probably get going. We're supposed to go down to Fishy Wishy for my 'job training.' At least they're saying I'll get some time off to go to the beach, but I still have to do the penguin project."

"Well, I'm sure it'll all be good. I'll call you tonight when we get back in from the beach."

Eliza groaned at the thought of spending the afternoon stuck in a fish shack while her friends were living it up at the beach.

"Okay, talk to you later." She hung up her cell phone and stared at a poster of a giant sting ray that hung over the bed. She was suddenly more curious about Billie than ever.

What was up with that girl? Had she been born with gills?

And if so, was she feeling as much a fish out of water in D.C. as Eliza was in Australia?

Fishy Wishy was everything Eliza had feared.

As she and Frank pulled up, she saw that it was an

overdone storefront shack on the main street in Sorrento. The street was a broad boulevard with the usual assortment of beach shops featuring bathing suits, souvenirs, and plenty of places to sit out and eat. The building was a low, one-story affair, with a faux-tiki top on the front and a big picture window. Out front were several tables on a patio that stretched onto the sidewalk.

The shack was open year-round with a skeleton staff, but as the weather turned warm they needed more people to service the increasing crowds that marked summer in Sorrento. That was where Eliza came in.

The shack itself was a lot like a McDonald's in layout but without the corporate slickness and flair. There was a counter facing the front, some tables inside, a bunch more outside, and an open kitchen in the back that mostly contained some freezers with fish and pre-cut frozen french fries—or chips as the Aussies say—and a bunch of deep fryers. There was a small station set up where fixings and buns could be added to sandwiches, but mostly what they served were fried foods, tossed into plastic baskets lined with wax paper.

"My parents bought this place back in the fifties, before Sorrento was even built up. They ran it, and every summer I worked here. This place is a real Echols family tradition, and we're proud to have you joining us," Frank said as he ushered Eliza into the store.

They walked up to the counter, where a quiet, slightly nerdy-looking guy came rushing up to greet Frank.

"Eliza, this is Steve. He's the manager, and he'll be supervising you and helping you get the lay of the land." Frank smiled and disappeared into a small office in the back.

Billie had explained via e-mail that Steve was a college student at the local TAFE—a kind of junior college or vocational school down here. He had worked at Fishy Wishy in high school and now was in charge of looking after the place when the Echolses weren't around, which was often. He gave her a quick tour and then offered her a uniform.

"That's about it. Here's a uniform that should fit you. Why don't you get changed in the bathroom, and we'll get you started at the fry station?"

Eliza took the hat, shirt, and pants into the bathroom and slid into them reluctantly. Once she was dressed, she took a look in the mirror and had to fight the urge to scream.

From bottom to top, Eliza saw the following:

Sneakers: Her own, and thus quite cute.

Pants: Red-and-white-striped pants. Red-and-white-striped *polyester* pants. Red-and-white-striped scratchy polyester pants that made a strange crinkling noise when she moved.

A shirt: A matching red-and-white-striped collared

shirt with what appeared to be mild discoloration in the armpits from a previous employee. It was clean, but that was small consolation.

A hat: Not just any hat. It was in the shape of a basket of fish and chips and had emblazoned across it the phrase: WHICH FISHY DO YOU WISHY?

It was all too humiliating for words. The only solace Eliza had was in the fact that there was little chance of her seeing anyone she knew from Melbourne and virtually no chance that any friends from back home would ever witness this.

Sometimes you just had to look on the bright side.

Eliza's first day on the job could be graciously described as an unmitigated disaster. Her first attempt at operating the fry station nearly burned the shack down when she knocked the saltshaker *into* the fryer. What ensued could only be compared to a science-class volcano she had made in middle school, what with the oil splashing all over everything until Steve stepped in and shut the thing down.

By the end of the day, her confidence had increased by a fraction—but that wasn't saying much.

The next several days followed a pattern. Each morning Frank or Estelle would drive her down to the village of Sorrento from the beach house. The house was on a small hill and had a nice view of the bay. The ride into town was only ten minutes or so, but Estelle pointed out that in the high season the traffic could stretch the trip into half an hour.

Eliza would get an hour or so on the beach before she had to come in for the lunch rush. Then she would work through until around five or six, when the sun would start to fade and they would shut the shack down. Steve would usually give her a lift back to the Echolses' on his way to night classes.

In the evenings, Eliza would watch TV with the twins, who, for two people with identical DNA, had remarkably different interests—they would argue as Nick insisted on animal programs and Sam demanded the Naked Brothers Band or the animated show *Kid Kelly*. If Eliza didn't feel like negotiating the TV viewing, she would chat on her computer and she would usually talk with Jess or Macca for a bit each night after everyone else had gone to bed. All in all, things weren't horrendous, but she was definitely missing some normal teenage company and was sorry not to be off having some amazing adventure like everyone else was.

"Eh, it's not so bad, I get to spend some time on the beach. I just miss the girls," she told Macca one night late that first week. She was actually looking forward to the end of break so she could at least be back with her friends.

"And me, too, right?"

Eliza could almost hear the laughter in his voice.

"Yes, and you, too," she admitted. They'd been talking regularly every day since the formal and by now were fairly well established as a couple. Which made the timing of this trip even more inauspicious.

"What about your penguin thing?"

"Right, that. It actually sounds fun—we're going to be tagging and monitoring baby penguins to make sure their population is growing the way that it's supposed to. We're going down there next week. Probably Thursday, but man, it's going to be a long bunch of days between now and then." She sighed, thinking of the fry baskets at the Fishy Wishy.

"Hey, listen, we have an expression down here: 'no worries.' Stay positive, okay?"

"Yeah, yeah. That's me—Polly Positive. But you guys also have a silly thing like an emu for a national animal, so I don't know how much I trust you."

Macca laughed at that one, and hearing him laugh, Eliza laughed, too. Funny, she thought, how just the sound of his laughing made her entire outlook brighten in an instant.

No worries, she decided. *None at all. For now, anyway...*

"Yes sir, I understand. The meal is seven dollars and fifty cents, not seven hundred and fifty dollars. I'll just reenter that."

Okay, so Eliza hadn't fully gotten the swing of the register, but she was improving. The customer paid and walked away.

Eliza leaned against the front counter of the Fishy Wishy and watched the people come and go from the tables outside. It was a Thursday, and she'd been told that the crowd didn't really pick up until Friday and the weekend. Then it got so crazy she wouldn't have a chance to rest, but for now she was just standing and watching people pass back and forth.

She glanced idly down the street and noticed a pack of guys her age walking along the boulevard. They were joking with one another and appeared to be headed toward the fish shack.

As they got closer she realized that one of the guys looked awfully familiar. Something about his gait...Way too familiar.

Is that? No way!

It was.

Macca.

It was Macca, and he was grinning so widely at her she thought he was going to swallow his own face. Eliza struggled to keep her cool, biting the inside of her lips so she wouldn't smile like a goon. Then she remembered the polyester stripes and the hat and just gave up. Cool was clearly out of the question.

Suddenly Macca was standing right in front of her.

She broke into a huge smile almost involuntarily.

"Excuse me, miss, you got anything good?"

"Depends. What are you looking for?" It was hard to be flirtatious while wearing an enormous french fry hat on her head, but she gave it her all.

"Howsabout a cute American in a fry-basket hat?"

Eliza blushed. "You're in luck, then. But what are you doing here?"

"Some of my mates and I were going for a surf out at Portsea, and I told them we had to stop by on our way."

"There's no surfing in Sorrento?" As excited as she was by Macca's unexpected drop-in, it was too sad that he was headed right out.

"Nah, you got Buckley's chance of catching a wave here. You're on the bay side of the peninsula. Head out to Portsea for the real breaks."

Eliza had no idea what he'd just said, but that didn't matter. She was thrilled to see him.

"What time do you get out of here?" he continued.

"I'm on until six, but then I have to be home by seven for dinner. The manager usually gives me a lift up there. I'm still on curfew from the Trinity Affair." Eliza managed to speak in capital letters to get her point across.

"Yeah, again, I'm real sorry about that."

"No! Don't be. I had a great time, and it was totally worth it. But you know, actions, consequences, etc., etc...."

"Well, tell you what, how about I pick you up at six and

I can give you a lift back to the Echolses' place, if that's all right with you and Mr. Bossman over there?"

"That'd be great," Eliza said. She tried not to appear too enthusiastic.

As expected, she failed utterly. But to be entirely truthful, she didn't much mind.

The rest of the afternoon went by in a flash, and before she knew it she was standing out front waiting for Macca to show. She was wiping down the outdoor tables with a sponge that had definitely seen better days when she saw a funky old dune buggy with a surfboard strapped across the open top cruise down the street. It pulled to a stop in front of her. Macca sat in the front seat and waved her in.

"This thing is so cool," she squealed, piling into the passenger's side eagerly. The wind rushed through her hair as they pulled out and headed off.

"It was my pop's back in the sixties when he started surfing, and we've kept it in running shape ever since. It's an old VW." Macca was proud of the buggy, she could tell. It was totally adorable.

"Doesn't look like any VW I've ever seen." Not that she was an expert on cars—not hardly—but she could recognize retro when she saw it. "I like it," she decided.

"We've got a bit of time before seven—want to go for a drive?"

"I don't know. If I'm late because I was riding around with you, I'm toast." The last thing she needed was more marks against her while she was struggling to get back into the Echolses' good graces.

"Don't worry, I'll have you back, I promise!"

Eliza thought for a moment…but *only* for a moment. When it came to Macca, she was completely and totally powerless to resist.

"Just make sure I'm back home on time, or it'll be both our butts, okay?"

"Trust me," and he turned up the radio and sped onto the main road toward Portsea.

A short time later they were parked overlooking a long stretch of beach with waves rolling in and a few sun-set surfers trying to catch last rides. The air had finally become warm, and she was now getting a sense of how nice the weather could be. She'd been able to work in short sleeves, and when the sun was out, she could even squeeze in some power tanning at the beach. Now the air was cooling as the late-afternoon rays began to fade to multicolored streaks on the horizon.

"It's beautiful. It looks so peaceful out there." Eliza thought she could sit there, in the car, drinking in the view indefinitely. If only that were an option.

"It is. But don't get fooled. There are some nasty rips. Harold Holt went missing just a couple beaches up."

"That's so sad. Was he a friend of yours?"

Macca smiled and shook his head. "Nope. He was a prime minister back in the sixties. Went for a swim one afternoon and then 'poof.'" He made a wavy gesture with his hands to demonstrate what "poof" meant.

"Wait. You mean to tell me that a prime minister just disappeared? What happened?" Eliza couldn't imagine something like that happening in D.C. Americans couldn't stand an unsolved mystery. That was why forensics shows were so popular.

"Nobody knows."

"Talk about 'no worries'! You guys really are relaxed down here! If the president went missing, there'd be years of investigations and movies and books and everything. Here? Nothing."

"Yep, no worries, and she'll be 'right, mate."

They sat quietly for a bit and just watched the waves roll in. It was nice to be with Macca. For a moment she could forget about having to be the proper daughter to her parents, or the proper houseguest to the Echolses'. For now, "no worries" was a philosophy that Eliza could definitely embrace.

Eventually time got the best of them, and they had to turn around and make their way back to the Echolses'. As they raced back along the road, Macca glanced quickly over at her and smiled.

"So, some mates and I are going down to Bells next week for a couple nights, and I was thinking, you should come."

"What's Bells?" Whatever it was, it sounded great.

"Bells Beach is some of the greatest surfing on the planet. It's down the great ocean road between Torquay and Lorne. If you come, I'll teach you to surf."

"Who says I don't already know how to surf?" she teased.

"You do?"

"There are lots of things you don't know about me," she said, poking him in the ribs. "But, no, I don't surf," she admitted. "I'd love a lesson from the master."

"Well, how about it, then? Can you get away for a couple days? We're going on Sunday afternoon, and I'll have you back for your field trip on Thursday." Macca's eyes twinkled in such a way that it almost killed her to have to decline.

"I really want to, but the Echolses would end me. I feel bad about everything that happened before and all, so I'm trying to be on my best behavior." She bit her lip. She hated the idea of missing out on prime one-on-one time with Macca. And learning to surf, too! Wasn't that the whole point of going abroad—to try her hand at new experiences?

She frowned, deep in thought. Finally, she continued. "I don't know. How about we talk Saturday, and I'll let you know for sure then? In the meantime, if you're staying down here, you can pick me up from work if you're free."

"It's not surfing," Macca said, conceding, "but I reckon it will have to do, for now."

It *definitely* wasn't surfing, though. And surfing was starting to sound like an opportunity not to be missed.

Chapter Sixteen

Billie knew from all of her S.A.S.S. guidebooks and supplementary materials that Georgetown was a historic area of D.C., but she was pleasantly surprised to discover, as she and Parker hopped off the bright red-and-silver Circulator bus—the bus spewing extremely un-eco-friendly fumes in every direction—that it was upscale and hip, as well. Trendy boutiques lined the cobblestone streets, and she could just imagine Eliza on a shopping spree after school or on the weekend.

For a moment, Billie had a small rush of self-doubt: the area was quite posh and she herself more the natural type, but then she decided that any group calling itself the Green Gorillas was probably pretty low-key. She glanced down at the note she'd scrawled to herself with the address of the group's meeting place. It was a coffeehouse called Drip, and if she was reading her Yahoo Maps printout correctly, it was right…over…

There! She gave herself a little mental high five. Slowly but surely, this Earth Mama was learning to adjust to life in the big city. "We found it," she said, grinning breathlessly at Parker.

He arched an eyebrow at her. "Was there any doubt?"

She laughed, and shrugged, not wanting to admit that her sense of direction was hardly her strongest quality. "Never mind," she said, starting forward.

She looked both ways before crossing the street—so confusing how Americans insisted on driving on the wrong side of the road—and they darted into the coffee shop, Billie ducking her head down to avoid a collision course with the oversized wooden coffee-mug sign swinging ominously over the doorway.

Upon stumbling into the shop, she realized she needn't have worried about being too "natural" for the Green Gorillas. Her eyes scanned the place—rickety, mismatched wooden furniture painted in bright primary colors, framed old-fashioned record covers hanging askew across the walls—and lit on a cluster of people about her own age huddled in the far corner. One guy in particular seemed

to be holding court at the makeshift "head" of two round tables that had been pushed together. He had dreadlocks sprouting off in every direction and was wearing a worn-in long-sleeved T-shirt that read I ♥ RECYCLING.

From alongside her, Parker poked her in the ribs. "Your kind of people, right?"

She didn't turn to look at him, but nodded her head just the same, wondering briefly if Parker, in fact, felt vaguely out of place in his typical preppy uniform of jeans and a pocket T-shirt. *Never mind that he actually wears "prep" well,* she thought.

The group at the table had to be the Green Gorillas, but just to be on the safe side, Billie nodded in the direction of a passing waitress. The woman looked briefly irked (or that could have just been the effect of her glaring eyebrow stud).

"Is that the—"

"Green Gorillas. They meet here every week," the waitress said shortly, then tottered off on matchstick legs in a blur of tattoos and black hair dye.

"Friendly," Parker murmured, mostly to himself. It made Billie smile.

Swallowing hard and gathering her courage, Billie made her way toward the back table. Any hopes she'd had of sidling up subtly, however, were dashed as she tripped on an uneven plank of flooring and careened directly into Mr. Dreadlocks himself.

She extricated herself from the arms of his chair and willed her face to return from tomato red to its natural hue. "Erm. Hi."

"Were you actually looking for the Green Gorillas, or did I just happen to sweep you off your feet without even trying?"

Dreadlocks grinned winningly, and Billie grew even more flustered. "Yes. I mean, no. I mean, sorry." She took a deep breath. "I didn't mean to crash into you. But I was looking for your group. A friend of mine at school—well, he's an exchange student and we do this internship together—I mean, I should explain, I'm from Melbourne—" Suddenly every word in the English language that Billie had ever known was spewing from her mouth at once. It wasn't pretty.

"Why don't we just start with the basics?" Dreadlocks asked, mercifully cutting her off. "I'm Adam." He stuck out a hand for her to shake.

"I'm Billie. And usually I'm a little more together than this. Not a lot, but a little." She smiled. "I'm doing the S.A.S.S. exchange program, and I intern for the Ritter campaign. But we haven't had the chance to do a whole lot of hands-on kind of stuff, so a friend suggested that I come by and check you guys out."

"Your friend is very wise," Adam said, his hair bobbing in time with his words.

"Thanks," Parker said loudly, stepping forward and

extending his own hand for Adam to shake. "I'm Parker. Otherwise known as Billie's 'friend.'"

Billie winced. She couldn't believe that she'd been so rude as to forget all about Parker in her tongue-twisted spazz-out. Thankfully, he seemed to be taking it okay.

Adam shook Parker's hand, then tilted backward and swept his hand across the table in a general sort of introduction. "This is Lisi, Meredith, Jordan, and Cal," he said, as a petite blonde in pigtails, a tall, cool brunette, a steel-jawed boy with blazing green eyes, and a tall, lanky guy whose freckles formed constellations across his cheeks shook their heads at her and otherwise waved their hellos in turn.

"Don't worry," Lisi said, smiling. "There won't be a test or anything."

"Thank goodness for that, mate!" Billie exclaimed, causing the table to break out in good-natured laughter.

Adam twisted in his seat and reached for a stray chair from a nearby table. "Sit," he said, dragging the chair over and pulling his own seat back to make room for Billie. He patted at the chairs invitingly.

After a brief glance at Parker and a questioning shrug of their respective shoulders, Billie and Parker decided to do just that, and happily.

As it turned out, Adam had mainly been crowned head of the Green Gorillas via family lineage, like a sort of eco-royalty. His older brother was big into environmentalism at Georgetown, where he was a freshman, and he had essentially appointed Adam leader of the 2.0 pack as a means of maintaining forward momentum.

The group's big plan for the spring was to stage a massive sit-in to protest the postponement of Proposition Seven. They were firm believers that putting the proposition on the back burner was just the first step in a bottomless pool of red tape that would result in nothing being done to clean the bay. For his part, Adam had been doing this for long enough that he knew how to pull in support from local media to maximize the impact and the attention that the group's protest would achieve.

"So you're pro-protest?" Billie asked. She was definitely starting to feel that she was, too, after all she'd learned through her research, but she wanted to hear Adam's take on the matter. Unlike Iris and everyone else she'd met at Ritter's office, he seemed like someone who cared about the environment on a pragmatic level. In other words, less talk-y, more do-y.

"It's the most immediate and impactful way of making our voices heard," Adam explained.

"And like I told you at school, the Green Gorillas are all about making their voices heard," Parker chimed in. "Some of the college outposts of the group have made waves for some particularly high-profile efforts."

Adam nodded grimly. "Obviously, we want to work with

administrators to the best that we can, but you know what they say about the squeaky wheel…"

Billie couldn't deny that. And despite the nagging feeling that Ritter might not appreciate her joining a group that was going to protest his policy, Billie was in—all in.

Luckily, Parker seemed to feel as galvanized as she did, and the two left the Green Gorillas' meeting buzzing with energy and anticipation—something she knew had nothing to do with the caffeine surging through their systems.

"That was…incredible," she gushed as they boarded a bus heading back to their neck of the woods. "I owe you a huge thanks for the hookup."

Well, not "hookup" hookup, she realized, blushing to herself and allowing a momentary mind movie of Adam's sparkling eyes. Maybe there was another reason for the tingling she felt all across the surface of her skin…

Unfortunately, back at school on Monday, Heather was nowhere to be found. Rumor had it that she'd caught an icky stomach bug that had been going around. Or maybe she was just suffering from the same vitamin-D deficiency that seemed to have taken hold of Billie herself.

Forced to put her need for girl talk on hold, Billie went for the next best thing. She tracked Parker down in the student newspaper office.

As usual, she found him in position behind his enormous computer monitor, engrossed in whatever his latest story was. The screen threw ghostly flickers of light across his face as he stared ahead, lost in thought. Billie almost hated to disturb him.

Almost. But not quite.

Giggling to herself softly, she tiptoed up behind him, snaking her hands lightly around his face and placing them firmly over his eyes. "Guess wh—"

Parker shouted "Whoa!" and jumped up from his seat, clearly startled.

Billie dropped her hands to her sides and stepped back sheepishly. "Did you guess?"

"I *guess* you almost gave me a heart attack!" Parker said, his voice stern, but his eyes twinkling. "Jeez."

"Sorry 'bout that." Billie tried to look contrite, but it was hard when the corners of her mouth still wanted to perk up into a grin. Parker was cute when he was scared half to death. "But...I have a great story idea for us!"

"Yeah?" Parker motioned for her to take a seat at the swivel chair next to his own. "If you're not exaggerating, then all is forgiven."

"I'm not exaggerating. At least, I don't think so," Billie assured him, settling down next to him and leaning forward with enthusiasm. "I was thinking we could do a profile on the Green Gorillas, you know? And the sit-in they're planning."

She *had* been thinking about it—all day Sunday while she was supposed to be working on homework, the thought

of the piece had played itself over and over in her mind.

The thought of the piece, and the piercing brightness of Adam's eyes.

Somehow, though, she didn't think the part about Adam's eyes was going to be the winning argument for Parker. So she'd decided to take a different tack. The activist tack. If she'd learned one thing about Parker since arriving in D.C., she knew how to hit him where he lived.

"The thing is"—she said, words pouring from her mouth in a heated rush—"the sit-in is something that anyone can get involved in, you know? And it's so proactive—like, just the one day, but a day of action. And talk about visibility! You remember what Adam said—the Gorillas' blog gets, like, hundreds of hits a day. Trust me—people will know about this protest. It's going to be so much more effective than all of those stupid mailings, e-mails, and endless, pointless 'research' that we've been doing over at Ritter's office. And you *know* we're not the only ones who are totally tired of the busywork." Her eyes glittered as she described the plan. She truly couldn't wait to pull it off.

"It definitely sounds like it could be big," Parker agreed.

Billie couldn't help but hear the slight note of reluctance in his voice. "But?"

"I just...wonder how Mr. Ritter is going to take it. The news of your involvement, I mean."

Billie's eyebrows squinched up. For her part, she'd been

trying not to think about that. "Maybe he'll be impressed that we're taking…um, initiative?" Her voice squeaked, a telltale giveaway that her confidence wasn't nearly as strong as she was hoping to project.

Parker shrugged. "Look," he said, "I think the sit-in is a good idea. I mean, heck, sign me up. But it's *possible* that Mr. Ritter would prefer something a little more off the grid. You know, quieter. Walk softly, and all that. Since you're basically protesting against his own office."

Billie slapped her palm against the desk. The horrible part was, of course, that Parker made sense. She'd have to be mad not to assume that the sit-in wouldn't ruffle some feathers.

But still. "We *have* been walking softly. Too softly. And the result is that the bay might never be cleaned."

Parker shook his head again. "I believe you. And like I say, I'm not disagreeing with you. But I've known the Ritters for a while now, and I think you might want to give Mr. Ritter the heads-up about it before D-day. And before you write it up for the paper."

Billie considered this for a moment. The notion of confronting Mr. Ritter was terrifying, even if it was the Right Thing to Do. For the time being, she decided to put the Mr. Ritter issue out of her mind. She'd get him to see it her way. Maybe he wouldn't ever really *embrace* the idea of the sit-in, but if nothing else, he'd understand where she was coming from.

She hoped.

But, yeah—for now, back burner. Because what Parker had just implied was much more exciting news.

"Meaning...you'll let me write it up for the paper?"

Parker nodded. "Who am I to stand in the way of free speech? Besides—here at the *Daily*, we're all about high... profile...ness..."

He was teasing her, of course, but Billie could see that through the faint smile, something was bothering him. Something having nothing at all to do with the paper, Proposition Seven, or anything remotely related to politics. She leaned forward, gazing at him steadily. "What's up?"

"Deadlines, you know," he said, waving her off.

Billie would not be put off. "You're in a Mood." Funny that she should know Parker well enough to recognize a Mood when she saw it, but there it was. Moodiness. "Give it up."

"It's nothing." Parker looked uncomfortable. He coughed, clearing his throat, and when he glanced at Billie again, his face was impassive. "You and Adam seemed to get along, huh?"

"Um, yeah, I guess," Billie said. She was confused. What did Adam have to do with Parker's Mood? Now she *really* needed some quality time with Heather. She'd never understand boys.

Parker sighed heavily, leaning forward and placing his

hands on his thighs. "Have you heard anything from Eliza lately? Has she…has she asked about me at all?"

The question lay between them, radioactive with meaning. Billie and Eliza had been e-mailing, of course, but lately Eliza hadn't mentioned one word about Parker—whatever that meant for their relationship hiatus. And Billie's Melbourne mates had reported that Eliza had fallen in with Jess and Nomes. It wasn't a bad thing—Billie was friendly enough with Jess and Nomes and thought they were cool girls, if a little rowdier than she and her mates were—it just meant that Eliza was probably keeping herself busy. Probably with boys—or maybe even one boy in particular. Billie swallowed. If there was one thing she suspected above all, it was that Eliza was probably off making good use of her "space" from Parker.

"No," she said finally. "I haven't heard anything. But"—she tried to cover—"I think the internship that she signed on for is loads more intense than ours. Like, she's out in the field mucking about all day. No time for messages back home."

Billie stood, resting her hands on her hips purposefully. Something needed to be done about the Mood situation, posthaste. But what? "There must be some place in this city that isn't soaked in partisanship, right?"

Parker blinked. "What do you mean?"

"Some place that the tourists go when they've had

enough with the Capitol Building, the Mall, the White House, and all of that."

"The zoo's pretty big," Parker confessed, after a thought-ful moment. "Especially when the weather's nice."

Billie glanced out the window at the sunny, crisp fall day. "As it is today," she said pointedly. "Decision made. We're going. After last period."

"To the *zoo*?" Parker asked, as though she'd suggested a brief jaunt to Pluto, or Narnia, or flat-out jet-setting back to Australia for a few hours.

"It sounds fun. You need fun." She narrowed her eyes at him, willing it to be so. "You are going to have fun."

The good news was, the National Zoo was definitely fun. So that was something.

Billie and Parker had meandered through the roll-ing paths in no particular rush, only to find themselves mesmerized by the giant panda habitat, of which the zoo seemed appropriately proud. Pandas of different ages—and levels of cleanliness, Billie noted casually—munched con-tentedly on large green leaves and generally ignored the fact that they were being ogled by masses of wide-eyed tourists.

"So, what's the deal?" Parker asked. He scratched at his nose and glanced down at the plaque that hung before them. "Is there such a thing as a non-giant panda? Like, a mini panda?"

"I reckon not," Billie said. She giggled, and tapped at the tall glass wall. A mama panda, extremely roly-poly and looking none too hyper, blinked sleepily. "I mean, other than baby giant pandas, I suppose." They'd already caught a glimpse of a baby panda being bottle-fed by a zoo official. Talk about cute overload. It was dead unbearable. But at least it'd had the desired effect of causing Parker to smile.

"Baby giant. That's an oxymoron," Parker observed.

"Always thinking like a writer," Billie said, shoving up against him. "Can't you take even an afternoon off?"

He shook his head ruefully. "I'm here, aren't I? I watched the whole feeding thing. With the bottle, and the…feeding."

"Don't even try to pretend you didn't love that," Billie threatened.

Parker shrugged, then smiled reluctantly. "Let's keep that to ourselves. It's not exactly manly, you know, getting all hyped up about baby bears."

"I'll take it to the grave," Billie swore. "And for what it's worth, pandas aren't actually bears." She held up the leaflet they'd picked up when they'd paid their admission to the zoo. "Let's check out the marsupials next. You know: the koalas or kangaroos."

"Native to the Australian region," Parker replied, raising an eyebrow. "You getting homesick?"

Billie looked around in surprise, realizing. "No," she said, shaking her head. "Not at all."

It was ironic that she should come literally halfway around the world, and here Parker was talking about koalas and kangaroos. She couldn't be farther away from Australia, here at the zoo. And yet for now, there was nowhere else she'd rather be.

Chapter Seventeen

From: billiesurf@email.com
To: elizarit@email.com
Subject: fish and chips

Hi there! How're you going?

Rumor has it you've been spotted behind the counter at Fishy Wishy. I can't believe my parents put you up to that! Well, chalk it up to yet another "culturally rich" experience.

It sounds like you guys have been getting on well, though, which is great. In fact, it may be more than I can say for myself and your parents.

Don't get me wrong—I'm hardly the rebellious type. But ever since the news broke about the Proposition Seven funding, I've been trying to find a way to reconcile my conscience with my work at your father's office. And what I have in mind may not be exactly what he was hoping for when he first signed off on my internship. . . .

Billie

"ELIZAAAAAAAA!!!!!!!!"

Eliza woke with a start. She'd been dreaming that little lollipop people were chasing her, yelling her name.

It wasn't hard to see where *that* dream had come from.

"EEEEEELIZA!!!"

Oh no…Those weren't lollipop people…

It was the twins. Eliza had to watch them Saturday morning while the Echolses went to brunch with some friends. Clearly, they were raring to go and now were pounding on the door to her room.

"Come on out and play." It was Nick. Or Sam. Or maybe both. It didn't matter right now.

"I'M UP! Give me five minutes and I'll be out."

She heard them start counting on the other side of the door.

"One Mississippi, Two Mississippi…"

The twins used to count using the one one-thousand method, but Eliza had taught them to use Mississippi, which they enjoyed much more and apparently made them quite the cause célèbre on the playground with their friends. At this hour, though, she didn't care how they counted, she just wished they would stop!

This is SO not right for a Saturday morning. Eliza swung her feet out of bed and rubbed her eyes. *This is going to be a very long day.*

"Oh, you've got to go!" Jess's voice rang through the phone.

Eliza lay on her back staring at the ceiling after a grueling day of babysitting the twins and then serving fish and chips. The rest of the family was now in the living room watching a movie while Eliza hid out in her room.

"I told Nomes, and she spat the dummy at the thought of you missing a trip to Bells with Macca. We decided; you're going," Jess said in a way that left little room for debate.

"I don't know. The Echolses will freak out, and I will *definitely* be grounded until the moment they put me on the plane back home." She thought back to her last e-mail from Billie and smiled ruefully at the irony of the two of them cranking up the parental worry-o-meter at almost exactly the same time. Coincidence? Or foregone conclusion?

Eliza rolled onto her side and held the phone against her ear with a pillow as she absentmindedly played with the fur on the giant purple stuffed dolphin on Billie's bed.

"Yeah, but you're going to miss out on the summer. You're not even going to get a Christmas barbecue. Bloody oath, you should go."

"I don't know, Jess. Running away seems...extreme."

"You are *not* running away. You're going on a little trip for a couple days. It's, I don't know, a cultural learning experience."

"I hear you but...I just don't know." There was only so far she could stretch the whole "learning experience" excuse, even in her own mind.

"Whatever. So are you bringing a swag...er, sleeping bag?"

"Oh! I haven't even thought about that. I don't have one, and I definitely can't ask the Echolses for one of theirs. I could probably swipe a blanket from the closet, though."

"Or you could use a tartan blanket by the name of Hamish to keep you warm."

Eliza could picture Jess's knowing grin even over the phone. "Shut up," she said, not really meaning it or minding the innuendo, and they both had a giggle. "All right, well, I'd better get to bed."

"Okay, but listen, I think you should go. What's the worst they could do?"

"Tell my parents. Tell S.A.S.S. Send me back home," Eliza ticked off the horrible possibilities. "You're a bad influence."

"That's for sure!" Jess said proudly.

Eliza laughed, and the girls said their good-byes.

After hanging up with Jess, Eliza was more conflicted than ever. To go, or not to go, that was the question.

She flopped backward on her bed and mentally hashed out the pros and cons of going away with Macca and his friends.

Pro: Macca is fun, and his friends will be, too. Between the Fishy Wishy and babysitting, I've been working my butt off, and deserve a little fun.

Con: The Echolses might not exactly see things my way.

Pro: Macca is hotness personified.

Con: I don't have any second chances left.

Pro: If Billie really goes through with the sit-in thing, my parents will have their hands full. Hers will, too, probably.

Con: Or they'll just lock us both up together and throw away they key.

Pro: You only live once.

She sat up, biting her lip. Then she reached for her cell phone.

Macca answered after only one ring. "What's it going to be?"

Eliza took a deep breath. "What time are you picking me up tomorrow?"

• • •

Eliza felt like a secret agent. After she showered and got dressed in the morning, she packed up her clothes and toiletries, a pair of very cute flip-flops, and a magazine or two. She stuffed everything into a backpack usually reserved for her schoolbooks or for carry-on when flying, and tossed it out the window. Steve was going to pick her up for work on the corner—she'd made special arrangements this morning so as to avoid arousing suspicion from the Echolses if they were to catch sight of her overnight bag.

Eliza grabbed a piece of toast as she passed through the kitchen and said a quick good-bye to the Echolses, trying her best to act nonchalant. She ducked around the side of the house, picked up the backpack from where it had landed in the garden, and went to the corner to wait for Steve.

The day dragged on forever. The nice weather seemed to have drawn people down to the beach a day earlier than usual, so the lunch rush was particularly busy. She shuffled back and forth between the tables and the counter, dropping off trays of fish and clearing and wiping tables when people left.

It was astonishing to Eliza what little regard people had for their manners when they were away from home. Customers would get irate over minor mistakes that were easy to fix—a vanilla milkshake instead of a chocolate one or two sides of slaw instead of three. It was shocking.

And then there was the overwhelming amount of garbage people would leave strewn about. Since spending so many hours in the backwaters of the bay, she had a new appreciation for the staggering amount of everyday junk that wound up floating in the water. No wonder her father was so passionate about the environment.

Maybe Billie's onto something with the whole sit-in—if it gets the bay cleaned faster, that is…

Regardless, even if Billie's intentions were noble, Eliza couldn't help but be glad that it was Billie rather than Eliza who was going to undercut her father's most recent decision.

Environmental issues aside, though, if the work at the Fishy Wishy had taught her anything, it was to have a whole lot more appreciation for waitstaff at restaurants.

She was a little surprised by how much into a zone she could get when doing this stuff. She'd never really had a job back home. She'd babysat before, but nothing with a uniform and cash registers. It was tough going, but she just kept thinking about two days of nonstop swimming and sunning at the beach with Macca, and she was able to "go to her happy place" and just get through it.

As much as she hated smelling like fish at the end of the day, she had to admit that on a day like today, things could get a lot worse. The weather was sunny and warm, and she got to be out in the open air (even if it was clearing tables) instead of cooped up in a classroom.

Eventually, the lunch rush gave way to the lull of the late

afternoon. Finally, there were only a couple of customers left sitting at the outside tables.

"Hey, Steve," Eliza called, walking back into the kitchen area.

"Yeah?"

"Things are pretty slow, and I've got everything cleaned up and put away. Do you think I could get out a little early? I'd love to catch a few extra rays before the sun goes down."

Steve gave everything a cursory eye.

"Tell you what, go back and refill all the napkin dispensers, and as soon as you're done with that, you can get changed and get out of here."

"Thanks so much," Eliza said, and went into the storage closet to grab packages of napkins.

"No worries, and Eliza?" Eliza's heart stopped for a second.

Has he caught on? I was being too perky, wasn't I? I knew it—excessive perk. Bad!

"You're doing a great job; you've really gotten the swing of it. I'm impressed, and I'll let Frank know."

She had a pang of guilt, knowing that she was about to let them down.

"Okay…" Eliza tried to keep her voice light. "Thanks, Steve."

After finishing with the napkins, Eliza pulled her backpack out from where she had stored it in the back of the restaurant and ducked into the bathroom to attempt a quick makeover. She jumped into her sundress, hoping that it hadn't gotten too wrinkled in her bag during her shift. She took out a brush and ran it through her hair until it was vaguely presentable and no longer pressed into the shape of an inverted fry basket. She put on a little lip gloss and a hint of shimmery eyeliner (enough to look good for the beach, but not so much that you'd look more suited for a nightclub), a hint of perfume, and checked her outfit. Finally feeling satisfied—or as satisfied as she was going to get—with things, she stepped out.

Eliza took a note she had written the night before from her bag and read it over once more.

Dear Frank and Estelle,

I know you're going to be upset with me for disappearing, but I wanted to let you know where I am. I have gone on a little camping trip up to Bells Beach with a couple of friends for two days.

I'm really sorry to have gone behind your back, but this was one opportunity that I didn't want to miss. Please don't be worried. I will be back on Wednesday and in plenty of time to go down to Prince Phillip Island with the family on Thursday.

Sincerely,
Eliza

She knew it wouldn't get her off the hook entirely, but at least she felt better than if she had just disappeared. She didn't want to wind up with her photo on the side of a milk carton. She slipped the note in the cash envelope that Steve dropped with Frank every Sunday night.

Eliza walked out front of Fishy Wishy and waited for Macca. She took a last look, patting down her dress and running a hand through her hair, then sat on a bench. She couldn't sit still, and her stomach had turned into a churning mass of butterflies. At least, she hoped they were butterflies and not the haddock sandwich she had had for lunch.

She tried to find the optimal position to be in so she would look just right when they arrived.

Sitting up, ankles crossed, looking at the ocean.

Nope…looks like I'm posing.

Standing, legs crossed, leaning on bench.

Nope—balance is off, can't stand still, will look like I am a crazy person.

Sitting, leaning back, reading a tabloid.

Perfect. Casual, but pretty.

Before long, two cars with surfboards strapped to the top pulled to a stop right in front of her bench. One was an old sedan and the other was Macca's dune buggy. Will, from the party at Trinity, and Annelise were in the front of the sedan, and squeezed in the back were a couple other guys and a girl. Macca, with a big grin, was driving the buggy by himself.

Without getting out, Macca called to her.

"Toss the bag in the back and hop in. We've got a ferry to catch!"

Eliza tossed her bag behind the seats in the buggy and got in and off they went.

About five minutes up the road was the Sorrento Pier and the car ferry that would take them across the head of Port Phillip Bay. They pulled into the loading lanes just as the cars started to load up.

After parking on the boat, they climbed out and headed up to the topmost deck to take in the sun and watch the sights as they crossed the bay. Everyone gathered at some seats, and Macca made the introductions.

"Will and Annelise you met." They all smiled and nodded at one another. "And this is Johnny and Whiz."

"Whiz?"

"Yeah," said the lankiest of the three, an academic-looking guy with spectacles. "It's really Will, but since he's Will"—he gestured to the broad-shouldered guy—"and I'm smarter, I'm Whiz."

"Aha. Do you guys all go to Geelong?"

"Just Johnny," Macca said. "Whiz is at Melbourne Grammar, and Will graduated from Geelong last year and

has been off jackarooing with Kat," and he gestured to the girl Will had his arm around, "at his family's station near South Australia."

"Jackarooing?"

"Being a farmhand," Will said. "Helping with the sheep and cattle."

"You're both jackaroos?"

"Technically, I'm a jillaroo. That's what they call the girls. I'm Kat," she said, "and you are the Yank we've heard so much about?"

"That's me," Eliza answered.

Soon the ferry shuddered as the engines revved up. The lines were cast off, and the boat pushed back from the pier heading out into the bay. Eliza, Macca, Will, Kat, Whiz, Annelise, and Johnny found spots at the railing where they could have a good view of the Mornington Peninsula.

The boat left Sorrento and soon was passing Portsea; farther out was Point Nepean, the very tip of the peninsula. There were freighter ships coming and going, and with the late-afternoon sun beginning to settle down in the sky, sailboats and cabin cruisers that had been out for the day were coming back into the expanse of Philip Bay.

The water was a luscious blue, and the late-afternoon sun made the ripples dance with light. It was so bright Eliza had to shield her eyes. Far off in the distance she could make out the tallest of the high-rises in Melbourne, and to the other side there was nothing but open sea with a sailboat heading off to points unknown.

"Look, hey, check it out!" called Kat from the other side of the deck.

They all rushed over to see several dolphins racing along the front of the boat. They playfully leaped out of the water, one following the next, then plunged back under, racing just out of the boat's reach.

As Eliza watched the dolphins and basked in the warm, afternoon sun, the guilt she had about running off from the Echolses melted away. She closed her eyes and smiled to herself when she felt Macca's hands on her hips as he leaned over her.

"Cool, aren't they?" he asked.

"Yeah, they're beautiful."

They watched as the dolphins danced back and forth in the water.

"Hey," Eliza said as she turned around. "Thanks so much for inviting me. I'm glad I'm getting to do all this. Your friends are really cool to be having me along." It wasn't exactly what she meant to say, but she somehow couldn't put it all into words. She hoped Macca would understand.

Macca smiled at her. "No worries."

Chapter Eighteen

From: elizarit@email.com
To: billiesurf@email.com
Subject: rebellion

Hi there! I'm going well—especially now that I've got the Aussie lingo down!

I'm sorry to hear that the internship isn't exactly everything you hoped it would be. Trust me—I get it. I thought doing fieldwork on the beach was going to be a good way to work on my tan. Turns out, not so much.

Still, though, the weather is finally turning, and I have

to say that I am really excited about the penguin project. Maybe it wasn't quite what I was expecting when I first applied to S.A.S.S., but talk about a once-in-a-lifetime experience!

I think the sit-in sounds really exciting. And I totally get your feeling like you might be letting my father down, but he's always after me to "take a stand for something I believe in"—which is what this is, right? I mean, time for him to put his money where his mouth is, I say.

Let me know how it goes. I've got my fingers crossed for you. And I'm glad that you've got Parker for backup, too. He's great.

Of course, I might not be the person that you want in your corner, since I'm doing a little rebelling of my own this weekend.

I won't fill you in on the details—wouldn't want to implicate you in this mess—but suffice it to say that this time tomorrow, your sit-in may very well be the last thing on all of our parents' minds....

More soon. Stay tuned!

Eliza

Billie returned home from the zoo that evening to an unusual sight. Or rather, an unusual *sound*: the strains of pleasant humming emanating from the kitchen.

After dropping her bag and jacket in Eliza's bedroom—homesick or no, it still wasn't quite feeling like *hers*–she

made her way toward the mysterious good mood. It was Mrs. Ritter, buzzing around the kitchen, occasionally lifting the lids off of pots and poking at vegetables in a bowl with a silver serving fork.

She looked up at the sound of Billie's footsteps. "Oh, hello," she said, her mouth twitching up ever so slightly into what Billie thought might actually be a smile. She inhaled deeply. "Doesn't dinner smell good?"

Despite the pots and general low-level commotion, Billie didn't actually smell anything. Well, anything that smelled liked food, anyway. As usual, the sharp scent of cleaning products cut through the air.

"What're we having?" she asked, somewhat nervous. Mrs. Ritter's razor-thin physique was not the result of a robust appetite, after all.

"Steamed cod fillet with broccoli."

"Broccoli?" She liked broccoli just fine. That was, when it was prepared with actual herbs and spices and other flavor-producing ingredients.

"Steamed broccoli," Mrs. Ritter confirmed.

Billie's heart sank. "Sounds…delicious." One thing she was homesick for: Marmite. And pavlova. And the occasional chocolate bar. Mrs. Ritter absolutely never served a dessert. She hadn't been too homesick since she'd arrived in D.C., but right about now she'd kill someone for a pressed peanut-butter-and-Nutella sandwich.

Okay, that was four things. But still.

"We're celebrating," Mrs. Ritter went on. "Mr. Ritter will be home soon, and we'll all have dinner together."

Billie perked up. "Celebrating?" That, at least, sounded promising. "Ace! What's the occasion?"

Mrs. Ritter pushed aside the dish she'd been fiddling with—a salad, from the looks of it—and sidled over to the kitchen table, pulling out a chair and settling in, leaning forward onto her elbows. Her eyes sparkled and Billie realized she looked almost giddy. Almost.

"Mr. Ritter was able to get some time off this weekend. We didn't want to say anything until we were sure."

Billie arched an eyebrow, still not entirely sure what this had to do with her. Were they leaving her alone for the weekend and heading off on a romantic holiday?

"We'll be going to Ocean City this weekend!" Mrs. Ritter burst out, her words coming in a rush. "You'll love it. Granted, it's the off-season and a *touch* cold, so you won't be able to swim, but we can still walk on the beach, and we'll be able to take the sailboat out—oh, and you'll get to try genuine Maryland crab cakes!"

It took a moment for what Mrs. Ritter was saying to sink in, so foreign to Billie was her genuine enthusiasm and bubbliness. But then it hit her: boating, the beach, and deep-fried crab cakes?

Billie was in. So in. Maybe not with the crabs, but with everything else, *definitely*.

Talk about aces.

• • •

The Ritters told Billie that she could bring a friend with her to the cottage. This begged the question of whom to ask.

It wasn't one she had to mull for long, of course, seeing as her close girlfriends could be counted on one finger.

She tracked Heather down outside of her locker the next afternoon.

"Busy plotting your next bold move of guerrilla war-fare?" Heather asked, smiling and flipping the combination to her locker, opening the door, and rummaging inside for some books.

"Hilarious, I'm sure," Billie said. "Anyway, no…no saving the world just now." She shrugged. "Other than typing up the content for the Ritter e-newsletter, that is. Just thinking, I suppose."

"Thinking? At school? Unnecessary." Heather laughed, fished out the books that she'd been looking for, and then slammed her locker door shut. "We'll have to put an end to that straightaway." She adopted a mock-Aussie accent for the word "straightaway," causing Billie to giggle.

She knew she and Heather would have a great time in Maryland. "About the weekend . . ." she began.

"What's going on?" Heather asked. "Am I going to be jealous of your wild social calendar?"

"Nope," Billie said, still smiling. "It's the same thing that you've got on. That is, if you want. Hear me out…"

Chapter Nineteen

From: billiesurf@email.com
To: elizarit@email.com
Subject: Re: rebellion

I appreciate being kept in the dark as to your "debauch-
erous" plans. That being said, I expect a full report once
you're back home safe and sound.

No news on the sit-in, but it sounds like you've got
enough excitement going on for the both of us. . . .

Billie

Barely forty minutes after leaving Sorrento, the ferry reached the other side of the bay at Queenscliff. Everyone piled back into the cars and headed off the boat, out of the harbor, and onto the main road.

They drove along, Eliza luxuriating in the feeling of the warm, early-evening breeze blowing through her hair. They drove through small towns and then through fields just inland. As they drove closer to the sea, Eliza could catch glimpses of the coastline. Interrupted only by low hills of scrub, there were long beaches stretching out of sight in both directions. The ocean looked calm and peaceful, with rows of waves gently crashing one after the next. The sky was huge above her, and the road stretched out in front of them.

After an hour, they pulled into a parking lot with a gas station, a grocery store, and a bottle shop—what they called a liquor store down here. Eliza went with the girls, Johnny, and Whiz to get food while Will and Macca filled the cars.

They bought several bags of food and sodas to keep them through a couple days, then popped next door to the bottle shop, where Will and Macca were picking up some beer. Once Macca had paid for the beer, they filled a cooler with ice, packed everything up, and headed back out onto the road out of town.

Soon they pulled off the main road onto a dirt track that wound along until they came to a clearing on a hillside overlooking a broad open beach. You could just make out the sea at this point as the sun had set and the last few rays of light were fading over the horizon.

The cars came to a stop, and everyone popped out. Eliza walked to the edge of the car park and looked out over the broad expanse of coastline framing a giant crescent-shaped bay. You could hear the waves breaking and the sounds of the last seabirds of the day. It was peaceful until Will shattered her private reverie.

"All right, me and Whiz are gonna find some wood for the fire and get that started. Macca and Johnny, you guys get the tents set up. Girls are on food and beverage detail. Right?" It wasn't so much a question as a command, and they all took to their task.

Eliza went to the back of the car and began unpacking bags and laying things out on a picnic table with the girls. This was a pretty easy job since they were mostly going to be eating burgers, hot dogs, and potato chips, but they made a nice spread of fixings for everyone and then watched as the boys piled the wood up for a fire.

Once everyone was done with the tasks at hand, Will took a small gas container from the back of his car and poured some diesel fuel on the logs and lit it with a dropped match.

Eliza was not, by any stretch of the imagination, a "camper." At summer camp she opted every time for things like weaving and movie night over hiking and canoeing. That being said, she knew enough that covering wood in

fuel and lighting was not the recommended method of starting a campfire. A fact that was promptly proven.

The match hit the wood pile and an enormous flash of flames enveloped the area, causing Will to leap back to save his eyebrows. Once the dramatic fireball burned off, the fire was actually burning very nicely, if a bit thick with black smoke.

"Subtle, mate, very subtle," Macca said to Will.

"What? We have a fire, don't we? So get stuffed! Now somebody toss me a stubby from the esky."

Johnny grabbed a beer from the Igloo cooler and tossed it to Will.

"Thanks, mate. Now let's get cooking. I'm starved!"

Later, after having eaten their fill, Johnny and Whiz brought out acoustic guitars and began to play. They had laid blankets out all around the fire pit, and everyone curled up, singing along.

The guys played a lot of songs that everyone knew the lyrics to. There were classics by bands that Eliza knew, like Green Day and Oasis, and each song seemed to capture her feelings of the moment, like some sort of movie sound track. Then the guys decided to do an Australian set in Eliza's honor, running through the best of AC/DC, INXS, Men at Work, and a host of Australian songs that she had no clue about.

"I am so out of my depth here. I know a couple songs

by AC/DC, but I have never even heard of some of these groups," Eliza whispered to Macca.

"Don't worry about it, babe. The fact is, most people don't know the words, either, just catch the tune and shout along." With that he turned to the others and asked, "Guys, is it the last train or the last plane out of Sydney in 'Khe Sanh'?"

It was clear to Eliza from the argument that broke out that nobody knew the answer, but that didn't stop everyone from joining in on a rousing chorus of Cold Chisel's classic song.

She lay with her head in Macca's lap looking up at his face, and slowly everyone disappeared from the fire until it was just the two of them huddled together under a blanket.

"Are you cold?" Macca asked, pulling the blanket up.

"Nah, the fire's warm, but I'm worried we're going to smell like human barbecues tomorrow."

"It's okay, we'll let everything air out. Besides, we're spending the day at the beach. I'm teaching you to surf tomorrow."

"You do realize that that will be a whole lot of wasted effort? You're a little nuts for thinking that you can teach this klutz to stand on a floating board, you know?" She poked him in the ribs.

"Ouch," Macca said with a laugh, and kissed her. "Just call me crazy, then."

"Crazy," she said, laughing herself.

And then she kissed him right back.

Eliza awoke completely disoriented. The sun was breaking over the hill across from her, and everything smelled of smoke from the night's fire, the last embers of which were still smoldering a few feet away. Macca was sound asleep, one arm draped across her, and she could see Whiz coming up out of the scrub with an armful of firewood.

Eliza slid out from under Macca's arm, wiped her eyes, and got up.

"Morning," Whiz said as he dumped the wood next to the fire pit.

Eliza blinked. "What time is it?"

"About seven-thirty or so. You want to grab the eggs, that bag with the bread and spreads, and the fry pan from the back of the car? I'll get the fire going, and we can cook up some brekkie."

"Sure." Eliza ducked into an empty tent, got dressed, and tried her best to get her hair under control, ultimately just pulling it back into a ponytail. She went and grabbed the supplies and came back.

Once the fire was going again, Whiz maneuvered the cooking rack onto some rocks over it and got the fry pan cooking. He put in some butter and sizzled some bread, making a kind of country toast.

While he cooked, people began stirring slowly, emerging from tents or from the blankets they had slept under. Eliza took some solace in realizing that everybody looked as rough as she felt.

Once the first couple slices were ready, Whiz pulled them out and offered one to Eliza. He then rooted around in the bag until he pulled out a jar of Vegemite and began spreading a thick layer of the stuff on his toast.

"You want some?"

"No, no thanks." She wrinkled her nose.

"Come on, it's the best way to start the day."

He seemed so earnest that Eliza acquiesced and spread a thin layer on one corner of her toast. She gingerly took a bite and made a face.

"Nope, no way."

"It's an Australian tradition."

"Yeah, well, I'm not Australian. Don't forget."

Macca was sitting up, wrapped in the blanket and rubbing his eyes by this point. Whiz poked him with his foot.

"Oi! Wake up, you lazy slacker! Brekkie's up, and your girl's complaining."

"Shut up," Macca said as he swatted Whiz's foot away.

"You guys sound so funny, I never get over it," Eliza said to Whiz as she nibbled at the safe area of her toast. "I mean funny in a good way. I love the Aussie accent. If I'm lucky, maybe I'll get a little bit of one by the time I go back."

"You think we sound funny? You're the one with the accent," he said. "You sound like a movie star or something."

Eliza laughed at that. It was the first time anyone had ever compared her to a movie actress. She decided that she could live with that.

The smell of a proper fried brekkie managed to rouse the rest of the group from slumber, and the next couple of hours were spent preparing eggs, coffee, and toast for people as they slowly emerged from their respective tents, sleeping bags, and blankets. Everyone was in a good mood, and the weather was beautiful—the early sun revealed a clear sky with a few high clouds glowing yellow in the morning light.

From up on the hillside they had an unobstructed view down to the beach. The guys could see the waves breaking and were talking about which break they wanted to hit first.

"Those down there are breaking nicely, and when the wind picks up, I bet we'll see some barrels off that left break," Whiz said, gesturing with his arm.

"Yeah, they look like they're closing out now, but give it a little time and they'll be sweet."

As they talked they pointed to different areas and used all sorts of terms Eliza had never heard before.

Surfing is a lot more complicated than I ever would have guessed, she thought as she dug her swimsuit out of her bag. *But at least there's one thing I know how to do—lie on the beach and soak in the sun. Finally!*

Once at a parking site, everyone climbed out and the guys pulled off their shirts, kicked off their sandals, and pulled their wet suits on over their swim shorts. Eliza realized she'd never seen a boy in a wet suit before, other than in the movies. They certainly were…formfitting. And Macca certainly had a…fit…form…

She hoped she wasn't drooling. Cool Americans with movie-star accents didn't drool.

"Zip me up?" Macca turned so that his back faced her, giving her access to the long zipper that ran down the back of the wet suit. Eliza briefly gathered her composure, then zipped him up.

They walked off down a path through the dunes. Each of the guys had a surfboard under his arm, as did Annelise, who wore a hot-pink wet suit. They also brought the cooler with drinks and a bunch of towels down with them.

Soon they arrived at a long curving crescent of beach with sand stretching from end to end. There were a handful of other people already out in the water surfing, but once they headed away from the path, they had a stretch to themselves.

The boys quickly dropped their things and ran into the water with Annelise and hopped on their boards, while Eliza and Kat laid out their blankets and began slathering on the suntan oil. Eliza pulled out a couple of tabloid magazines she'd brought along. She had discovered that they had an Australian version of *People* called *Who*, and they loved their *Hello* magazine, though all of the royalty gossip was a bit beyond her. She put on her earphones, but she chose to watch the others surf for a while before settling in with the latest in celebrity news.

After an hour, Eliza had begun to thoroughly bake and needed to stretch her legs and cool off some.

"You want to go put our feet in the water?" she asked Kat.

"Yeah, that'd be good."

They walked down by the water and stuck their toes into the surf. Eliza felt goose bumps up and down her legs as the water swirled around her ankles. It was chilly, for sure, but not nearly as bad as the Atlantic would be this time of year; after a moment, it even felt cool and refreshing.

"Macca really likes you. I've known him and the guys a long time. I just get the sense he's into you."

"You think?" Eliza asked, trying to play it cool, even though she wanted to jump up and down and shake Kat by the shoulders, demanding details.

"Yeah, for sure."

"He's great. It's just too bad that I only have the semester here. I wish I could stay longer." Not only for Macca, of course, but he was definitely a large part of it.

"Why don't you?"

"I have to get back to the States at the end of the semester and see my family, finish school. I've got college SATs to start thinking about." All true. But none of which was nearly as exciting as hanging out in the Australian surf with cute boys.

Kat shrugged. "That's a lot of pressure." She gestured toward the expanse of blue that stretched before them. "At least you're here, now."

"True." Eliza smiled. "Very true."

She was here, now. And she was determined to make the most of it while she could.

"Oh, man, it is absolutely spectacular out there. We are totally getting you up on a board after lunch," Macca said to Eliza with a grin as he toweled off his hair, his wet suit peeled down to his waist.

"We'll see," Eliza responded, trying not to stare too hard.

"Come on, everyone to the cars. I'm puckish, and it's time to grab some lunch."

They drove into Torquay, parked, and walked around Surf City Plaza, sort of the world headquarters of surfing. All the famous surf companies (with which Eliza was now well acquainted from looking at Billie's posters) were based

here, and there were a ton of surf shops and restaurants.

They found an open place that looked out toward the beach and scarfed down some food. The guys were starving from spending all morning in the water, and all they could talk about was catching this wave and that and who'd had the best ride.

"So, Eliza, Macca's gonna get you out there, right?" Will asked between bites of his sandwich.

"I don't know. I'm guessing he's overestimating his abilities as a teacher."

"Easy, people," Macca protested. "My abilities and I will be just fine. I guarantee I'll have her riding big waves like a legend in no time." Macca bit into his sandwich with gusto.

"We'll see," Eliza said with a devilish grin.

She wasn't sure she'd be a natural surfer, but she was looking forward to her private lesson. Another glance at Macca made her stomach do a quick flip.

Actually, she thought, *maybe the private lesson can't come soon enough…*

Eliza successfully wriggled into Annelise's wet suit—an exercise that caused her to bend into any number of enormously unflattering poses that she was glad no one had witnessed. She joined the guys at the water's edge, looking out at the waves.

"Come on, we'll take Johnny's long board, which is nice

and easy, and we'll get you up on a wave by the end of the day."

"Easier said than done," Eliza said doubtfully.

"Trust me. You just have to feel the wave and go with it. You'll get it."

"Um, I'm not sure you understand what I'm saying. I'm not someone who really 'feels' waves. Usually I feel things like 'sleepy' or 'thirsty,' you know?" She shot him a grin to show him that she was kidding. Mostly.

"Don't worry, it'll be great. Besides, when you fall, it's just water." Macca seemed so confident that there was no way for Eliza to disagree. Now," he went on, "stop making excuses and let's go!"

After a few graceless hours in the water, Eliza had managed to lock down a routine of sorts:

Step 1: Paddle your arms really hard when Macca says "Go."

Step 2: Hop up on the board when Macca yells "Up."

Step 3: Wave your arms around frantically like a windmill.

Step 4: Careen into the water.

It wasn't quite surfing, but it was something.

Eventually she started getting the hang of it. That was to say, she got the hang of those four steps. *Paddle, hop up, freak out, fall over.* At least she finally stopped looking like she was being attacked by a swarm of bees each time she

hopped back up onto the board. Soon she could even stay up on it for a few seconds and, yes, even "feel" the waves carrying her along.

The best part, though, was when they would take a break to catch her breath. She would climb up to sit on the board, and Macca would climb on behind her, resting his palms on her shoulders as their feet drifted in the surf. She would lean back against him until she felt up to another go. They'd wait for the right wave, Eliza lying on the board and Macca floating next to her, his hand on the small of her back until he would yell "Go!"

Eliza would paddle furiously and then hop up onto the board and, once in a while, the wave would catch the board and begin pushing it toward the shore. And there would be Macca, catching her eye, a smile on his face as big as the one on Eliza's.

Chapter Twenty

Ocean City was nothing at all like Surf City, back home, but it took Billie only about thirty seconds to decide that she'd take it, regardless.

"What do you think?" Mr. Ritter asked, beaming at Billie as he grappled with a complicated set of knotty things.

"It's a beaut." She wasn't sure whether she meant the sunny, chilly afternoon, the view of Northside Park in the distance, the Ritters' sailboat—or all three—but she decided that it didn't matter. *All of the above, definitely. Absolutely.* She turned to Heather. "Right?"

Heather nodded happily. "That's for sure." She slurped eagerly at a Diet Coke and tilted her head backward into the sun.

When Billie had first raised the suggestion to Heather of her joining them for the weekend, her friend hadn't hesitated for a moment. So after a short drive down on Friday morning, here they were, bobbing peacefully along, soaking in the warmth of the sun and admiring the glittering surface of the bay. Even Mrs. Ritter looked totally relaxed and at home, her face content underneath enormous designer sunnies.

"We love to come down here on weekends when we can. And Eliza practically lives here in the summer," Mr. Ritter went on. He was fiddling with the boat's sails in a manner that seemed to be called "jibbing"—not that Billie knew what that meant.

Billie propped herself up on her elbows and unzipped her fleece hoodie. "Eliza comes here on her own?" She couldn't imagine that. Her parents' place in Sorrento was great, and sure, yeah, she and her mates hung out there all the time—but not alone. Billie's parents were laid-back, but not *that* laid-back.

She suddenly wondered just how Eliza's cunning plan was working out. She hadn't heard anything from down under, but in this case, she wasn't convinced that no news was good news.

"She's very mature for her age," Mrs. Ritter chimed in. "Grew up quickly with a father in the public eye. Very poised. You know."

Billie wasn't so convinced that Eliza was as grown-up as all that. More like, good at keeping up appearances. At least, from the little she'd heard about her American twin. And now, all of those years of playing at perfect were finally starting to catch up with her. Still, Billie only nodded. What did she really know, after all? "I'm sure," she said.

She sat up suddenly. "Are those people picnicking?" she asked, delighted, taking in the blankets dotting the landscape of the park.

Mr. Ritter nodded. "Sure are. Don't worry—we've got a basket in the cooler." He indicated the storage space underneath the deck of the boat. "Are you hungry?"

"Not yet, actually," Billie said, realizing that it was the truth. "I'm happy just to stay out here on the water for a bit longer. We're in no rush, right? It's just a holiday weekend?"

"No rush," Mr. Ritter confirmed. "None at all."

Billie decided that she liked the sound of that.

"Do the twins even know who the Orioles are?" Heather asked, laughing.

Billie glanced down at her shopping bag spilling over with Orioles paraphernalia: two pennants, two T-shirts, two

refrigerator magnets, two bumper stickers. It had been a busy Saturday afternoon.

"And are your parents really going to let them stick both of those on the car?" Heather pointed to the stickers.

"We do have two cars," Billie said defensively. It was actually somewhat of a sticking point for her. She'd been after them for ages now either to give one up or at least trade one in for a hybrid. "Anyway, you don't know what it's like having twin brothers. It's a constant competition. The only way around it is to buy two of everything."

"Hence the excess baggage. Never underestimate the power of a good bribe, huh?" Heather shrugged. "Hey, I'm not the one who's going to have to stuff all of that mess into a suitcase when it's time to go home."

Billie was silent for a moment. It was true, her time in D.C. was finite. They were more than halfway through the exchange by now, but it still felt as though she had just arrived yesterday. She hoped the second half of the semester didn't whiz by as quickly as the first had, but she had an idea that she wasn't going to get that lucky. There were some things over which she simply had no control.

She didn't want to think about going home. Even if she was missing the twins. That would change the moment she had to break up one of their famous quarrels.

"Well," she said, deliberately changing the subject. "It's not as if your mother needs more fish sauce." She nodded toward Heather's own parcel, which was admittedly half the size of her own.

Heather glanced at her, completely deadpan. "You can never have too much fish sauce, Billie."

At that, Billie had to laugh.

Billie thought if she took one more bite of pasta, she'd explode. She pushed her plate away from her and toward the middle of the table, the edge of it catching on the red-and-white-checkered plastic tablecloth. She smoothed the "cloth" and settled back into her seat. "I'm full," she announced, patting at her stomach.

Mr. Ritter chuckled heartily. "Then you're in trouble, missy."

Billie's eyes widened in alarm. "Why's that?"

"Because dinner was only a warm-up," he said. "We've still got a whole dessert sampler coming."

Billie groaned. "We never should have let you order for the table!"

"When in Rome," Mr. Ritter pointed out.

Heather reached across the table and refilled her glass with sparkling water. "Rest. It'll be at least three minutes before the next course comes out."

"The shrimp cocktail here is fantastic," Mrs. Ritter said, nibbling daintily at the edge of a crab cake and clutching at a wine glass.

"So far, everything's been fantastic," Heather said. "Thanks so much for having me—for having us this weekend." She flushed, her expression earnest.

"Glad to do it," Mr. Ritter said. "I'm just sorry I don't have more time at home to spend with you, Billie. My hours are so long."

Billie waved her hand at him. "'Course they are. I completely understand. Besides"—she glanced at Heather—"I've kept busy."

"That's right. I've been meaning to ask you about the internship. The program is new," Mr. Ritter said. "This is the first year that we've taken on S.A.S.S. students. We'd love to get your input, hear how you think things are going."

Billie paused for an awkward beat. She and Heather exchanged a look. She wasn't sure what tack to take here, so she settled on, well...*tact*. Honesty, but tactful honesty.

"The truth is..." she said, fiddling nervously with her butter knife. "I just wonder if we could...you know...be doing more?"

Silence fell across the table.

"You know we're huge supporters of Proposition Seven," she went on, her words coming too fast for the thoughts in her head, "but since funding for that has been put on hold, the internship...it's a lot of, you know, e-mailing, and *mail*-mailing, and I just wonder if there isn't...a way to, you know, get out there. Really take action."

Mrs. Ritter coughed lightly.

"I think what Billie is saying," Heather jumped in, "is that maybe she'd like to get out more, you know—from behind the computer screen and such."

"Exactly," Billie chimed in. "I've found a great group—the Green Gorillas. And they're planning a sit-in to support—"

At this point Mrs. Ritter made a dramatic choking sound, sending a light spray of her white wine over the table. Mr. Ritter reached over and patted her gently on the back. After a moment, she was breathing regularly again.

"Do you…know of them?" Billie ventured, hesitant.

"We do," Mr. Ritter said shortly. "I'm curious how you found them."

"Uh, a friend suggested that I pay them a visit," she said, hazarding another quick look at Heather. "Because of how I was wanting to get involved and stuff. And that's when I heard about the sit-in…" She trailed off, realizing that the Ritters were bound to have a different opinion of the sit-in from her own.

"It's a protest against the postponed funding of Proposition Seven," she admitted, lowering her gaze.

Mrs. Ritter's face went white.

"I'm sorry…" Billie stammered. "Honestly, I knew you'd probably be upset that I was protesting against the EPA, but I was hoping that you'd support me standing up for something I believe in."

Mr. Ritter sighed. "You couldn't have known, Billie, but the Green Gorillas are a very aggressive team."

"What have they done?" Billie asked nervously. "Aggressive" didn't sound good. Maybe they'd had some sort of history with violent protests or the like. She shivered at the thought.

"They're extremely loud. Their protests garner a lot of negative publicity."

Billie's chin dropped into her chest. "That's it?" That didn't sound very aggressive to her. But what did she know? This whole world was completely new to her.

"That's more than *it*," Mrs. Ritter jumped in. "That's quite enough. It's like those PETA volunteers who throw paint on fur-clad celebrities—it's negative publicity for the EPA."

"Well, yes, I can see that," Billie sputtered, desperate, "but I guess I just assumed—"

"You assumed wrong," Mrs. Ritter snapped.

Billie looked helplessly to Mr. Ritter, hoping for some sort of reprieve, but it was clearly not to be found. His face had turned very red, in stark contrast to his bone-white knuckles, which gripped the edge of the table tightly.

Parker had been right, she realized. This wasn't going to go down well.

"I'm sorry," Billie said quietly, looking down. "I made a mistake."

Even though in her heart of hearts, she really didn't believe that it had been a mistake. Not at all.

"No harm done," Mr. Ritter said, looking as though he

was really trying to believe that. After a moment of consideration, he added, "I hope they weren't counting on you for the sit-in."

Billie took a long swig of her water, hoping in vain to postpone the inevitable. Even if she did drop out of the sit-in—was that really what she wanted?—there were other considerations to take into account.

"Well," she said finally, "I suppose they'd be fine without me. But Parker had"—she winced, wanting to bite back the words—"told me that they were planning to run my article on the protest in the school paper. I mean, if I wrote it."

"No." Mr. Ritter banged his palm down flat against the table.

"I'm sorry?" Billie was so unused to this sort of display of anger—from one of the Ritters, no less—that she thought she might be hearing him wrong. Studying his trembling face, however, there was no mistaking his tone.

"That's out of the question."

Her face flamed. Much as she hated the idea of disappointing Mr. Ritter, she couldn't believe he'd truly try to stifle her. "That's free speech," she replied.

"Mr. Ritter needs to distance himself from the Green Gorillas," Mrs. Ritter insisted. "Which means that you do, too. End of story."

Heather kicked at Billie's ankle underneath the table, indicating that the conversation was over, at least for the

time being. Tempers were flaring, and if things continued on in this direction, it would only get worse. It was no use. She would have to concede the battle.

For now, anyway.

The waiter arrived at the table, depositing an enormous silver platter laden with desserts. Everyone shifted in their seats uncomfortably.

Talk about a waste of resources, Billie thought. It didn't matter whether it was dessert or not; she had completely and totally lost her appetite.

Chapter Twenty-One

"I think that's a day for me. If I get one more noseful of saltwater, I'm going to be sick for a week," Eliza said to Macca as they treaded water.

"Oh, come on! You're just getting the swing of it."

"I know, and it's great, but it's getting late in the afternoon, and I want you to be able to surf on your own. We'll get some time tomorrow, right?"

"All right, I'll be in in a bit. You did great."

"That might be overstating it just a smidge, but I'll settle for all right." With that, she turned and began paddling in toward shore, letting a small wave carry her most of the way.

Once back on the beach, she set down Johnny's long board, shimmied out of the wet suit, and stretched out on her towel while the other girls dished about people Eliza didn't know. She watched the waves as the swells got bigger in the late afternoon and the wind coming off the beach made them curl over into rolling barrels of water. The guys would seemingly disappear into the froth, and suddenly a flash of wet suit would appear, and there they would be, standing tall on their surfboards, with the wave chasing them along. She wasn't sure, but it crossed her mind that this could be paradise.

As the sun started setting, the golden light of the end of day caught the spray off the waves, and one by one the guys in the water trickled onto the beach, until finally they were all lying in the sand watching a few people catch the last waves of the day.

"I'm famished!" Will stated at last. "Let's get out of here and make some dinner."

No one could argue with that plan.

When they reached the site, everyone went back into action as they had the night before. Collecting wood, setting up tents, laying out food. Before long Whiz was bent over a pile of wood and coaxing along the fire while Will muscled into place the large stones on which to balance the grill.

Eliza was chopping tomatoes on a slab of wood when the flash of headlights caught her eye. A car pulled off the main road and headed down the short track to the campsite. As it neared, she could see that it was a Victoria State Police car. She didn't think much of its approach.

That is, until it pulled directly up to their site.

The troopers flicked on the spotlight and shined it on the group. Eliza blinked, puzzled. What could the officers want?

Apparently she wasn't the only one wondering. As the two cops exited the car and came closer, the kids—all of those in Eliza's party, as well as a bunch who were not—gathered, curious to see what was up.

"Good evening. Could we see everyone's identification?" The trooper looked impatient with the whole scene.

"Is there a problem, Officer?" Macca asked, stepping forward and clearly trying to appear mature and responsible.

"Just get your identification."

Eliza grabbed her bag out from under the edge of the tent and pulled out her passport as one of the cops walked up to her. He shined his flashlight at her face as he took the passport and looked at her name and photo before calling to his partner.

They weren't shining the flashlight on anyone else's face. Why were they shining the flashlight on her face?

Eliza was starting to get a very bad feeling.

This bad feeling was confirmed by the next words out of the officer's mouth. "This is her, Bob."

Eliza's heart fell. They're here for me. She was humiliated, and terrified, in equal measure.

"Young lady, you've caused quite a bit of consterna-
tion, do you know that? The state police were notified of
a missing person because of you." The officer no longer
looked impatient, but seeing as he now looked angry, this
development was not necessarily an improvement.

Someone from behind her giggled, and Eliza could feel
her face burning with embarrassment. She looked around,
hoping to find a large rock or something she could crawl
under and die. Everything had been so perfect, and now it
was perfectly ruined. She was certain Macca would never
talk to her again.

"Why don't you grab your things and say your good-
byes."

"This is ridiculous. Couldn't we just make a call and
let the Echolses know where I am, and that I'm fine? You
know, clear this all up?" Eliza sputtered, searching for a
way out.

"You are a minor who was reported missing by your
custodians, and thus we have to return you to their care.
Grab your things and we're going. This is not up for debate.
As for the rest of you, consider this a warning: we catch a
beer in the hands of anyone under the age of eighteen and
you're all going to get written up. Got it?"

There were meek nods of understanding, and a few

irritated grumbles from the other campers. Eliza hurried to her tent and quickly grabbed her few things, trying to avoid catching the eye of any of the others and wishing that something, anything (meteor? tidal wave? earthquake?) would happen so that this moment would just end. Finally she had her things, and as she turned to go, Macca came up to her and grabbed her arm.

"I'm so sorry, Macca. I ruined everything and, well, I don't know—"

"Hey, don't worry about it. We had a good time, and besides, 'round here getting taken away in a divvy van is a badge of honor. I'll call you tomorrow, okay?"

Eliza wanted to cry. How could he be so nice, so cool about this? She forced a smile and a nod. For the first time in a long time, she was feeling very far from home.

"Seriously, don't worry about it. Okay?"

"Okay," Eliza said as he gave her a hug. *Of course* she would worry about it. In fact, she planned to do nothing *but* worry about it for the immediate and foreseeable future. She couldn't believe she'd been so dumb as to run off with her boyfriend. She couldn't believe she'd risked her spot on the S.A.S.S. exchange. She couldn't believe that she'd let her adventurous side get the best of her.

And most of all, she couldn't believe that she'd been picked up by the police.

It was all she could do not to collapse into hysterics in

front of Macca and all of his friends. It was through sheer determination only that she managed to maintain her composure.

"All right, time to go," said the cop as he put his hand on Eliza's shoulder and turned her back to the car.

She got in the backseat and waved at them as the car pulled away. Eliza turned and looked out the back window of the car until it turned onto the main road and headed back toward Sorrento.

A couple of hours later they drove off the ferry and into Sorrento. The closer they got to the Echolses' house, the more anxious Eliza became. She really didn't know what she was going to say to them. There had been an APB put out on her. This was beginning to feel like a Lifetime made-for-TV movie.

Had they called her parents? They would be mortified. Her dad was always worried about public opinion, and he never wanted to shed any negative light on the EPA or to take away from the work he was doing. This was exactly the type of situation he would not want. His daughter, in the back of a police car, in a foreign country.

Please let there be traffic....

Eliza prayed for anything to prolong the ride and put off the inevitable confrontation with the Echolses.

• • •

Traffic, it seemed, was not in the cards. It wasn't long before the police cruiser headed up the road on the last leg of their journey from Bells Beach and turned into the Echolses' driveway. The officers got out and opened the door to let Eliza out. They walked her up the front path and rang the bell. As they waited for someone to answer the door, Eliza could see people looking out the windows of the houses across the street, wondering what the police were doing there. She felt another wash of shame at the embarrassment this was probably causing the Echolses, but she didn't have long to think about this before Frank opened the door.

"I believe this belongs to you?" one of the officers said to Frank.

"Yes, Officer, thank you very much for bringing her back. We're very sorry for any inconvenience. Aren't we, Eliza?" Frank's expression was impassive, but his voice was firm.

"Um…Yes?" Eliza choked on her words. "Yes," she repeated, strong this time. "I'm sorry for causing a problem."

"No problem at all, Mr. Echols, that's what we're here for. Now, Ms. Ritter, I trust this will be the last we hear of you? If it is not, then we can revoke your visa and put you on a plane back to the States. Are we clear?"

"Yes, sir." They could do that? Eliza vowed to spend the remainder of her semester holed up in Billie's bedroom

doing crossword puzzles and reading the classics of literature. Since she'd probably be grounded in perpetuity, anyway.

"Good. Now you folks have a good night."

"Thank you again, Officer," said Frank as he closed the door behind Eliza. He turned to her. "Let's go to the kitchen. We need to have a chat."

Eliza nodded solemnly, and followed him through the living room and into the kitchen, where Mrs. Echols was sitting at the kitchen table with a teakettle. She looked very…stressed. Eliza sat at the end of the table and waited while Frank prepared himself a cup of tea and sat across from her.

The room was silent for a moment, and Eliza found herself wishing again for a nice, random natural disaster to save her from the horribleness of it all.

Frank sighed. "Eliza, I don't know what to do about you. You had us really scared. Do you know that? We didn't even have the heart to call your parents, not being able to tell them if you were okay or not."

"I—" Eliza mumbled, but she didn't get to finish the thought.

"I don't know what got into you, but the idea of running away was a very, very stupid one. Frankly, I am inclined to pack your bags and put you on the next flight back to the States," Frank declared.

Eliza went white. This was her worst nightmare, playing

out before her eyes. She'd be sent home, away from her new friends, and Macca—and worst of all, she'd be letting the Echolses and her parents down. It was the absolute worst outcome to her S.A.S.S. exchange that she could possibly imagine.

"I'm so sorry," she said, her voice breaking as tears welled in her eyes. "I know I messed up. I didn't mean to let you down; it's just, you know, I wanted to make the most of my time here in Australia." Eliza was crying freely now. She sniffled and looked up at the Echolses meekly. "Please don't send me home. I'll write ten more reports for my internship. I'll babysit every single night. I will lock myself in my bedroom whenever I'm not at school. Whatever you want. Just...*please*, don't send me home."

For a moment, no one said anything. Eliza could hear her heart pounding in her ears.

Finally, Frank spoke. "We are not going to do that," he said quietly.

Eliza allowed herself a deep exhale.

"However," he went on, "we are letting you stay only on some conditions."

Eliza nodded gravely. Conditions were fine. She could do conditions.

Frank took a long sip of his tea. "First, you are going to have to sit with Estelle every Sunday to make a schedule for the coming week. This is a schedule you are going to stick to. No ifs, ands, or buts.

"Second, you are going to complete the penguin project on Thursday and work the remainder of your shifts this week at the Fishy Wishy. *And* you are going to apologize to Steve. Because of your selfish behavior, other people had to take up the slack. Who do you think had to cover your shift when you disappeared?"

Eliza nodded. It hadn't occurred to her that in addition to worrying the Echolses, her disappearance was inconveniencing Steve.

"Finally, you may keep your mobile, but you are going to adhere to a strict schedule. You cannot be on the phone after ten P.M. or during school hours—and that includes text messages. Are we clear?"

"Yes," Eliza said, wiping at her cheeks as her tears began to dry. She would spend the rest of her days communicating solely via smoke signal if it meant that she could stay.

"Eliza," Estelle said, "you have no idea how worried we were. You just vanished, and though we had your note, we didn't know where you were or who you were with. I am personally very hurt that you've felt it necessary to take such advantage of our kindness. We have tried to provide you with a very comfortable, friendly environment and to give you a good learning experience. But you've treated our home like a youth hostel, a place you can come and go from with little or no regard for the rest of the family. You are a part of this household, and as such you should respect the other members of the home the same way you would like them to respect you."

Eliza had no answer. Estelle was right, and she knew it.

"Now dump your clothes in the washing machine and go get a shower and into bed. I think you've had quite enough for today."

Eliza had to agree.

Eliza did as she was told. As she washed her hair in the shower, she thought about everything that she had experienced so far and how different she felt today than when she'd arrived a couple of months earlier. She had learned to pitch a tent. She had learned to *surf*! Well, sort of. Her friends from D.C. would never believe it. But the truth was that any worries about being too sheltered and protected in D.C. were long since forgotten. She'd had her fair share of adventure. Probably just a little more than she'd care to repeat for a while.

She knew that the Echolses had a point and that, in skipping out, she had crossed a line. She deserved punishment—but what if she wasn't allowed to spend time with Jess and her friends anymore?

What if she wasn't allowed to see Macca anymore?

Even if Macca and Jess weren't the best influences, she'd miss spending time with them.

She dried off, changed into a tank top and shorts, and

climbed into bed. She was staring at the ceiling, contemplative, when there was a knock at the door.

"Eliza?" It was Estelle's voice.

"Come in."

The door opened, and Estelle came in with a tray of tea and a couple of cookies. She put the tray down on the bedside table, took the chair from the desk and pulled it up next to the bed, and sat down.

"I thought you might like a snack before bed."

Eliza was, in fact, starving. She reached for a cookie.

"Thank you. They picked me up right before dinner."

"Well, this should hold you until the morning."

Eliza chewed thoughtfully, considering her next statement.

"Estelle?"

"Yes?"

"I'm really sorry." It wasn't much, but it was honest.

"I know, dear," Estelle replied as she poured the tea into the cup. "I think we've all been there, and I can't say I don't understand, but you have to think about our position. Your parents wouldn't be too pleased to find out we had no idea where their daughter was, don't you think?"

"I know...I just didn't want to miss out on...well, on everything, you know?"

"By 'everything,' do you mean the boy from the college formal?" Estelle peered at her slyly.

Eliza blushed. "Yeah, Macca. Well, Hamish MacGreggor, but everyone calls him Macca."

"Maybe this boy isn't the best influence on you right now?" Estelle suggested gently. "He had to have known that you weren't meant to be sneaking out, and yet he encouraged you to run off with him."

Eliza didn't have a response to that. Macca was hardly a bad boy—more like a sweetheart—but she could see where Estelle might have a different opinion on the matter. Besides, sweetheart or no, he *had* been the one to suggest running off together for the weekend. Not that Eliza had needed much convincing.

"You'll learn," Estelle said with authority. "Bad boys aren't all they're cracked up to be. Watch your step." She smiled gently, taking some of the sting out of her words.

Eliza nodded. "I will. I promise."

She meant it, she realized. She was going to watch her step. She wasn't going to do anything more to jeopardize her time in Australia. It was a promise to Estelle, but more than that?

It was a promise to herself.

Chapter Twenty-Two

From: elizarit@email.com
To: billiesurf@email.com
Subject: walkabout

Okay, truth time. My Bonnie-and-Clyde routine wasn't exactly the brightest idea I've ever had.

Here's the thing—I know you're friends with Parker, so I hope it's not weird for you to hear this, but the truth is that I have fallen head over heels in like with a boy I met down here. His name is Macca, and he asked me to go away with him to Bells Beach.

I knew your parents would kill me if they found out, but I couldn't say no. I mean, you only live once, right?

Needless to say, your parents freaked. They even sent the police after me! Talk about humiliating.

But once I got home, and we got to talking, I have to say—they were pretty cool. We've got some new rules set up for the remainder of my stay, but they aren't going to tell my parents about what happened. Personally, I can't believe it. It's not exactly "all's well that ends well," but I will take what I can get—trust me.

So when you have a chance, you have to fill me in on your latest adventures. Have you told my father about the sit-in yet? How did he react?

No matter what happens, just keep the image of me in the backseat of a divvy van fresh in your mind—it couldn't POSSIBLY be worst than that, could it?

Eliza

The drive back to D.C. was suffocating. The air was thick and heavy with tension, like wet cotton. Billie gazed longingly out the car window as they whizzed along silently, watching the scenery float past in a fuzzy gray blur. That was the way things felt in her head: Fuzzy. Gray. Blurry.

No one spoke.

They dropped Heather at her house, then headed back to their own. As Mr. Ritter pulled the car into the driveway, Billie scrabbled at the door handle. She couldn't spring

fast enough from inside the contained atmosphere of the car out into the fresh air. Once outside, the air enveloped her, cold and welcome despite the humidity. She stood, taking in deep, steady breaths, aware that she possibly seemed like a psychotic yogi. It didn't matter.

Mr. Ritter coughed to himself, pocketing his car keys, and strode into the house. Mrs. Ritter paused, eyeing Billie's impromptu meditation. "Are you coming in?"

Billie paused for a moment, then shook her head. "In a bit." In this sort of mood, there was only one way to lift the fog. "I think I'll have a short walk," she said as she buttoned her coat around her.

Mrs. Ritter nodded and followed her husband inside.

Billie started out, then pulled out her cell phone and dialed.

An hour later, Billie and Parker were seated in front of two steaming cups of coffee at their favorite hangout in Adams Morgan. She'd been grateful when, upon hearing the story of her disastrous weekend, he'd insisted that they meet up. Just being around him was calming.

She sipped at her drink, and then sighed heavily.

Parker placed a reassuring hand on her shoulder, stopping her in her tracks. It was a warm hand, and it felt quite nice on her shoulder, truth be told.

"It's not as bad as it seems right now," he said with quiet certainty.

"Not as bad? How could it possibly be worse? Wait—don't answer that. I don't want you to jinx me." She certainly couldn't afford a jinx. In fact, the ways things were going, she realized she herself might actually be the jinx.

She inhaled sharply again. "It's just…I'm so humiliated," she went on. "I mean, I admire Mr. Ritter so much. I came here expressly to work for him! And all I've done is to let him down." She glanced down at her feet. "That's not even the worst part," she added, reluctant.

"No?" Parker prodded.

Billie shook her head, miserable. "The worst thing?" She lowered her voice like it was a secret. Which, maybe it actually was. "The worst part…is that I think he's wrong." She looked away. "I really do."

Her eyes widened with guilt. This was heresy, treason of the highest order. She almost couldn't believe the words coming out of her mouth. Almost.

Parker was silent for a minute, compounding Billie's guilt. Surely he thought she was a terrible person. Shallow, naïve, and self-centered. Surely he was sorry he'd come to her rescue.

There was a sound from Parker's direction. For a moment, it was muffled, but then Billie realized…it was… was it—*laughter*?

It was! It was muffled, choked, and sputtering, to be sure, but it was laughter, nonetheless. He was laughing. At her abject pain and humiliation. At her.

She stiffened. "It's not funny."

"No, of course not," Parker agreed, drawing himself up taller and clearly trying to pull himself together. The corners of his mouth twitched, giving him away.

"It's not!" Billie swatted at him with her gnawed-down fingernails. "Quit it."

Parker shook his head and wiped at the tears that were forming in the corners of his eyes. "You're right. I'm sorry. I swear, I'm not laughing at you, I'm laughing *with* you... Or, I would be, if you were laughing." He cocked his head at her thoughtfully. "Are you sure you don't want to try laughing?"

She giggled. She couldn't help it.

"See?" Parker smirked at her. Then he grew more serious. "I understand why you feel bad, I honestly do, but the truth is that you have strong convictions. And you owe it to yourself—and to Mr. Ritter—to be true to those convictions. I'm sure, at the end of the day, that he'd agree with me. He'd rather see you fight for your beliefs than go along with him just to get along. He has to admire your passion."

Parker leaned closer to her, holding her gaze with his own. "I know I do."

Suddenly Parker's features took on a softened expression, and he leaned in toward her. It almost looked like—well, like he was going in for a pash!

Billie'd barely had time to process the realization when

Parker's lips were pressing against hers. She was so taken aback that she opened her mouth to protest, causing their teeth to clang together awkwardly. "Ouch," she said, righting herself, and banging her forehead against his in the process.

"Ow, indeed," Parker said, rubbing at his forehead wryly. "That wasn't the smoothest kiss I've ever had." He looked slightly embarrassed.

Billie hadn't had enough snogs in her lifetime to really compare notes, so instead she concentrated on willing the fiery blush creeping up her neck back to her normal flesh tone and her heartbeat back down to a normal rhythm. She was completely caught between wanting him to kiss her again and knowing he shouldn't.

"What was that?" she asked, once she'd regained some semblance of composure. It was all she could manage; Parker's unexpected advance had pulled the words right off of the tip of her tongue.

"I…" Parker looked uncertain. "That was a kiss?"

"No, I mean, that much, I understood," Billie said, increasingly flustered. "But…why?"

"What do you mean, why?" Parker looked extremely confused. "Billie, I like you. I thought you liked me. Don't you think it means something that I'm the person you called to talk about what was going on with you and Mr. Ritter?"

"*What?* No. At least, I don't think so…." Billie said,

confused. Did it? "Or, I mean, of course I like you," she added hastily, seeing the slightly hurt look on Parker's face. "But just as a *friend.* I mean, I called you as a friend. I wouldn't make, you know, a move, on someone else's boyfriend—especially not someone whose house I'm currently living in."

And that was it: the whole truth. It didn't matter whether or not she and Parker had chemistry (which, if she was going to be really, truly honest with herself, they did). He was Eliza's boyfriend, even if they were on a sort-of break. It didn't matter that Eliza was off flirting with another boy down in Melbourne; Billie didn't think that Parker knew about Macca, but she sure wasn't going to be the one to tell him.

Which meant, then, that Parker was strictly off-limits.

Even if he *was* a good kisser.

"I don't know what's going on with Eliza and me right now," Parker ventured, looking embarrassed and vulnerable.

Billie bit her lip. "Maybe that's another great reason why you shouldn't be getting involved with anyone else," she pointed out gently.

She knew she was right.

Why, then, did she want nothing more than for Parker to kiss her again?

Parker's eyes narrowed. "Is this about Adam?" His voice was low.

"What?" Billie couldn't believe it—Parker almost sounded…could he be…*jealous*?

"It's not about Adam," she said.

In the moment, she knew it was true. Adam was cute, and just thinking about him made her blush, sure, but kissing Parker had sent a surge of electricity down her spine. Even as inexperienced as she was, she had the distinct feeling that electricity trumped blushing.

"So, does that mean you're not going to bring him to Mr. Ritter's gala fund-raiser?" Parker went on.

Billie looked at him. "Parker, we're working the fund-raiser. It's hardly like a date-type situation." Or so she'd thought. It would never have occurred to her to bring a date to the banquet

"I guess not," Parker said, looking pensive. After a beat, he stood. He offered her a crooked smile. "I think I'm going to go home now, if you don't mind. I'd like to preserve what little dignity I have left. Are you all right getting back by yourself?" He pulled on his coat and zipped it up.

Billie nodded, wishing as she did that she could make him understand that he had nothing to be embarrassed about. She watched as he gathered his things and left the café, as his figure grew smaller and smaller in the distance. She wished that she could do the same. Wished that she could just outright disappear. That seemed the only solution to the tangled mess she'd created.

Unfortunately, she wasn't going to up and disappear,

much as she might want to. She was stuck with the mess. And she'd have to be the one to clean it up. One way or another.

Sunday was unbearable, with everyone going wildly out of their way to pretend that everything was 100 percent perfect and hunky-dory. Mr. Ritter made eggs for breakfast, and while Mrs. Ritter of course didn't do much more than push them around her plate, the uncomfortable group settled themselves around the breakfast table and did everything in their respective power to be cheerful and bright.

When Billie finally escaped the breakfast table and got Heather on the phone, her friend was unsympathetic to her latest tale of woe.

"Um, I'm sorry, Billie, but duh! Did you not realize that Parker totally has the hots for you?"

Huh? Was it possible? Had Parker really had feelings for her all along—and everybody knew it except for Billie?

She really *did* have a lot to learn about guys, it seemed.

Still, she protested weakly. "Not the hots," she insisted. "More like…the warms."

Heather sniffed into the phone. "Whatever. He lurves you. Own it, sister."

"Lesson learned, I guess," Billie said. "But he's Eliza's boyfriend. Kind of. It's too weird."

"Fair enough, but didn't you say that Eliza was dating someone in Australia?" Heather asked.

"Yeah, but still…Now that she and I are pen pals, I just don't know." Could she e-mail Eliza about it? Was that too awkward?

Heather sighed. "Okay. I guess it's not a bad idea to proceed with caution. But you two would be so cute together."

"Thanks for the vote of confidence," Billie said. "Now all you have to do is come up with the perfect way for me to broach the topic with Eliza."

"I'll work on it." Billie could hear the doubt in her friend's voice.

"See? You don't have a clue how to handle the situation, either," Billie pointed out, her stomach sinking slightly. For a moment there, she'd allowed herself the hope that Heather would be able to sort this all out in a way that meant more e-mails from Eliza *and* more kisses from Parker. But no such luck, apparently.

"You don't need to rub it in. I'm on your side." Heather paused, and Billie could almost hear her friend twirling a dark curl around her fingertip. "So what are you going to do about the sit-in, then?"

"What are my choices?"

"I guess…either do it and write the article, or don't?"

Billie had been so distraught at the way things had gone with Mr. Ritter that it hadn't even occurred to her

that there were still decisions to be made regarding the Green Gorillas.

"I'll save a space for you in the paper, if you decide that you want to go through with it," Heather said kindly.

"I just don't know." She really didn't. Billie realized that this was the perfect example of a lose-lose situation. If she did go through with the sit-in—never mind the article—Mr. Ritter would never forgive her.

But if she chickened out? Backed down from what she believed in?

Well, if that happened, she just might never forgive herself.

Chapter Twenty-Three

"Well, that didn't turn out as expected, did it?" Jess asked with a grin as she settled onto her seat next to Eliza and Nomes in Mrs. Carroll's class Monday morning.

It was the first time Eliza had seen Jess after the incident with the police. They had talked, but Eliza hadn't gotten much time on the phone between finishing her shifts at Fishy Wishy, spending a whole day on the penguin project, and babysitting the twins. For the rest of the past week in Sorrento, every second of her life had felt like it was under surveillance.

Being back in Melbourne in the familiar halls of school

and around her peers was, well, *comforting*. She would never have guessed that a time would come when she was dying to go back to school, but there it was.

"You can say that again," Eliza said, looking around the classroom. "Did people hear about it?" She couldn't decide if the looks she'd gotten in the hallway on her way to class that morning were a figment of her imagination or not.

"Everyone is awful impressed, I reckon," Jess confirmed. "You're the first person we know to run halfway across the state of Victoria only to be tracked by the cops and dragged back."

"And that's a good thing?" Eliza wondered.

"Zazza—this country was founded by a bunch of convicts. Heck, our national hero is Ned Kelly, and he was hanged for being an outlaw! I think you earned yourself a fair bit of street cred with that stunt."

"You guys are a little nuts; you know that, right?" Eliza asked.

"Yep. So," Jess said, leaning over her desk, "did you kiiiisssss Macca and snuggle up on the beach?"

"Shush," Eliza said. "I don't kiss and tell."

"Oh, come on, 'fess up! We demand all the gory details."

Eliza managed to contain herself for a full second before bursting out, "Okay, fine! We kissed!"

"And?"

"And we snuggled on the beach. I even learned how to surf!"

"That's awesome," Nomes chimed in. "I bet it was so much fun."

Eliza smiled. "Yeah, it was pretty great."

"So," Nomes continued, "what did the Echolses say? Did they kill you?"

"It was awful when the cops brought me back, but I have to say, Estelle has been pretty cool. Of course, she thinks that Macca is a bad influence."

"Oh, please. Did you tell her that he was practically a puppy dog?" Jess joked.

"Somehow, I thought it would be best to just agree with her and leave it at that." Eliza smirked. "Anyhow, we worked it out. I told them I would keep to their schedule, and I made up for the work I missed at the Fishy Wishy. I had to promise that I would spend every Sunday with the family— and I can't miss any more sessions of the internship. But I think I earned some brownie points when I brought the twins with me to visit the penguins. Apparently they love penguins. Who knew?"

"But what about Saturdays?" asked Jess.

"That's the good part. Except for days when I have the internship, I've been given Saturday afternoons and Saturday evenings free, so long as I'm back by ten. And I have to let them know my plans in advance. They realized

that their rules were a little bit strict, so we decided to meet in the middle."

The girls all decided that that wasn't so bad.

"But what about Macca?" Jess wanted to know. "How did you guys leave things?"

"Well," Eliza continued, "the thing is, I like Macca—a lot—he's funny and cute and sweet. But he knows what a close call the trip to Bells Beach was. I mean, I could have been sent home, and then what? I wanted more adventure while I was down here, but I think that was maybe *too* much adventure. I do not need to be spending more time in the back of police cars. If my parents found out, I'd be locked away in a tower forever once I got home. Which is what I explained to Macca the day after the ordeal."

"So how did he take it?" Jess asked.

Eliza shrugged. "He understood. We haven't talked in a few days, though." She quickly changed the subject, grinning and pointing at Jess. "You're part of the problem. You know that, right?" She wagged her finger. "You totally egged me on, even knowing it was a hugely bad idea for me to run off with Macca."

Jess widened her eyes innocently. "*Moi?* I just provided advice! You were the one—"

Jess didn't get a chance to finish her thought. She was interrupted by the shushing of Mrs. Carroll and the start of first period.

"Girls! How about we all take our seats and open our notebooks?"

Eliza smiled as Jess settled back in her seat. "Saved by the bell," she said. "Lucky you."

After classes ended, she made a plan with the girls for Saturday and then boarded a tram down to the ocean for her internship. She watched the city go by out the window. Tree-lined boulevards gave way to commercial parks, and finally the tram was coasting along the side of the bay.

With summer coming, it was staying light longer, and the afternoon sun was catching the waves, making Eliza squint. She imagined being back out on the long board and feeling the swells rising and falling below her. She smiled and decided that spending some more time with her feet in the water, even if it was for science, might not be the worst.

The tram pulled up to her stop, and Eliza got off. She crossed the road and headed down to an old pier where Mr. Winstone and a couple of the other interns were getting their gear ready.

"Good afternoon, Ms. Ritter!" called Mr. Winstone. "It's so nice to have you with us."

"It's nice to see you, too, Mr. Winstone."

"I heard that we had some adventures over spring break and that you'll be gracing us with your presence

each and every session for the remainder of the semester."

"That is correct."

"Well, we're very happy to have you. Why don't you put on some bibs, and we'll go check out some tidal pools."

Eliza dropped her stuff on the pier and wrestled on a pair of oversized rubber bibs. She tightened the straps until they were as comfortable as they were going to get. She grabbed a net and a few jars and followed the team off the pier and into the water.

She spent the next couple of hours chasing little bugs and invertebrates around tide pools. She managed to get far more water into her bibs, it would seem, than critters into jars. She debated briefly just pouring the contents of the bibs into a jar but ultimately decided that thinking about what was swimming around her toes was not a good idea. Instead, she would look at the water and think about the fact that this was the same water that flowed out of the bay and all the way back to Bells Beach.

Eventually, as the sun sank low on the horizon, Mr. Winstone called everyone back to the pier and collected their sample jars. As Eliza sat on the concrete drying her feet, Mr. Winstone came up to her.

"So, Ms. Ritter, how was your first day back?"

"Actually, it really wasn't that bad."

He chuckled. "Well, that's good to hear. I assume the excuses are going to be a thing of the past?"

"Yes, sir," replied Eliza.

"Excellent. Have a good night and get home safe, Ms. Ritter."

"Thanks. I will."

Eliza gathered her things and headed back toward the street. The Echolses were going to be picking her up, and as she rounded the corner of a warehouse, she looked for their car, but it wasn't there.

Instead, parked at the curb, was a very familiar dune buggy; leaning against the dune buggy was a very familiar guy with a very big grin on his face.

"Macca!" Eliza yelled as she ran over toward him.

"Hey, you. How's botany treating you?"

"It's biology, you big dope, and it's treating me just fine. Which is more than I can say for you!"

"What? What did I do?"

"You haven't called!"

"I know, I'm sorry. I was afraid that if I tried to get in touch, you'd be in even more trouble. And once I decided that I had to see you, I wanted to surprise you!"

"Yeah, well, you succeeded." Honestly, though, she didn't mind. It was the best kind of surprise.

They smiled at each other. Eliza still felt embarrassed, wondering what Macca must think of her. Surprise or no, maybe his feelings had changed. Finally, he broke the silence.

"So, are you going to get in?"

Macca walked around to the driver's side of the car.

"I can't. The Echolses are picking me up."

"Don't worry about it, it's all taken care of," Macca said with a grin.

"What does that mean?"

"It means I worked it out with them. I stopped by there looking for you after school, and Estelle was home. I told her that I was really sorry about everything and I didn't mean any disrespect, but that I really wanted to see you again. She said I should come pick you up on the condition I took you straight home. So get in the car; otherwise, we'll be late and we're going to be up the creek without a paddle."

Eliza smiled until her cheeks hurt. She tossed her stuff in the back of the buggy and swung into the passenger's-side seat. Macca settled in behind the wheel, started the car, and pulled out.

As the car sped off down the boulevard, Eliza looked at Macca and then at the bay passing along the side of the road. She thought about where she was. She was ten thousand miles from home—literally. If you dug a hole through the Earth from Washington, D.C., you'd probably come out right around Melbourne.

Yet despite that enormous distance, she was feeling like this place was a home for her. The stores that had seemed so different when she first arrived now were familiar. The streets and names she knew and they felt comforting. That being said, she also was aware that she was going to have to go home before long. The end of the semester was not so far in the distance that it was inconceivable.

Going home meant back to her parents and friends. How would she be able to explain everything she had seen and done? She could show pictures and tell stories, but they hadn't *been* there.

But at this moment, with the wind in her hair and the setting sun on her face, Eliza couldn't imagine wanting to be anywhere else.

Well, maybe back at Bells, she thought with a smile as she glanced over at Macca. She knew this relationship would be at an end soon and she was fine with that, but for the moment, this very moment, it wasn't a bad thing. She was okay with living in this moment.

They had driven a couple of miles and were approaching the boardwalk in St. Kilda when Macca suddenly pulled the buggy over.

"What's the matter?" Eliza asked.

"There's something I've got to do," Macca answered.

"What's that?"

"This."

Macca leaned in and kissed her.

Chapter Twenty-Four

From: elizarit@email.com

To: billiesurf@email.com

Subject: Parker

Hey there! I know I've been quiet this week—it's been busy here!

What can I say? I've been making amends for all of my scandalous exploits. Thankfully your parents believe in second—and third!—chances.

I heard that you've been spending a lot of time with

Parker, especially down at the newspaper office, and I just wanted to thank you for taking such good care of him while I've been away. I know I haven't been as good about keeping in touch with him as I could have been. Maybe I've just taken for granted that I could do what I wanted while I was away and that he would still be waiting for me when I got back. But a lot has happened since I've been in Australia, and I think Parker deserves some honesty from me.

Believe it or not, I told him all about Macca, and even though I think it wasn't easy for him to hear, he was cool about it.

One reason I think he was able to take it in stride: it seems he's had his eye on someone while I've been away, too....

I have to admit, when he first told me how close you guys had become, I was jealous. But it makes sense. I mean, I know you're great—so no wonder Parker agrees. And speaking of second chances—I'm not going to encourage you to get together with Parker, but I promise to do my part to keep things as unweird as possible in the event that there is a genuine romance blooming. Who am I to stand in the way, after all?

Maybe I'm oversharing. What can I say? I feel like after living in my shoes—or at least, my bedroom—all this time, you probably know me pretty well. I know I've got a new appreciation for you and your wholesome, outdoorsy lifestyle that you've got down here. :P

I bet you're itching to get back to it. Myself, I can't believe we only have a month left!

Write soon.

Eliza

The banquet to benefit the EPA may have been work for Billie and her intern colleagues, but that didn't mean it wasn't fun. Billie had to admit—however grudgingly—that five hundred dollars a plate covered a lot of flair.

The party was held at the Top of the Town, a hall overlooking all of the city's major monuments. Every time Billie happened to catch a glance out of one of the ceiling-to-floor picture windows, she was rendered breathless all over again.

She had to admit, she had an idea that she was having a similar effect on the male volunteer population. She wasn't one to fuss too much over her appearance, but she knew that the floor-length, black halter gown she'd bought for the event showcased her petite waist and slender arms to their best. And her sophisticated low ponytail and clean, buff-colored manicure was surprisingly muss-free, thanks to Fiona-belle's collaborative attentions. The waitstaff certainly seemed to take notice of her as they made their rounds through the grand ballroom, keeping champagne flutes overflowing and making sure no one was without a shrimp samosa, salmon pinwheel, or stuffed mushroom.

She was glad to be keeping busy, whether by performing actual intern duties or by chowing down on finger food. It helped in her efforts to circumvent Parker, whom she'd been studiously avoiding since her arrival. His parents were good friends of the Ritters, so of course he'd arrived with them. He was hard to miss, tall and broad-shouldered in his tux, but they'd managed to avoid any run-ins since the awkward kiss, and Billie wasn't looking to break that streak anytime soon.

She allowed herself to dwell momentarily on the last e-mail she'd received from Eliza. It was gracious of Eliza essentially to give Billie the go-ahead to date Parker, and Billie genuinely appreciated the gesture.

But what if it was too late?

She'd blown Parker off when he'd tried to kiss her, and even told him that she didn't think she could get involved with someone who'd dated Eliza. For all she knew, she'd made a very convincing argument. Even if Eliza *had* spoken to him and told him about her relationship with Macca, who knew what frame of mind Parker was in right now? He was probably over Billie, having written her off as too naïve to be worth another thought.

It was sad, really, when you thought about it—her first kiss and her last kiss, one and the same.

At least she wouldn't have to talk to him for the next hour or so, when she'd be manning a table for the silent auction. Iris had plucked her out of the crowd when her shift came up, leading her by the elbow to a table with a

photo of a hybrid car and a sheet for writing down auction bids.

The car was one of the most expensive auction items, and though Mr. Ritter had plenty of supporters with deep pockets, Billie found her table to be less crowded than some of those around her. Therefore, she had nowhere to hide when Mr. and Mrs. Ritter wandered up with a group of friends in tow.

"Hello, Billie," Mrs. Ritter said. Billie couldn't help but notice that, for once, Mrs. Ritter's smile seemed actually to reach her eyes, which sparkled their reflection of her lake-blue silk dress. Clearly, tonight Mrs. Ritter was in her element. It suited her.

"Hi," Billie said, smiling back. The situation was definitely still strained at home, but she owed it to Iris, to S.A.S.S, and even to herself to be professional tonight. "Are you interested in the car?"

"If everyone drove hybrid, carbon emissions would be significantly reduced," Mr. Ritter said. "I've been trying to get my wife to agree to go hybrid for ages."

Mrs. Ritter only rolled her eyes. "Safety first, darling."

"Right," Billie mumbled. She swallowed hard, not sure if, after everything that had happened, she had it in her to say what was on her mind.

She glanced to the right and saw that, for the first time all evening, Parker was looking directly at her. He had to know how hard it was for her to face Mr. Ritter. And what was it he had said when they'd had coffee? *He has to admire your passion. I know I do.*

She didn't know whether or not Mr. Ritter admired her passion. But she hoped, at least, that he would appreciate her honesty.

"You know," she said, glancing first into Mrs. Ritter's eyes, and then directly at Mr. Ritter, "hybrids are fantastic, but electric cars offer an even lighter carbon footprint."

Mrs. Ritter frowned. "Electric cars aren't really market viable right now," she said.

Billie shook her head. "Actually, Nissan recently unveiled a five-year plan for their product development that placed a high emphasis on electric cars. It's only the wave of the *future* if we refuse to embrace it *today.*"

Mrs. Ritter raised her eyebrow, stepping aside so one of her friends could place a bid on the car. She was silent.

Mr. Ritter, however, burst out laughing. Billie looked up at him, startled. "You're right, of course," he said, noticing her curious expression. "You're also the first person to contradict my wife—or me—in years."

Billie looked down. "I'm sorry," she said.

Mr. Ritter tilted his body so that he could look her directly in the eye. "Don't be," he said. "Don't be."

Later that evening, Billie was coming out of the restroom, marveling at the contradiction of the tiny, individually wrapped cosmetics and toiletries that were all labeled

"organic," in the ladies' lounge, when she bumped directly into Mr. Ritter again. Talk about mortifying. He must think she was a total clod.

"Having a good time?" Mr. Ritter asked. She didn't think he was asking just about the evening.

"I am," Billie said, considering. "But—I wanted to tell you…" She paused.

Mr. Ritter widened his eyes, questioning.

"I…I think I'm going to do the sit-in. With the Green Gorillas. And, um, the article for the Fairlawn paper." She couldn't deny the thrill she got at thinking about protesting alongside the other Green Gorillas.

"Are you." It wasn't a question.

"Yes?" Billie squared her shoulders. "Yes." It wasn't a question, either.

But Mr. Ritter surprised her, stepping forward. "Good," he said firmly.

"Good?" Billie was confused.

Mr. Ritter sighed. "The truth is, Billie, you actually remind me a lot of myself when I was your age. I was very idealistic. Once upon a time, I would have been the one pushing for electric cars, insisting hybrid engineering wasn't enough."

"What happened?"

"Reality happened," he said, looking thoughtful. "I'm part of the system now, and in order to make things happen, I need to work *within* the system." He smiled. "You'll see."

Billie shrugged. "I sort of hope I don't. See, that is."

He smiled. "I sort of hope you don't, either. And that's what youth is for—idealism. So I hope you have a great time with your protest. And that you change a lot of people's minds about Proposition Seven. I'd love to have a budget increase that allowed us to move forward with the cleanup more quickly."

Billie grinned. "I'd love that, too."

Billie had barely made it down the hallway when she felt a tap at her shoulder and whirled around. This time, it was Parker. He smelled like high-end shampoo and sports deodorant. He really was attractive. It was a shame she'd had to push him away. There was no way that he was still interested in her—no matter what Eliza may or may not have said to him. Boys had very fragile egos—she'd read that in a magazine once.

"Was that what I thought it was?" he asked, incredulous.

"Depends what you thought it was."

"It sure looked like Mr. Ritter playing nice with you," he said.

Billie nodded proudly. "Yup. Said I reminded him of himself. All filled with good intentions and the like."

"You are," Parker said. "You're the quintessential do-gooder. Not to mention—you clean up pretty nice, too."

She blushed. "Thanks. All of the makeup is organic."

Parker laughed. "I wasn't worried. Besides, Fiona told me about your makeover. She said that she and Annabelle basically pinned you down and forced a curling iron on you."

"Just about. But I rather like the results, I have to say. When were you talking to her?"

"We danced for a bit before it was time for her to man her auction station," Parker confessed.

Now it was Billie's turn to raise her eyebrows. "Really?" As much as she assumed that Parker was well over his feelings for her, she hadn't thought he'd be so quick to move on to another bird.

"Really. She's actually quite funny once you pry her away from her ball and chain."

"I'll have to take your word for it," Billie decided. "I guess I hadn't thought that she was exactly your type."

"And what would you know about my type?" Parker asked, his eyes twinkling.

This was it: the moment of truth. She had to just go for it. Didn't she?

"Eliza—" she said, almost choking on the name.

Parker held up a hand. "I spoke to her. We're not together anymore. And I told her…" He trailed off, looking slightly embarrassed.

"Yes?" Billie's stomach flipped. Could he be about to say what she hoped he was about to say?

"I told her that I had feelings for you," he said, the words coming out in a rush. "And she was okay with it."

Forget flipping—her stomach was doing a full-on back handspring. Billie wanted to jump up and down and giggle like a little girl.

Instead, she managed to maintain her composure. "Really," she said. "Are you sure you wouldn't rather have another dance with Fiona?" She grinned to show him that she was only kidding.

Parker smiled in a way that made the corners of his eyes crinkle up adorably. "You're cute when you're jealous," he said. "Actually," he went on, "you're pretty much always cute."

Swoon. It was all Billie could do not to melt into a puddle right there on the ballroom floor. She channeled all of her energy into remaining upright and returning Parker's steady gaze.

"So," Parker said, breaking into her thoughts. "You've got a few weeks left of your semester abroad. The banquet has come and gone. Proposition Seven is on hold, despite our best efforts. What now?"

Billie giggled. He was right—so much had happened. And yet, she wasn't too concerned. There was still the Green Gorillas, the sit-in and article...and lots of other causes. She wasn't done fighting. Not by a long shot. Mr.

Ritter seemed to respect Billie's sticking to her convictions. So she was just going to keep right on doing so. And best of all? She'd have Parker at her side while she did.

"I'm sure we'll think of something," she said to Parker, stepping forward and letting him take her hand in his own. "No worries."

He leaned forward to kiss her, pausing only to brush a wisp of hair off of her forehead. "No worries, indeed," he agreed.

And then they didn't say anything at all.

From: billiesurf@email.com
To: elizarit@email.com
Subject: almost home!

Well, your father's banquet has come and gone! I imagine you're used to these bashes by now, but I can tell you, my feet are screaming. Those peep-toe stilettos might have been gorj, but give me a pair of comfortable trainers any day. If there's one thing I'm learning here in D.C., it's that I know what I like, what I believe in, and what works for me.

And I can't believe I'm talking about this with you, but I have to thank you for whatever it was that you said to Parker. I obviously don't know him nearly as well as you do, but I know he appreciated hearing from you. And I'm glad for the chance to get to know him better during my time here.

You'd be surprised how much people respect a little bit of honesty and straightforwardness. I know *I* was.

It seems strange that we've swapped places this semester; we know so much about *each other's life* even though we've never met in person. Thanks for agreeing to do the exchange. Let's make a pact to get the absolute most out of our last few weeks—me up over, and you down under.

What do you think?

Billie

From: elizarit@email.com
To: billiesurf@email.com
Subject: Re: almost home!

I'm glad you made it through one of the dreaded banquets. The only thing worse than those are the benefit concerts with Tibetan yak singers or some such.

As for me, I've had my share of excitement. I totally know what you mean about feeling like we know each other but don't know each other. I feel a deep kinship with anyone who ever had to put on a Fishy Wishy fry hat!

I know I did the right thing in being straight with Parker,

and honestly, I think it's great that you guys clicked.

I can also be straight with you: as much as I hate the thought, I know things with Macca—like the semester— are going to have to end eventually. Even so, I'm going to enjoy the last weeks here. Who knows? Maybe in a couple years you'll be up for doing a university exchange!

I'd like to spend some more time down under—if you're willing to head back up over, that is!

Eliza